The Ironbridg

By Robert Herrick

ISBN 978-0-9957933-1-6

www.robertherrick.co.uk

robertherrickwriter@gmail.com

WHARFAGE PUBLISHING

Text copyright 2015 Robert Herrick
All Rights Reserved

Copyright © 2015 Robert Herrick
Wharfage Publishing

The right of Robert Herrick to be identified as the author of this work has been asserted by him in accordance with the Copyright, Designs and Patents Act, 1988.
This book is a work of fiction. Names, characters, brands and incidents are either the product of the author's imagination or are used fictitiously. Any resemblance to real persons, living or dead, is purely coincidental

This book is sold subject to the conditions that shall not, by way of trade or otherwise, be lent, resold, hired out, or otherwise circulated without the author's prior consent in any form of binding or cover other than which it is published and without similar condition being imposed on the subsequent purchase.

Cover design: Lynne Herrick
Cover original photograph: Robert Herrick

To my Sue for her unswerving support

With thanks to so many people, you know who you are, if I missed you, I'm sorry.
Angie, Lynne, Chloe, Alex, Alison, Jayne, Betty, Elaine, Heather, Ylva, Wendy, Selena, Ian, Terry and Ron.

With thanks to the following organisations: -
Severn Valley Railway
York Railway Museum
Telford Libraries
WEA (Workers Educational Association
Story – Robert McKee
The Alliance of Independent Authors (ALLi)

Table of Contents

Part 1:

The Ironbridge Gorge 1942

Chapter 1: Coalbrookdale by night

Chapter 2: Fishing Trip

Chapter 3: The Storm

Chapter 4: After the Storm

Chapter 5: Director's Cut

Chapter 6: Harris

Chapter 7: Open door

Chapter 8: A Jug to Remember

Chapter 9: Coney Island

Chapter 10: On the Mend

Chapter 11: The First, First Friday Club Meeting

Chapter 12: The Horse and the Lady

Chapter 13: Under the Albert

Chapter 14: A Job for Harris

Chapter 15: Do Not Flush

Chapter 16: Her Ladyship

Chapter 17: Second First Friday Club Meeting

Chapter 18: Don't Touch

Chapter 19: Penny a Fish

Chapter 20: The Third First Friday Club meeting

Chapter 21: Under the Albert

Chapter 22: Tom Gets Them In

Chapter 24: Night Ride

Chapter 25: Reburying the Coins

Chapter 26: Emergency Meeting of the First Friday Club

Chapter 27: The Spiv comes knocking

Chapter 28: Deep Water

Part 2: 2015 in Telford

Chapter 1: Meeting Joan

Chapter 2: Secrets

Chapter 3: Short Trousers

Chapter 4: Falling Down

Chapter 5: Archived Newspapers

Chapter 6: The Specialist

Chapter 7: A Walk to Benthall

Chapter 8: Above the Sundial

Chapter 9: Second Clue

Chapter 10: Sarah and Precious

Chapter 11: That Robin

Chapter 12: Trainspotting

Chapter 13: Knock First

Chapter 14: York by Train

Chapter 15: 440 Yards

Chapter 16: Harris' Confession

Chapter 17: Where's Joan?

Chapter 18: The News

Chapter 19: Under the Frog Clock

Chapter 20: How may I help

Part 3: Around and around

Chapter 1: Warning – the beginning.

Chapter 2: The beginning of the End

Chapter 3: Different people?

Chapter 4: All aboard

Epilogue

Part 1:

The Ironbridge Gorge 1942

Chapter 1: Coalbrookdale by night
Late Friday 19th of June 1942

Slumped against the bridge parapet, head bowed, hands on knees, he fought the urge to throw up. Torment gnawed at his guts, as he willed the pills to kick in.

He began to feel safe, hidden in the impenetrable darkness. The industrial tumult surrounding him, reminded him of the chaotic skirmishes he had fought with his mates. He missed them badly, even though he was safe here. No bombs, bullets or screams. He knew if he could stick it out, the incessant cacophony would eventually sooth his raw edges and usher him towards the oblivion of sleep.

The elongated thump of a stamping press began a counterpoint; its regular percussive beat redolent of a solemn funeral march. He felt the earth tremor beneath his boots in time to the hammers blows.

The muscular heft of his prized trophy Luger felt good in his hand. Standing to attention, he raised the pistol above his head, and then paused solemnly before firing a volley of unheard shots. 'For you boys,' he shouted, as he saluted the night sky.

Desultory moonlight reflected weakly from smooth steel rails that stretched out towards the Works. He visualised the haphazard piles of scrap metals, coal, coke and sand, dumped around the lower pool. The pool and sluices had once powered the Works but now lay derelict. The Works were hazardous by daylight and lethal in the blackout. Only the foolish ventured into the yard after dusk.

Irritably, he rummaged through his pockets for a match. He struck it three times against the parapet before it flared. Protecting the fledgling flame with his cupped hands, he lit the cigarette lodged between his lips. The flickering flame illuminating his troubled face. Phosphorous and tobacco fumes mingled above his head as he tossed the spent match and took a drag.

'I thought I might find you here, lovely boy.'

He straightened and stared towards the voice.

'Cat got your tongue, pretty boy?'

His head spun, *how can he see me? Bugger it's the fag!* Ripping the cigarette from his lips, he threw it toward the voice. It landed well short, bouncing across the track bed, sparks spluttering from its tip.

A cone of light sliced through the darkness finding his face and drilling into his eyes, making his eyelids snap shut. Squinting to shield his eyes, he blinked towards the brightness. *He must be tall by the height of the light*, he thought.

Backlit against the lighter sky, a large head and shoulders rocked metonymically towards him. *He's huge*, he thought.

'You should never have come back, lovely boy. Going to take your punishment like a man, are you?'

'But I ...'

'I'll teach you to mess with my missus.'

'You've got it wrong ...'

'When I've finished, even your mother won't recognise you.'

Gravel crunched under heavy boots as his deliberate, confident footfalls advanced. The smaller man judged the torch to be maybe forty feet away. Any logical thoughts began to dissolve in a torrent of panic. Where were his mates? They had saved him from the Germans, but where were they now? His knee's buckled.

From somewhere deep within him a voice began to chant with growing conviction.

'Hold him down, you Zulu warrior,

Hold him down, you Zulu Chief, Chief, Chief,'

The chant transported him back to his combat camp training. The recollection began to dispel his fear.

'Use whatever advantages you have, there are no rules. It's him or you, no prizes for coming second. You will be victorious or dead,' barked the drill sergeant in his ear.

'Is that you, China?' He said, as he gained confidence.

The beam stopped. He had his attention. *Now, to rattle the big man*, he thought.

'June, you mean. I've got to tell you China, she's dirty in the sack is your missus. Begging for it, couldn't get enough!' He said, reaching for the pistol in his waist band. '*How many left,*' he wondered. China silently rocked from side to side, his rage growing inside

China blew an elongated whistle blast that sliced through the darkness. His blood ran cold at the eerie sound

'Follow me boys,' China bellowed, as he wheeled around exalting invisible soldiers behind him, to do their worst. Inclining his torso, he charged with the ferocity of an enraged Pamplona bull.

The smaller man held his ground impassively as the torch beam shrank towards the inevitable melee. Raising the pistol, he delayed until the last moment before squeezing the trigger. CRACK, click, click. '*Shit, empty.*'

Instinctively, he feinted right and dodged left. China adjusted to his left but failed to react a second time, his momentum carrying him forward only to fall at the other man's feet. Franticly he drove his knee into China's back and simultaneously seized his head in an arm lock. To his surprise and disappointment, the big man offered no resistance. The first shot, his last bullet, had felled China.

He felt for a pulse. Satisfied he rolled the big man onto his back, blood oozed from his chest. He felt nothing as he stared down at China's impassive blood splattered face.

A trophy, why not? He pulled the whistle and cord over the big man's head and pocketed it. Heaving China's body upright, he toppled it over the wall. Crashing through undergrowth, China's body plunged into the sluice, detonating a huge splash. He picked up the smashed torch and tossed it towards the body. Shaking a bent fag from its crushed packet he nonchalantly lit it with the embers of his discarded cigarette. Exhaling he smiled to no one.

Relaxing against the wall, he closed his eyes. A picture flooded into his mind's eye. Prominently hung on their classroom wall had been a print 'Coalbrookdale by Night'. It had impressed his young mind. He had lost himself in the fantastical fires raging through the picture's heart. He had marvelled at insignificant men and horses that emphasised the scene's monstrous scale. Transfixed, he heard the pandemonium, sensed the searing heat and smelt the sweet stench of scorched earth. With satisfaction, he speculated that the artist had probably sketched the outline from somewhere near where he stood. He nodded to himself in confirmation.

Nonchalantly he flicked the glowing fag end into the air. His dispassionate eyes traced its lazy arc. The voices, now subdued, spoke to him in whispers. They were pleased with him.

The works hooter announced the start of the ten till six shift. *'Time to visit June,'* he mused. Turning away, he crossed the bridge without a thought for China, steeped in the sluice below.

Chapter 2: Fishing Trip
Saturday 20th to Sunday 21st of June 1942

Jackson Hailstone turned his good eye towards George and Bill, who slouched on the bench beside him. The early summer sun shone fitfully, between banks of dense cloud.

'Any gossip?' he said, to no one in particular, as he fussed Nipper. His mother named him Jackson but everyone in the Bridge knew him as Jack the lad, Jack to his face.

'China's missus is playing away,' George said, raising his eyebrows.

'Never,' Bill said, his eyes opening wide. 'Who would be that daft?' Jack and George turned puzzled expressions towards him.

'Don't get me wrong,' Bill said, realising he had been misunderstood. 'She's a looker alright, but who'd risk tangling with China's?'

'Where did you hear?' Jack said, to George casually.

'China himself, at the pub last night,' George said.

'You're joking,' Jack said. 'Tell me you're joking.'

'Sat on his own in the corner, drunk as a lord he was. This was about eight thirty and he was due on the ten till six shift, what a state to go to work. When he left, he blew that whistle of his and then started mumbling, 'Over the top my boys' and 'Follow me I know where the bastard is.' Then he staggered through the doors waving his arms. God knows what he was on about.'

'What, the whistle he blows to start the fishing comps?'

'Yes, they say it's from the trenches, never without it, hangs round his neck on a lanyard.'

'A sergeant, wasn't he?' Jack said.

'Too true, hard as nails. There were rumours he'd shoot his own men if they wouldn't go over the top,' George said, absent-mindedly adjusting his cap. 'Wouldn't want to get the wrong side of China.'

They stared at their boots as the conversations ended abruptly. After a respectful silence, Bill put his arm around Jack's shoulder and said, in a confidential manner,

'She's your sort, isn't she, Jack?'

'Any skirt's his sort.' George said, chuckling.

'Nice pair, too.' Bill said, cupping his broad hands across his chest. Jack looked away, striving to avoid a reaction.

'Younger than China, isn't she?' Bill said, thoughtfully, hoping Jack would bite.

George eventually filled the silence, 'Not born in the Bridge, was she?'

'From away wasn't she?' added Bill, turning towards Jack.

14

Jack glanced up the line, hoping to catch sight of their recalcitrant train and change the subject.

All three wore the railwayman's uniform of overalls, peaked caps and scuffed, black boots. Bill and George worked in protected trades, avoiding the war. Jack had not been so lucky. The fourth member of the party hid amongst the shadows behind Jack's legs, a rotund and off-white Jack Russell, who answered to 'Nipper'.

The group would have made an interesting photograph. George on the left; tall and angular, sporting an impressive comb-over of fire red hair. Between him and Jack sat Bill. By contrast to George, Bill appeared almost spherical. A broad leather belt defining his equator, abandoned buckle holes plotted his flourishing waistline. To those who knew him, the belt served as a barometer to his state of mind - one thumb inserted casually: relaxed; clutched by both hands and twisted back and fore: agitated; jerked tighter by a hole or two: anger.

George and Bill sat close together almost touching. Jack sat slightly to one side, his piercing grey-blue eyes staring uncompromisingly into the lens. His open smile and carefree demeanour granted him the look of a younger man.

At school, Jack had hated reading: words swarmed into jumbles across the page that only he could see. Miss Stanwick held him back in her class as his friends and twin brother Robert progressed through the school. A black Victorian dunce's hat emblazoned with a white capital D stared at him from its shelf below a print of 'Coalbrookdale at night'. By rights, he should have been made to wear it. Fortunately, Miss Stanwick believed an intelligent boy lived inside him somewhere and decided not to discourage his debut.

*****

'Great watching other people work,' Bill said, staring towards the goods yard, where two of the lads danced around as they struggled to unload a frisky bullock.

'About time those two pulled their weight,' George said, jutting his chin forward dismissively.

Their train clanked into the platform, the locomotive slowed and eased to a stop at the water tower. The First Friday boys, as they would become known, threw their baskets and fishing paraphernalia into the guard's van and strolled along the corridor towards the compartments.

Doors slammed, whistles blew, coaches were heaved as the grimy engine took up the slack. Bill and George rushed to take possession of an empty compartment and sat simultaneously side by side like school kids. Jack dropped heavily onto the sagging seat opposite, disturbing cloud of dust particles, which rose and twinkled as they climbed through sunbeams towards the ceiling.

'Open the window, let's get some air,' George said, looking towards Jack.

'What did your last servant die of?' Jack said, reaching for the window catch.

'Now then gentlemen, fishing club rules, a little decorum if you please,' Bill joked.

'Bollocks,' George said, with a wink to Bill.

Bill and George had grown up in the same street and attended the same blue-bricked church school. They often made comments simultaneously, or acknowledged empathy with a nod. Physically spectacularly different, they were as attuned mentally as identical twins.

Bill began a private game of I spy. *'I spy a pub,'* he started, with the Station Hotel on his left, before twisting right just in time to glimpse the open back door of the Old Vaults. Across the bridge, he spied the top floors of the Tontine Hotel. Then between the White Brickle chimneys, he spied the lime-washed courtyard at the White Hart. He imagined endless pints of best bitter lined up on the bar, before spotting the drinking trinity, the Talbot, the Swan and the Rodney standing together along the Wharfage. He then visualised the Crown and the White Horse, nestling out of sight, on top of the Gorge. Looking right across the river, he spotted The Valley Hotel and finally The Meadow. Raising an invisible pint glass in salute, he could almost feel the quenching beer lubricating his arid throat. *Ah, that first pint, always the best*, he thought. Although they all enjoyed a pint, George considered himself the most committed to the art of drinking, though he conceded that the others were not far behind.

Jack grinned to himself, eyes half closed, recalling conquests both real and imagined, mostly enjoyed along Sunnyside: the park; the shuts and jittys; the rowing club, gardens, orchards and pubs. Jack the lad, a man for all terrains.

Gazing down at the river, Bill examined moored boats, fishing stands, eddies, pools, boys skimming waste tiles, swans, ducks and more boys under the Albert bridge, swinging from the rope. The sight of the rope spun him back to the childhood thrill of swinging in a wide arc above the river. *The bee's knees*, he thought. Secured high in the bridge girders the rope hung down over the river, tantalisingly just out of reach from the bank. A second, modest rope allowed the swinging rope to be pulled within reach. Bill recalled that daring and skill were required to swing and stay dry. Missing a push off against the bank twice in succession doomed the swinger to an inevitable soaking. Bereft of momentum, the hapless swinger hung helpless above deep water. The inevitable soaking waited: the only variable was for how long. Bill shivered as he recalled the shock of flailing about in freezing water.

Nipper lay under the seat, her muzzle twitching languidly in appreciation of aromas sucked through the open window. The power station grew at each click from the rails until it loomed above them, blotting out everything but the sky directly above them. Smoke erupted from massive chimneys and stained the pale blue sky grey. The inline stacks reminded Jack of the funnels of giant ocean liner, straining to break its moorings.

Passing bedraggled coal wagons leaning in sagging lines, they entered Buildwas Junction. Existing only as two lines that cross here in a no man's land devoid of roads, houses, pubs, and shops, the weary traveller has only two options, change trains or continue.

'Dig for Victory', 'Careless talk costs lives', 'Keep it under your hat' demanded station posters of their captive audience.

'Why does China think she's playing away?' Jack said, addressing his question to the middle distance with casual disinterest. Bill and George shared a 'who does he think he's kidding' glance.

'She's wearing perfume; she's out when China's working nights; she's singing. She's giving him the cold shoulder. I think that's what he said,' George said, privately thinking it didn't add up too much.

'So, he's not caught her at it?' Jack asked, evenly.

'No,' George said. 'Why are you asking?'

'No reason,' Jack said, as he gazed distractedly through the dirty window.

Coney Island came and went without comment. Jack enjoyed fishing from the island, though more than fish were landed on dark evenings. Jack's eyes twinkled at the thought.

Picking up speed, the train rolled past Buildwas Abbey ruins and began to skirt the Severn's floodplain. Wide fields of pasture offered unobstructed views of the Severn remorselessly eroding its squat, sandy banks.

18

'Sandy Beach,' Bill said, the others nodded in recognition, wistful smiles playing across their faces.

'The rock, remember that?' Jack said, through a nervous grin.

'Don't remember it being that far from the bank,' Bill said, furrowing his forehead.

'It's always been there,' George said.

'I know, it can't have moved, I just thought,' Bill said, wishing he had said nothing.

'You were brave if you jumped off the top,' Jack said, with a wistful glance.

'Or stupid,' George said.

'And you weren't stupid were you George?' Jack observed dryly.

'Now, now, children, club rules please,' Bill said, fearing a minor skirmish.

'So, what would China do, if he caught her out?' Jack said, to the seat back between Bill and George. Another glance passed between Bill and George.

'They hushed it up, but on New Year's Eve a few years ago China pulped that travelling salesman type who got fresh with June,' Bill said, as stared impassively over Jack's head at a framed photograph of Chester.

'I'd say he'd do pretty much the same, or worse, if he caught whoever it is,' George said, staring knowingly at Jack.

'Do you remember his first wife,' Jack said, looking through the window.

'No, we were only kids, but someone said she took their lads off back to her family in Ireland. China was in the trenches,' Bill said.

'Tasty with his fists is our China,' George said, adopting a southpaw stance. 'Boxed a bit at home as well, I'm told.' They stared at their boots in silence.

In and out of Cressage station they rode, now only a mile of steady climb separating them from Cound Halt, their destination. Standing untidily amongst their randomly dumped fishing tackle, they wistfully watched the train coast towards the horizon as silence fell.

'Quite a view, isn't it?' Jack said, admiring the sweeping curve of the Severn below them - a vast glinting ribbon that connected the eastern and western horizons, whilst dividing the pastoral landscape into north and south.

'Best view in Salop,' George said, inspiring nods of agreement.

'Even better with a pint,' Bill said, glancing over his shoulder at the Inn. He bet himself the view from the bar would be magnificent.

'No time for a pint,' George said, sensing where Bill would prefer to be.

'It's a bit late for old Seth, let's hope the ferry's still running,' George said, casting a concerned glance down at a tired looking punt, its reflection shimmering in an eddy.

'Whistle him, Bill,' George said.

Bill's shoulders rose as he sucked in his belly preparatory to producing a prodigious whistle through his gappy front teeth.

'Come on Seth,' George shouted.

'Another whistle,' Bill said, his eyes seeking approval.

Before Bill could derive further satisfaction, Seth appeared from a nearby copse. His sleepy yawn and stretch told its own story.

Here the restless Severn widened and became placid, an ideal ferrying spot. As loading commenced, Nipper watched nervously as the punt rocked erratically. Splitting the load would have been prudent, but there had been no time for second thoughts, let alone second trips. With everything aboard, the punt sat so low in the river that Nipper could lick nervously at her reflection. As Jack picked her up, she began to practice doggy paddle in mid-air.

Lucky to be alive, Jack had found Nipper on a railway embankment tied up in a hessian sack and left for dead. Nipper's ears were small, neat and pointy, though one hung down as if broken. Nipper habitually tilted her head to one side, conjuring a bogus impression of intelligence. 'Don't be fooled,' Jack would say. 'She's thinking about her next meal. The fat little thing could eat for England.'

Once safely on the far bank, Bill stole a resigned look at the Inn before following the others upstream along the fisherman's path towards their favourite pegs. The uneven path proved uncomfortable to navigate as basket corners dug into soft flesh. Insects buzzed and annoyed. Evening sunrays shone beneath dense leaf canopies, illuminating tree trunks in vivid oranges and reds. A nothing sort of day had transformed into a wonderful summer's evening.

Floats bobbed satisfyingly in pools of reflected sunset. Twilight lingered, prolonged by banter, laughter and bottled beer. Jack's stories entertained them long after the beer ran out. Eventually sleep silenced him.

Chapter 3: The Storm
The following morning

Dawn arrived unseen. Wrapped snugly in duffle coats the First Friday Boys slept on soundly. Jack woke first, tentatively opening his eyes into the new day's tepid sun. Standing groggily, he shifted his weight to alternate legs, hoping to breathe life into his sleeping feet. Nipper looked on impassively as Jack searched the landscape for a suitable place to perform his morning ablutions. A tump in the corner of a nearby field caught his eye. Marooned on a headland and surrounded by Broom bushes it appeared perfect.

Leaving the others to catch fish in their dreams, he hastened towards it, adopting a slightly crouching walk inspired by a rumbling stomach. Completing his constitutional, Jack stood to hoist his trousers. The combined treachery of the slope, loose soil and mutinous trousers sent Jack head over heels down the tump and under a bush. Recovering briskly, he checked no one had witnessed his acrobatics. Satisfied his honour, as a railwayman and an angler, had not been compromised, he relaxed. It occurred to him that the incident had the makings of a good story. *A few embellishments and a little fine-tuning, it could work well*, he speculated.

'What are you up to, Nipper?'

Nipper ignored him, as she dug furiously, half hidden in her excavation. Stooping, Jack caught sight of a roughly circular object half covered with loose soil. He picked it up and rubbed it vigorously on his duffle coat sleeve, applying spit, he rubbed it again; the soft irregular shape began to shine. Encouraged, he rubbed even more vigorously until it spun from his grip, landing near Nipper's back end. Moving Nipper to one side gently with his boot, he stooped to recover it and found two more coins. Within minutes, he had found sufficient coins to fill two duffle coat pockets.

Animated, he strode back, imagining regaling Bill and George with his new story. His return to the riverbank proved anticlimactic however, as both men were utterly absorbed watching the rapid movements of George's fishing line. Jack could see, by the curvature of the rod, that George had hooked a sizeable fish. Abandoning his rod, Bill slithered down the bank brandishing his landing net. The fish fought ferociously. Finally, after much gut straining, rod bending and reel spinning, George manoeuvred his catch into shallow water. Bill eventually landed the prize carp, but not before he had been soaked by several spectacular tail splashes.

Jack glanced casually over his shoulder towards his own rod, which to his astonishment had begun to twitch violently. He ran. The rod toppled from its stand and jerked toward the river. Agonisingly he watched as his prized bamboo rod slid down the bank and into the river. It floated towards the reeds, pulled he suspected by another large carp. *Amongst the 'one that got away' stories circulating the fishing club, this will take the biscuit,* he thought.

Bill and George chuckled and derided Jack's vain attempts to retrieve his rod without getting soaked. He threw stones near the rod, dragged branches across it, and swore at it, all to no avail. Finally, Jack accepted the inevitable and stripped down to his underclothes. Accompanied by mocking wolf whistles he waded into the river. As a strong swimmer, he could easily have swum the short distance, but Jack had decided to wade, in the hope of remaining half dry. As he stepped gingerly off the bank the cold water rose to his knees. Feeling increasingly confident of avoiding a complete ducking, he took another tentative step. Unfortunately, the riverbed dropped away, leaving him waist deep before his foot found the bottom. Cold and dispirited, Jack turned for encouragement to find George and Bill hanging on to each other in fits of silent laughter. To add insult to injury, George suggested that they could probably have hooked it with Bill's rod and pulled it to the bank. Though fervently denied by Bill and George, Jack suspected that their helpful suggestion had occurred to them before he had waded in. They had just forgotten to mention it, deliberately…

Jack tiptoed cautiously towards the bank. Having reached dry land, he bowed graciously, acknowledging the rapturous standing ovation offered by his tear-stained audience.

Jack stepped unsteadily into his dry overalls and pulled them over his wet long johns. The unaccustomed weight of the abandoned duffle coat jogged his memory. Holding the coat aloft in triumph he announced:

'Hey lads, guess what I've found.'

'A GWR duffle,' George said, wondering what the real answer would be.

'Well, I found loads of old coins.'

'Come on, play the game, there's no time for your stories, we've a fish to catch,' Bill said, as George dismissed Jack with a disbelieving head jerk. Frustrated, Jack produced a fistful of coins.

'Beauties, aren't they?'

'Where did you get those?' Bill said.

'Well, I went for a tom tit, while you two were still driving z's into the sky and well, to cut a long story sideways ....'

'Please do!' George said, cutting Jack off.

'Let's hear him out George.'

Jack warmed to his task. 'I know it's hard to believe, but I fell over and found them. They were in some sort of animals' tunnel,' Jack sensed the others were not buying his story. 'Well, tell the truth, I didn't find them,' pained looks passed between George and Bill, 'Nipper did!'

'Let's get this straight,' Bill said. 'You expect us to believe that when you went to powder your nose, Nipper here found the coins.'

'You must think we came up the Severn in a rickshaw,' George said, glancing over at Bill.

'Look, I'll show you where, if you don't believe me,' Jack said, pointing towards the tump, Bill and George followed half-heartedly.'

Jack handed them each a coin as they stood around the base of the tump.

'You know, I'm almost sure these are Roman, and gold I'm guessing,' Bill said, turning a coin over in his hand.

'Well, it makes sense. Wroxeter, the old Roman city, is just 'up along', it can't be much more than a mile here.' George said, spinning a coin.

'I wish we could spend them, they'd keep us in beer for life,' Bill said, beaming from ear to ear.

'They'd be worth a few quid, melted down,' George said, nodding his agreement.

'But we could lose the lot if we don't do this right.' Jack paused and then responded to George's questioning glance. 'It's private land here. I bet they're not ours to sell.'

'Aren't they the King's or the country's or something?'

'Whatever it is, we won't see any money out of it,' George sneered, in resignation.

'That's right, the war effort would have them off us, you know, "dig for glory" and all of that rot,' Bill said, in support of George.

'Gentlemen, I have a suggestion. Why don't we put them in my snap bag and shove them back in the hole? We could leave them here while we work something out?' Jack looked from one to the other for agreement. 'They'd be safe here for another two thousand years I'm thinking.'

Bill and George nodded their grudging approval.

'O.K. as long as we don't step in your doings,' George said, looking suspiciously around the tump.

'Lads, it's looking black over Bill's mother's,' Bill said, pointing to a bank of black clouds massing in the west.

'Best get to some shelter before it pours down,' Jack said, as he hurriedly funnelled the coins into his snap bag and rammed it into the tunnel.

'Let's catch the next service,' George suggested. Jack shivered his agreement, river water collecting in his boots. Packing up began in earnest, mixed with plenty of banter at Jack's expense.

Dumping their fishing gear on the platform, they slumped down inside the primitive shelter. Jack shivered between them, his back and shoulders hunched against damp underclothes.

Dark clouds merged into an impenetrable blanket, an eerie half-light settled around them. Heavy raindrops splashed random penny sized circles across the platform planking. Nipper retreated behind Jack's legs. Within seconds, a downpour of African proportions blurred their vision as the horizon disappeared. A sense of boyish excitement gripped the three castaways, marooned, but dry, in their rudimentary shelter. Spellbound, they gazed open mouthed as the deluge drummed deafeningly across the corrugated iron roof. Communication subsided into admiring nods, exaggerated eyebrow raises and silent whistles. Nipper barked as the wheezing locomotive broke through the curtain of rain and shuddered to a halt.

Why couldn't it be late for once, Jack thought. *Still, now I won't be the only one who's wet. By the time we get this lot aboard we'll all be soaked.*

Rivulets of rain streaked the grimy windows. Crows perched on sagging telegraph wires, bobbing and cawing raucously, apparently oblivious of the deluge. Conversation stalled. Recent events left them unsure of their next move; small talk had dried up long ago.

Chuffs of escaping steam and smoke echoed around the Gorge as the engine slowed. In a few short minutes, they would be back in the Bridge.

Opinions should be voiced, tactics discussed, agreement reached, Jack thought.

'Anyone know what a tontine is?' Jack asked.

'They serve a good pint there,' George said, winking at Bill.

'What else?'

'There's a good snooker table upstairs,' George said, smirking to Bill.

27

'But, what does it mean?' persisted Jack.

'There's Tontine Hill. 'That' a street?' Bill said, being deliberately obtuse at Jack's expense.

'I can see I'll have to tell you,' Jack said, appraising blank faces. 'Well, a Tontine is an agreement between a group of investors. They would put equal shares into a scheme, draw dividends as it developed, then eventually the surviving investor gets the lot!'

'Very interesting, professor, but how does that affect the price of cod?'

Ignoring George, Jack explained, 'Well, we could have a Tontine between us three.'

'Sounds mad to me.'

'Don't listen to him Jack,' Bill said, giving George a telling glance. 'How would it work?'

'Well, as I see it, the coins would be our secret investment. We would meet say, once a month until we figure out how to sell the coins.'

'What if we never find out?' said George.

'I don't think that would happen but, like a Tontine, the last surviving investor would pass the secret down to their eldest son and so on.' Jack said, not really understanding how it would work in practice but not wishing to back down.

The platform glided into view followed by squealing brakes, escaping steam and shouts of 'Ironbridge and Broseley'. Hands shook in agreement; they would meet on the first Friday of each month at the Station Hotel, straight from work, no excuses. The 'First Friday Boys' were born.

'Remember lads, like the poster says: "careless talk...".'

28

Rainwater lay in broad puddles around the station. Nipper, distinctly unimpressed, circumnavigated them where she could. Those she could not avoid, she crossed, employing the high stepping strides of a dressage horse. Thunder and lightning rolled around the Gorge as impenetrable clouds extinguished any hope of a sunset.

No fishing tonight, Jack thought.

Chapter 4: After the Storm
Monday 22nd June 1942

Opening the front door, Jack breathed in the mustiness of damp morning air. Eyeing the destruction wrought by yesterday's storm, he shuffled passed climbing roses torn from walls around his front door. Broken stemmed flowers and smashed seedlings lay prone in the flowerbeds. At the garden gate, he turned his back to the destruction, consigning it to the future when he would find time to repair the damage.

He sauntered down Bridge Bank towards the railway and the river. His first glimpse of the Severn, confirmed the storm's magnitude. Yesterday, its translucent waters flowed sedately under the bridge; within hours, the storm had transformed the Severn into a torrent. Suspended clay sucked from sodden fields stained its waters orange. Massive half-submerged tree trunks floated through its boiling surface.

Invalided from active service with the REME six months ago, Jack had returned to the railway, not to his previous job as a fitter, but as a lowly linesman: a job he could do with only the sight in one eye. Jack's length spanned the seven miles of single track between Lindley in the east and Buildwas Junction in the west. It ran through the dense industrial landscape of the Gorge for two miles but the remainder meandered through endlessly deep countryside.

Jack occupied a lowly position within Great Western Railway, but between the boundaries of his [its] length, seven miles long and 60 foot wide, he ruled. King Jack held the power of life and death over all living things within this kingdom. He farmed it for himself, while performing his duties on behalf of the GWR. His linesman's job paid poorly but Jack lived comfortably enough for a widower, thanks to the produce from his kingdom. Mushrooms, blackberries, pea and bean canes, rabbits, pheasants and pigeons all helped to enrich his life. He traded with train crews, who kicked lump coal from the footplate for his winter fires and transported his larger produce in the engine's tender. In exchange, he gave them mushrooms for their breakfast, canes for their gardens and the odd rabbit for the pot. Jack enjoyed the fleeting company of passing train crews, who waved or shouted greetings. Happy in his own company, the solitude suited him down to the ground.

Jack also benefited from all manner of items lost through carriage windows, discarded or dropped from bridges, fallen from wagons or thrown over boundary walls. His finds were usually of little value - mainly hats, scarves and handkerchiefs - though he had once found a pair of silk knickers and, another time, a salesman's sample case of perfume.

31

As a lad of ten, he made his first find as he took a short cut to school through a railway cutting. A cardboard box lay invitingly near the track. He had been about to kick it, his foot poised to take the penalty kick - the goal would win the cup for his beloved Wanderers – when the baby cried out. He ran as fast as his legs would carry him to Tunes Crossing, where he told the crossing keeper's wife. She took charge and sent Jack off to school; he had forgotten the incident before he reached the school gates. Jack eventually received a commendation from the GWR, a gesture that would guarantee his lifelong interest in the railway.

The tracks allowed him freedom to move unobserved throughout the Gorge by day or night, a covert route to clandestine rendezvous. Nipper understood the King's command of 'Hide!'. At the word, she faded into the undergrowth until the King's low whistle called her back to his side. Her hiding skills were called upon in the presence of visiting GWR inspectors and assignations with local ladies.

Jack savoured the wonderful aroma of fresh bread wafting through the bakery's back door. He imagined his favourite meal: fresh bread with hunks of cheese, washed down with cold tea and for pudding more bread slathered with Golden Syrup. A battered tin of the sweet liquid nestled inside his knapsack: though it was difficult to come by, he always found a way around the rationing. Barter usually worked.

Twenty past seven already, he announced. Jack prided himself on his ability to estimate time. He carried his father's pocket watch, though only to check the accuracy of his estimates. The watch, a veteran of sixty years' hard labour, its case scratched and dented though the movement kept good time.

Jack's interest in estimating time had started as a competition between him and Robert. Their father's battered watch refereed the contest. Jack refined his skill during his lifetime in the Gorge. Robert had gone, the battered watch had remained. Nipper could also tell time, though only time for food.

Timetabled trains passing through his kingdom provided the starting point for his estimates. Experience allowed him to factor the timetable relative to his position along the line. Regular goods trains to and from the power station also helped. Skilfully he identified and interpreted shift change hooters issuing from works along Moneyside. Screams and shouts from children at play before and after school or at playtime also helped his estimates. He listened for the quarters chimed by church clocks as they competed against the sounds of industry that echoed around the Gorge. Rich odours also played a part. Hops and malt from brew houses, chlorine from the gas works and bacon fried at local hotels, were all factored in.

The river and railway ran integral parallel paths through his life. Never veering more than a hundred yards apart, the river and railway followed each other through the Gorge's geological squeeze. Almost every notable event in Jack's life had started or ended between the boundaries of the far riverbank and the railway's fence line.

Reaching his kingdom at Ironbridge level crossing, he headed down the line to the west and into the prevailing wind. Nodding up to Jim in the signal box, he received a grudging nod in return. Passing the Victorian coach that served as the station mess and tearoom, he glanced in to see smiles and steaming mugs of tea. Oh, how he wished he could join them.

Peering up at the soot stained bridge, he thought of the childhood games he and his gang had played here. The unusual bridge crossed the rails at an angle, sloping steeply towards the river. In its heyday, it had carried clay from the levels over the rails and into the White Brickle to be manufactured into pipes and bricks.

Jack pressed on towards the next quarter milepost and the viaduct. He cleaned out two gullies blocked by an accumulation of leaves, twigs and branches washed down by the storm. Reaching the western boundary of his length, he turned to retrace his steps in his customary zigzag pattern.

Must be a quarter to nine, he thought, hearing the sounds of energetic children, their shouts distorting across the river. The strident ringing of the school hand bell cut through the happy sounds, signalling the start of another school day. *No, I'm ten minutes out, it must be nine o clock,* he concluded, visualising bright eyed children forming class lines across the glistening playground.

Returning to Ironbridge station, he nodded greetings to the station staff. His kingdom grew wider at stations, where platforms, sidings and goods yards stood together. He thought of them as islands within his kingdom, islands which failed to recognise his authority. Duty done, appearances kept up, he embraced the thought of solitude and strode eastwards towards Jackfield and his own company. The footplate crew of a local goods train waved as they clanked past, he waved back. Once he would have envied them.

Damage to the line had been minimal, a couple of blocked culverts and a tree down but nothing serious. Nipper lagged well behind. *Will she ever lose her fear of this place*, Jack wondered, as he watched the hackles rise along her back.

'Come on Nipper, it's fine.'

Nipper, head bowed, eyes fixed straight ahead, reluctantly plodded forward. Jack glanced up the bank to the place where he had rescued her. Two runts of a litter tied into a hessian sack, thrown down the bank from the bridge and left to die. Nipper survived, her brother did not.

Nipper recovered the lost ground and led the way towards their favourite meal stop.

'Time for snap, Nip?'

Nipper's tail twitched in recognition. She sat, eyes trained on the food bag. It had become customary that Nipper would be offered the last mouthful of whatever food they had. Nipper drooled, as she waited impatiently for Jack to finish: woe betides him, should he forget. Nipper snaffled the piece of bread, before optimistically searching for more.

Chapter 5: Director's Cut

Jack visualised his life as a black and white movie, shot, scripted, and edited in his head. He wrote and rewrote the script, shot new scenes and edited as he inspected the rails. The director in his head spoke in an American accent, but they were Jack's words. He explained his life without allowing the camera to wander into its darker corners. Scenes could be reshot until he achieved the correct tenor: his actions justified, his lines honed, his looks shot in soft focus.

He meticulously scripted each scene with the truth, Jack's truth. Some scenes were already in the can, though he speculated that given the passage of time, he would reshoot them through a less claustrophobic lens. He supposed that some scenes would survive as shot, but that others would involve subtle changes given the benefit of time, insight and clouding of memory.

The first scene is set at Ironbridge railway station in 1915. His father is waiting for the train that would take him and many others to war. He has set the camera well back, capturing the spectacle of flapping bunting and cheering crowds crammed onto every vantage point. Sunlight pushed shadows across the set; the camera closes in, moving at speed along the track. A blur of sleepers flash through the shot before the camera comes to rests, the steaming engine that fills the lens.

Focusing along the platform the camera captures steam and shimmering heat, before picking out groups of smiling jubilant men crowded into each compartment. Doors bang closed, a shrill whistle blows, many flags fly. The crowd cheers to an echo, subdued only by the engine's hissing departure. The carriages disappear into a wall of steam. The camera holds on the rear coach as it fades into infinity. Jack and his twin Robert stand and stare.

Jack had also scripted a more recent wartime scene, based on his own experiences of just a year ago. It features Jack and his pals on leave in a small North African town. It is their last night of a forty-eight-hour pass; they are determined to make the evening memorable. They are pictured setting off towards their favourite bar in the souk. Framed by narrow streets they stride out, arms around shoulders. Copious bottles of beer and wine cement their comradeship, keeping their fear of death at bay.

Jack is then seen alone in a shabby toilet. Hearing a disturbance from the bar, he hurriedly buttons his fly and sprints towards the sounds of shouts and breaking glass. Bursting back into the bar he is immediately absorbed into a melee of brawling bodies. A meaty fist catches him before he understands who is friend or foe. Staggering to his feet he grabs the nearest shoulder and wrenches it towards him, his fist raised ready to inflict damage. His opponent's face spins into focus; Jack's fist drops in mid-flight as he comes face to face with his twin brother, Robert. They hug and backslap each other, an oasis in the midst of flailing arms and legs. So bizarre are their actions that the mass brawl paused in bewilderment.

Tommies and Anzacs are seen toasting each other's health until they can no longer stand. For a few precious hours amidst a deadly war, the twins are united again. They part outside the bar, unsure if they will ever meet again. No edit required.

Jack continued to polish other key turning points in his life, though he had been unable to shoot one particular scene to his satisfaction. No matter how often he reshot the scene, the final minutes retained a pervasive whiff of desertion.

Jack established the first shot using a long lens which captured endless arrow straight rails cutting through undulating fields, hedgerows and bubbling streams. The backdrop is of bleak countryside blanketed in hoar frost, backlit by a low, diffuse sun struggling to rise. The camera closes, revealing Jack in his twenties stamping his feet and blowing streams of white breath across his cupped hands.

A billycan hangs above on an impromptu fire alongside the wagon he is repairing. Smoke and steam rise into the low, leaden sky that leans heavily against the landscape beneath. A distant whistle signals a change of tempo. Jack's open face furrows as an engine grinds to a halt alongside him. A smutted, sweaty-browed fireman leans from the cab and waves him to come over.

'Report to the station, URGENT,' is the fireman's line, delivered while pointing, wild-eyed, back towards the Bridge. In the foreground an agitated Jack empties his billycan over the fire and kicks out the embers. The goods train clanks away in the background. The camera emphasises Jack's isolation, as he runs into a stark foreboding landscape and fades to a speck before reaching the horizon.

A delivery lorry stands waiting in the station yard. The frantic driver waves Jack to join him in the cab. Jack recognises concerned faces.

What do they know? Can it be that bad?

Sweeping through the yard gates, the lorry scatters dried leaves and paper into the air.

'Jack, your wife is in hospital, the baby's come too soon.' The driver says, as they rush through the hospital's pillared gates.

The Matron intercepts Jack as he runs along seemingly endless, echoing, white-tiled corridors.

'Mister Hailstone, Mister Hailstone, please follow me.'

She directs him brusquely into her office.

'Sit down, please,' she says, motioning towards a chair.

'I'll stand, thank you.'

'I'm afraid I have bad news,' she says, waiting for Jack to look up from the floor, before she continues. 'I'm sorry to inform you that your wife died earlier this morning due to complications during childbirth.'

She pauses to allow the enormity to sink in. Jack stares at the walls for what appears to be an eternity.

'You have a baby son, Mister Hailstone.'

No answer.

'He is premature and is well below our discharge weight. We will look after him here until he gains weight.'

Jack continues his stare.

'I need to see my wife.'

'If you are sure.'

'Yes, I'm sure. I need to say goodbye.'

Jack is seen disappearing behind a large white curtain. He re-emerges moments later doubled up with grief, tears streaming down his ashen face.

At this point, Jack's film version becomes difficult to shoot.

'Will you see your son, Mister Hailstone?' The Matron beseeches, as Jack disappeared from view.

Even with the passage of time, he has been unable to produce the scene as he wishes to view it. His script has been written and rewritten a hundred times and more, but no form of words can disguise the guilt he holds inside. There are no scenes of his son's adoption by Ellen's childless sister or his christening as Thomas.

It has taken many years but now Jack has begun to shoot new scenes. Adopting a documentary style, they capture the sunlight of long summer Sundays. Tom, now sixteen, plays the starring role. So far, so good.

Chapter 6: Harris
Tuesday 23rd June 1942

Jack disliked muggy summer days and so it pleased him when a refreshing drizzle drifted in. He marvelled at the agility of twittering Swallows that swooped low catching insects forced down by the weather. Emerging from the railway cutting, he stood on the adjoining embankment hoping to catch a breath of breeze. Why he decided to splash his boots in such an exposed spot he never really understood. Enjoying the relief of the moment, he idly scanned the fence line below the embankment, as he buttoned his fly, something registered at the edge of his vision, *the sole of a shoe maybe?*

He edged his way down the embankment towards the object protruding from thick undergrowth. Closer inspection confirmed his first thought: a shoe. Forced into a double take, he realised, to his horror that a sock protruded from the shoe and disappeared into the cuff of a trouser leg. Fearing the worst, Jack moved closer, but in doing so lost his footing on the cross slope. After several attempts to regain his balance, he fell, landing far too close to the corpse for comfort. Recoiling, he scrambled hurriedly upright only to lose his balance again, forcing him to take an involuntary step backwards onto the corpse's leg. The corpse screamed and contorted with pain.

Jack dragged the man into the open. He appeared to be in his early thirties. Dressed in good quality country clothes and brogues, he lay blinking wildly up at Jack.

'Where am I?' he said, trying to focus through half opened eyes.

Jack found himself trying to place his accent. Not local he thought. *Lowland Scots*, he guessed.

'Half way to nowhere, mate,' Jack said, attempting a joke. 'You're near Coalport.'

The man stared blankly back at Jack, as if attempting to understand a foreign language.

'What do they call you?' Jack asked

'Me,' he said, his voice just audible.

'Jack.' Jack said, offering his hand.

'Who me, I'm Jack,' the injured man said.

'No, I'm Jack, who are you?' Jack gave up, 'Got to get you up that bank. Can you stand?'

'I'll try.' He said, as he tried his injured leg and stumbled.

With his back to the embankment, Jack grabbed under his armpits and heaved. The man helped by pushing with his good leg. Eventually, they managed to synchronise their efforts and inched towards the rails. Finally, they topped the embankment and collapsed against a sand bunker, fighting for breath.

The injured man's eyes rolled out of sight under his eyelids as his head lolled. As Jack wrestled him upright, the man's head swung in a lazy arc, revealing a nasty swelling across the right temple. *How did I miss that?* Jack wondered.

Holding him upright, Jack probed for information without success. Using his free hand Jack searched the injured man as he drifted in and out of consciousness. His only find, a clipped return ticket from Worcester to Birkenhead, appeared from the depths of his jacket pocket. No wallet, no coins, no ration book, no identity book, no watch, no rings. With twenty minutes to wait, Jack's mind drifted towards the Sherlock Holmes stories he admired so much. He wondered what Holmes would have made of this nameless man, devoid of memory. *Could he be a German spy or a deserter? Had he been attempting to commit suicide? Could he be a homosexual or a bigamist maybe? Could he be on the run from the police or the army?* He doubted the truth of any of his speculations, though the war made all of them possible. *What did Holmes say? 'When you have eliminated the impossible, the rest, however improbable, is the truth.' It was something like that, anyway.*

This was a real live mystery, an opportunity too good to miss. Jack found himself drawn in. He needed to solve the puzzle. He believed, given time, he would.

Jack shook the man into vague consciousness.

'Listen, this is the plan. A goods train will pass in a few minutes.' Jack said, checking he understood before continuing. 'I'll flag it, to stop, then we'll ride to Ironbridge.'

Almost imperceptibly, the man nodded his battered head in acknowledgement.

'Leave the talking to me, understand?' Jack said, looking for any sort of recognition. 'When we get to the Bridge, I'll work out what to do. Remember, leave the talking to me.'

He nodded, distress etched across his haggard face.

'Look, Ironbridge is a town, but it gossips like a hamlet,' Jack said, getting to his feet. Looking down at the injured man, he continued, 'By tomorrow everyone within a mile of the Bridge will know about this.'

Jack flagged down the train. The guard's van came to a halt within twenty feet of them. *So far, so good*, thought Jack. The guard appeared from his cosy cabin scratching his head, puzzled by the unscheduled stop.

'What's up, Jack?' The guard shouted. 'Wow, he looks in a bad way!'

'He's not too bad, just shook up. Give me a hand, will you?'

Once inside the van, the stranger lost consciousness. The guard looked towards Jack for an explanation.

'Who's this, then?'

'Billy, meet my nephew, Harris.' Jack improvised.

'Not much of a family resemblance,' the guard said, looking for facial similarities and finding none.

'He's down from Scotland to visit.'

The guard nodded tentatively. Jack sensed he should give Billy a little more to chew on.

'Keep it quiet,' Jack said, tapping the side of his nose in a confidential manner. Billy looked puzzled.

'I'll be in big trouble from his mother if she finds out.' Jack said. Sensing Billy's scepticism, Jack put his arm around him and whispered, 'between you and me mate, it's a bit complicated. You know families.'

Billy nodded knowingly: 'Say no more.'

Jack relaxed until Billy asked, 'How did he get like this,' looking down thoughtfully at Harris. 'With you looking out for him and all?'

Good point, acknowledged Jack, *How, do I answer that*? Jack decided to answer as vaguely as possible allowing maximum room for manoeuvre. *Down there for dancing*, he thought, as he glanced at his boots.

'You're right. First time I take him out, he comes an absolute cropper,' Jack said, shrugging his shoulders as if to say, 'Just my luck.'

He's not buying it, he's close to smelling a rat, Jack thought.

'Picture it,' Jack said, putting his arm around Billy's shoulder again. 'I'm checking the keys, when I spot a loose one. So, I grab the key hammer and give it a whack. Except Harris here doesn't know the drill. He stands right behind me and cops my backswing on the side of his head, bosh. Down he goes like a sack of spuds and disappears over the embankment.'

Jack's sense of the dramatic encouraged him to produce a rolling action with his hand. 'If he hadn't been hurt, it would have been bloody funny!'

The two men shared a grin. *That was a close shave*, Jack thought, as he ran the back of his hand across his perspiring forehead. The goods train rumbled into Ironbridge station where, with some difficulty, they lifted Harris onto the platform.

'You should go to the hospital,' Jack said, studying the head injury.

'I feel fine, truly,' he said, wincing. 'I hate hospitals; they're full of sick people. I'll be fine by the morning.'

'What shall we do with you then?'

'Jack, I'm in your hands. I'd prefer to stay out of sight until I recover, if that's at all possible.'

'It's my cottage then.'

'Thank you.'

'When we've got settled in, I'll go down to the cop shop and see if anyone's been reported missing.'

'I'm sure they will have more important things to do. After all there must be thousands of displaced people due to the war. I wouldn't concern yourself, I'm sure it will all become clear by tomorrow.'

Jack nodded and went to borrow a goods cart from the yard. He liked Harris. Why, he couldn't say. Jack sidled towards two lads sitting on the goods yard wall.

'Give us a hand to push this barrow up the bank will you.'

They looked unenthusiastically back at Jack.

'Come on, got to get my nephew up to the cottage.'

They slid from the wall and began to slope away, ignoring Jack.

'Look, I know who you are and your school.' He had their attention. 'Help and I won't tell the school board you've been bunking off.'

After ten minutes of hard graft, they rested at Jack's garden gate, breathing heavily unable to speak. Jack threw the lads a tanner for their trouble: in short order, they were running down Bridge bank to spend it.

'Did you know those boys?'

'I know their faces.' Jack said, with a smirk.

'And which school they attended?'

'Not exactly, but there's only two in the Bridge and one in Coalbrookdale and one in Jackfield and ….'

'Do I take it you have no idea, then?'

Jack shrugged his shoulders and beamed his innocent smile. 'Come on then, let's get you into the cottage.'

Jack hauled Harris upright and, in a madcap three-legged race, propelled him towards the front door. They stepped clumsily around the prone roses before Jack shouldered the door and ducked under the threshold into the scullery. Harris wrinkled his nose involuntarily at the stale cabbage smell that inhabited the cottage.

'Best leave the door open,' Jack said, wedging it open with Nipper's bowl. 'Sit in my chair, and put your leg up on this stool,' he added, as he dragged a stool across the quarry tiles. 'I'll call at the doctor's surgery and arrange for him to call.'

'That won't be necessary, my injuries will heal. Besides, I haven't a bean,' Harris said, as he patted his pockets.

'You should see the quack. Look, I can find the fee.'

'How would I pay you back?' Harris said. 'Let's just see how I progress.'

'Maybe I'll call on the doctor tomorrow then.' Conversation eluded them as Nipper's mellifluous snores took centre stage.

Harris swivelled uncomfortably in the chair and asked, 'Jack, you don't know me, do you?'

'No, why?'

'You called me Harris.'

'Billy was getting suspicious!'

'But why Harris? Is that my name?'

'It's in your jacket,' Jack said, smiling impishly. 'All you posh boys have your names in your clothes. My brother did, when he went to Cambridge.'

Struggling upright in the chair, Harris pulled his lapel to one side. His weary face dissolved into a grin as the penny dropped.

'Jack, you're either very stupid or extremely quick witted. 'Harris' is printed on the maker's label!'

'Distinctive don't you think? It's a version of Harry, to my mind.'

'If you're so clever, what's my surname then?'

'It's next to your Christian name.'

Harris glanced down at the label and then, incredulously, back to Jack.

'My surname can't be "Tweed" for pity's sake.'

'What's your real name then? Harris Tweed sounds good to me.'

Harris shaped to answer, but a stab of pain stopped him.

'Must get back to work. Don't run away,' Jack said, with a wink.

'Before you go, will you find something for me to urinate into?'

Jack disappeared through the back door, returning with a chipped enamel bowl and a broom that had seen better days.

'Hope it's big enough,' Jack said, raising the battered bowl. 'Try this broom as a crutch if you need to move.' Jack demonstrated by turning the broom upside down and positioned the worn bristles under his armpit. Harris grimaced weakly and nodded his approval.

'Got to go,' said Jack, leaning the broom against the chair and placing the bowl at Harris's feet. Jack patted Harris's shoulder and made for the door.

Chapter 7: Open door
Later, Monday 22nd June 1942

Jack could not put his finger on it, but something about Harris reminded him of Robert, his twin. He did not look, talk or move like him: maybe he just filled the void Robert had left behind. It felt right somehow for him to be here at the cottage.

Arriving at the station yard, he decided to ask a few questions. *How could he ask questions, without giving anything away,* he thought? Be subtle. Though subtlety usually failed him, he would give it a go.

'Brushing air aye?' Jack said, with a smirk, hoping to provoke a little banter with the young, slightly cocky porter.

'Pine needles between the slabs, Station Master's orders,' the lad said, with mannerisms that suggested his disgust at being ordered to undertake such a meaningless task.

'How come?'

'A heap of trees got stored here at Christmas,' the lad said. 'From the Wye Valley.'

'He's got a point then; those needles have been there for six months.'

'You can't see them in the cracks. Waste of bloody time.'

The porter glanced up towards the grand houses on the opposite bank.

'For the Sunnysiders. Left loads of needles, they did!'

A wave of pigeons took to the air, smacking their wings as they climbed skywards, spooked by something only pigeons understood. Jack felt he had achieved some sort of rapport with the lad and risked a question.

'You on afternoons, yesterday?'

'What's it to you?' the lad said, as a mock challenge.

Jack smiled, though he felt like boxing the lad's ears for his cheek.

'Many on the evening train?'

'No one got off if that's what you mean.'

'Nobody? I'd been expecting someone see. He didn't show up.'

'There were a couple of blokes I'd never seen before, in the front carriage,' the lad said. 'Sounded like they were from the smoke.'

'How so?'

'Easy really, the one leans out the door window and asks, with a proper cockney accent, can he get back to London from here. I tell him he can, but he's best staying on till Shrewsbury. Plenty from there, I told him.'

'You gave him some good advice there,' Hoping the complement would pay dividends. 'Anything else?'

49

'Well, I had to shut the last carriage door.'

'Open, was it?'

'No - on the half latch with the window down.'

'How's that?'

'Could be someone got out at Jackfield halt and didn't bang it hard enough.'

'Ask the guard?'

'No, by the time I spotted it, they were due to leave. It was all I could do to close it proper.'

'You did well, then.'

'Thinking about it, the other chap asked did I know of a Mr Chubb from round here somewhere. I told him I thought he lived in one of the big houses over by,' he said, pointing towards Sunnyside.

'Thanks Jim, you were no help at all,' Jack said, shaking his head, feigning a show of disinterest.

'Who's this relative of yours, then?'

'Blimey, news travels fast!' Jack smacked his cap on his thigh and flipped it onto his head as a sign of amazement. 'Jim, it's been good talking to you mate but I must be getting along.'

Jack glanced down at his boots still shaking his head. 'I tell you what,' he said, glancing back up at Jim. 'You wait a while and the waggle-tongue wagers round the Bridge will tell you all about my nephew. That way you'll know more than me!'

'Spoilsport,' Jim said to Jack's back as he strode away.

I think I know who didn't close the door, thought Jack. *The question is, did he fall, did he jump or could he have been pushed?*

50

Chapter 8: A Jug to Remember
Evening 22nd June 1942

Jack, hampered by his tool bag, snap bag and a large jug of beer, barged through the heavy cottage door.

'One pint or two?' Jack announced.

Harris woke with a start blinking wildly, orienting himself. Jack dropped the bags in the corner and placed the jug reverentially on the table.

'Well then, who are you? Worked it out yet?' Jack said, pouring flat beer into two glasses. 'A beer may lubricate your memory,' Jack said, as he passed Harris a glass. 'Cheers.'

'Your health,' Harris said, through a grimace.

Nipper whimpered and twitched as she dreamed next to the range. The room filled with a vague odour of singed hair. Jack pulled the rag rug she lay on until she slid clear of the spitting fire. She slept throughout the manoeuvre.

'Before we chat about what you've remembered, we need to sort out our family connections so we're singing from the same hymn sheet,' Jack said, nodding seriously at Harris.

'Won't that sound fishy?' Harris said, looking at Jack who did not appear to understand, 'after all I have no memory.'

'But they will expect you to remember important details like family as you regain your memory.'

'But what if I don't,' Harris said, almost to himself.

'Well, you must have remembered something during the day?' Jack said, attempting to counter his apathy.

'Nothing, absolutely nothing,' Harris said, shrugging his shoulders apologetically.

'Look, I've always wanted to try something,' Jack said.

'Try something?' Harris turned to Jack with a quizzical expression.

'Use Sherlock Holmes's deduction.'

'You are pulling my leg? You must be.'

'Not at all. My Dad used to read me the stories. I loved the observation and deduction parts.'

'You would require a Watson character for authenticity?'

'You see, you have remembered something: Watson!'

'I'm not Watson.'

'No, you remembered "Watson", I meant.'

'Oh, I see,' Harris said, a little crestfallen. 'All afternoon, I've endeavoured to remember my life before today.'

'Let's hear it then.'

'Don't expect too much.'

'Stop stalling.' Jack said, with a placatory half smile.

'I remember how to sweep the floor, boil a kettle, etcetera. The problem is, I have no recollection of when I last did either!' Harris thought of another example. 'I can read and write, so I've been to school, but which school I couldn't tell you.' Showing signs of frustration, Harris continued, 'None of the Christian names I can remember feel like they belong to me.' He paused as if defeated. 'Jack, I know you better than I know myself.' He stared vacantly at his injured leg.

'Well, let's see if Holmes can help.' Jack struck what he thought to be a Holmes-like pose, all concentration and intensity.

'I don't imagine it can do any harm, assuming you don't use Watson's methods,' Harris said, with a raised eyebrow. 'Watson always got it wrong.'

'Let's start with your clothes,' Jack said, as he mimed peering through a magnifying glass. 'As a general point, your clothes are cut in a country style; they are well made and expensive. Clothing of this quality is not available in the Bridge. The jacket has leather elbow patches and a shotgun butt patch on the right shoulder: both are recent additions.'

'Pray, what inferences do you draw from your observations, Mister Holmes?'

'I deduce you are right-handed and have recently taken up shooting. You have reason to use your elbows a great deal, possibly at a desk. You have, or had, money. I don't know how much, but certainly more than me! I would also deduce you are a town dweller who aspires to country pursuits.'

'That speaks volumes, I'm sure.' Harris said, his expression lightening as a mocking grin played across his face.

'I admit it's inconclusive,' Jack said, smoking an imaginary, long-stemmed Broseley clay pipe. 'Let's study you, now.'

Jack threw his head back theatrically. Picking up Harris's right hand he began to examine it.

'You've a farmer's tan, which highlights the white band around your finger, where until recently you wore a ring.' Jack narrowed his eyes as he got into character. 'There's also an indentation in the skin which suggests the ring fitted tightly, almost certainly making it difficult to remove. It assuredly didn't fall off.' Jack looked up with obvious satisfaction.

'Pray, what conclusion do you draw Mister Holmes?' Harris felt the groove in his finger. 'Could I, perhaps, be a married man?'

'I doubt that, as it's not your ring finger.' Jack warmed to his task. 'Also, there's a less pronounced but still visible band around your left wrist, where presumably you wore a watch.'

Harris rubbed his wrist as he stared blankly. 'I have no recollection of a watch.'

'There are two possible explanations. You may have pawned your watch and ring to raise funds, or you could have been robbed.'

'Do you honestly believe that?'

'No, not really, but it does fit. There is more!'

Jack lifted a mirror from the wall and handed it to Harris. 'Study your face, do you notice anything?'

'What? Excluding the fact that I'm a rather handsome chap,' he grinned. 'I appear to have two of everything I should have two of, plus a mouth and nose. All pretty normal I would suggest, Mister Holmes.'

'Do you notice anything about your top lip?'

Harris glanced into the mirror and shrugged his shoulders.

'If you study the beard stubble above your lip, you will notice it is of uniform length, whereas the rest of your beard stubble is of varying lengths, suggesting a well-established moustache had been removed recently. I also notice your skin is lighter there, which further supports the proposition.'

'Yes, I see what you mean but is your conclusion correct? Surely, it could happen naturally, couldn't it? Even if you are correct, I don't understand how it helps.'

'I must admit neither do I, but there's something else. You may be able to see it in the mirror. Look, your hair is cut in several lengths. I would say you have been subjected to a crude hair cut recently, it's definitely not a barber's craftsmanship.'

'So, Mister Holmes, or may I call you Sherlock? What conclusion do you draw from your observations?'

'Unlike the real Holmes, I can only suggest that you were given a cheap haircut, which I hope you didn't pay for. If you did, you were robbed.'

Uncontrolled laughter filled the cottage; Nipper woke with a start and slunk behind Jack's chair. An uneasy silence settled as Jack's thoughts crystallised. He attempted to disguise his concern by lightening the mood.

'It's just a bit of fun, let's forget it. How is your leg bearing up?'

Harris twisted his hand from side to side in response, 'So so. It's improving I think.'

Jack's mind kept returning to his observations and deductions. *The missing ring and watch. The missing moustache. The poorly cut hair. Surely, Harris had attempted to hide his identity. But, from whom and why? Had he really lost his memory?*

'Maybe you'll get up the stairs in a day or two. You can have the box room.'

'I'll be fine to sleep here for now,' Harris said, patting the arm of Jack's chair.

'Some pot luck?' Jack said, glancing at Harris before ladling from the pot onto enamel plates. 'After this,' Jack said, handing Harris a plate, 'I'll be off out, for a spot of night fishing. I feel lucky tonight.'

'What are you hoping to catch?'

'Anything really.'

Chapter 9: Coney Island
Evening Thursday 25th June 1942

Jack grabbed his fishing gear from the garden shed and shut the sagging door. He thought for the hundredth time, *I should repair this door before it falls apart, though maybe it'll last a little longer?*

Pushing through the squeaky back gate, Jack and Nipper set off for the river with a spring in their steps. To save the toll they followed the railway west towards the Albert Bridge and crossed it high above the Severn. The sun slid below the horizon leaving Jack's world bathed in twilight. Scrambling down the railway embankment, he moved stealthily to the rear of the rowing club. Standing silently in the shadows, he satisfied himself that there were no prying eyes.

No, I've never found the right one, not since my Ellen, he could hear himself replying to anyone who enquired. He had no desire to marry again, far from it. Women, in his way of thinking, were wonderful creatures, but designed to be taken in small, exciting doses. He believed the excitement he sought disappeared with marriage.

Thoughts of his youthful adventures conjured a wistful smile. That day on the caterpillar ride at a seaside fairground, *where was it, could it have been Barmouth?* The ride had featured a cover that cut out all the daylight. He seemed to remember it slid over the riders on hoops.

'Around and around she goes

In the dark, nobody knows

Around and around she goes

Under the cover, anything goes,' called the fairground lad, as he randomly deployed the cover.

Jack and his girl crept back into the fairground after it closed. Jack dropped the lad two shiny half crowns in exchange for a long ride with the hood over, no questions asked. Jack and his adventurous girl rode around and around and up and down in darkness and nobody knew.

There were disasters though, along with his triumphs. A disaster that on recollection sent shivers down his spine, involved the use of the Benthall Edge Ferry. Little more than a punt, it crossed the Severn alongside the Albert rail bridge. The ferryman propelled it by pulling a rope attached to an overhead cable or punting it with a pole depending on river conditions. Jack borrowed the ferry after it closed one evening. It would be ideal for his first date with a new woman from away. Something different, something exciting he hoped.

All had gone well initially; though later, she had become extremely enthusiastic, coming close to capsizing the punt. As Jack came up for air, he found to his horror that the ferry had detached from its mooring and drifted into midstream far from the wire. He searched for the pole but the ferryman had taken the precaution of removing it. Turning unsteadily, his trousers around his ankles, he eyed the riverbank wistfully.

There was no alternative but to get into the river and kick the craft downstream towards the bank. Gasping for breath, he eventually got them to safety and clambered thankfully up the bank. Tethering the craft securely, he thanked his lucky stars that nothing worse had happened. Surprised and still breathless, he found her standing very close behind him, admiring his river-soaked frame. She wanted to thank him, again!

*****

Coney Island had always been his favourite assignation destination. Not that the others were not good, they were all good, but Coney Island would always be special. Setting off from the rowing club under the cover of darkness, he would show off his prowess as an oarsman as he moved effortlessly up stream. His enjoyment derived from the opportunity to control the tempo and direction of the evening. Jack enjoyed, anticipating each detail and running each stage through his mind, until perfect.

He also enjoyed the thrill of the chase and prided himself on his ability to discover what each woman wanted. He believed they would tell him in their own way, he just had to watch and listen. His preference had been to satisfy his date first, it seemed to work for him and them. After all, he thought, there had been no complaints. Jack also believed in the fine balance between a willing daring woman and a willing demanding woman. He credited himself with the ability to spot the difference on most occasions, though not always.

Jack's eye accustomed itself to the growing darkness. Some people in the Bridge thought him a shirker. After all, he looked fine. Why wasn't he in uniform, they would ask behind his back. Only he and the army board knew the true extent of his injuries. He did not want to feel less than whole or pitied as an invalid.

Banishing thoughts of his injury he began to think about the new woman he would meet in a few minutes. They had met in the baker's a week ago and strolled together up to Broseley, while she chatted away thirteen to the dozen. Eventually, she agreed to meet him under the Albert. Jack thought she could be a nurse or a barmaid. He liked the straightforward types. An incomer, he was not sure where from. Wherever it was they had lost out: she was a real cracker.

Finding the chain and lock he deftly inserted his copy key and manipulated it until, with a light click, it sprung open. Crouching on the rough boarded landing stage, he slid the chain through the securing ring and then stepped into the boat. Placing the oars in the rowlocks, he settled himself, then, with a few powerful strokes, he propelled the boat to the far bank. Nipper watched from the safety of the rowing club steps. Jack pulled hard into the base of the Albert, its abutments towering above him, blotting out the moonlight. A sticky humid day had faded into sultry evening. Perfect, he thought.

A nervous but excited whisper asked, 'Jack, is that you?'

'Yes, can you see your way down the bank?'

'I think so.'

'Come to the edge. Don't be worried, I'll help you.'

He extended his hand encouragingly. She appeared nervous as she stared into the gloom and the boat below.

'It's perfectly safe, I've done this hundreds of times before,' Jack said, as encouragement, but then regretted his lack of tact. Realising his error, he attempted a recovery. 'Don't worry, I've been messing about in boats on the river here since I was a lad,' he said, staying close to the truth.

He guided her into the boat and then to the rear seat.

'Would you like a blanket?' He said, placing the blanket on her knees before she could reply. *A nifty ice-breaker, all part of the plan*, Jack thought. Returning to the oars he began to row powerfully against the current, watched admiringly by what he hoped would be his latest conquest. He enjoyed the intimacy of their private world.

She appeared to enjoy the ease with which they could chat, sitting face to face, as he rowed. His plan involved rowing to Coney Island. Local folklore had it that rabbits were bred there centuries ago. With any luck, he planned to be mimicking the rabbits, and not by eating grass.

Rowing had many advantages, Jack thought: if conversation stalled, the rhythmic progression of rowing helped to fill the void. Each stroke started with a muffled slap as the blades cut into the river accompanied by a slight squeak from the rowlocks as he pulled on the oars. The bow rose and ploughed through the current, issuing a subtle whoosh, followed by the pattering rain of water droplets shed from the oar tips as they swung back to start the cycle once more.

'So, what do you do Jack?' She said, surprising him that she had taken the initiative.

'I work for the GWR.'

'I know that much, what do you do?'

'How do you know? I can't remember telling you,' he said with an eyebrow raise of surprise.

'I've been asking around; you'll be surprised what I know about you,' she said, pulling the rug from her knees before folding and stowing it behind her.

'What do you know?'

'You're called Jackson, Jack for short. You're a widower. You have a son who doesn't live with you. You have a mysterious lodger. You were demobilised from the war, no one knows why. You were wild and dangerous before the war. You were a bit of a lad, a lady's man......'

'Whoa, hold your horses there, enough ....'

'Jack, am I safe with you?'

'Of course, you are, I wouldn't hurt a fly.' Jack said, giving her what he hoped would be a reassuring smile. She returned the smile in her own crooked way.

Within ten minutes, they reached the power station bridge, his first landmark. Its girders silhouetted against the moonlit sky reminded him of the bridges of small town America he had seen in black and white films. Beyond the bridge, they could make out the squat brooding pumping house. Jack described how the blackout had spoilt the strange lighting effects. How in the past a ghoulish light would have reflected haphazardly through the myriad of small panes that made up the massive windows.

A low hum of electric motors pulsed from the bowels of the building adding to the eerie atmosphere he attempted to create. He pointed to twelve giant pipes, just visible in the dusk. They protruded from the building's foundations before arcing below the river's shiny surface. When the pumps sucked water from the river, whirlpools formed around the pipes, giving the impression that the boat and occupants could be sucked from the river's surface.

The whole effect could be disturbing for Jack's women. They would draw themselves in and look to him for reassurance, which he would willingly bestow, all part of the plan. Having offered her reassurance and flashing her his best smile, he rowed further upstream towards the oasis of Coney Island.

Jack manoeuvred the boat into placid water and beached smoothly on a small sand bar. He helped her step onto dry land, *so far so good*, he thought. She clung to him, trembling with relief, or excitement, he could not tell. Jack spread the blanket across the sand in the boat's lea. He had planned meticulously and enjoyed the anticipation of being subtly in control. He anticipated that they would lie down on the rug and chat comfortably, as they stared through the overhanging branches towards the stars and moon.

He glanced at her face, to his surprise, she appeared unfazed by the journey or the isolation of the island. He had worked hard to create an atmosphere where she felt reliant upon him, allowing him to dictate the pace and direction of the assignation. She, however, had not read the script and appeared extremely comfortable and a little excited by the situation. Pulling away from him, she fixed him with a wicked leer and began to undress. Swaying to an imaginary big band, she removed her blouse and bra. Naked from the waist, she proudly displayed her breasts. Jack trembled with a heady mixture of excitement and concern. He had lost the initiative. He had not planned for this.

She glided sensuously towards him, swaying to the music in her head. Jack took mental steps backwards as she drew close. Not unlike a rabbit caught in a lamper's light, he found himself rooted to the spot. Leaning heavily against him, she threaded her arms around his neck before pulling him slowly towards the rug and enveloping him in the longest kiss he had ever experienced.

She missed the eerie coracle bobbing silently past on the current. Jack nodded to the poacher, the poacher nodded back. They were both where they should not be, doing things they should not do. Nothing would be said.

Jack's women were often reflective on the return journey, watching Jack for signs of reassurance. The journey could be pleasant enough, though subdued, neither party committing themselves. This evening had been different: she chatted all the way back, he couldn't get a word in edgewise. She complimented him on his rowing technique, though he would have preferred to be complimented on other aspects of the evening. When it came to their goodbyes, she gave him a sloppy kiss and pinched his bum with such gusto the boat rocked. Jack helped her safely onto the bank and turned to go.

'Jack, I'm sorry, I don't want to hurt your feelings, but I don't think I can do this again.'

Surprised, Jack attempted to disguise his inward sigh of relief.

'You see my hubby, Reg, well he's due home, on leave.'

Jesus, I didn't need to know his name, Jack cringed.

'He's been wounded, I'm not sure how badly yet.'

Hell, I feel bad enough already, don't go on. Please, go home missus.

'Of course, if he can't do it, if you know what I mean,' she said, raising the hem of her dress. 'I'll come looking for you Jack, for a bit of extra.'

With a wink, she disappeared into the blackness.

Not if I see you coming first, he thought, pulling hard on the oars.

Chapter 10: On the Mend
Monday 29th June 1942

As his injuries healed, Harris progressed from Jack's broom to a gnarled walking stick loaned by George. Filling two stomachs and finding clothes for Harris with one ration book severely dented Jack's wage packet, leaving little money for the pub. Jack made ends meet by the use of his own currency: rabbits. Most tradesmen in the Bridge were amenable to a spot of barter and happily accepted rabbits in trade for under-the-counter items. Although Jack would not have admitted to anyone else, he enjoyed his enforced evenings at the cottage. Supper invariably came from the pot over the range, though occasionally he endured a burnt offering especially cremated by Harris.

After clearing away and washing the pots, they habitually settled by the fire. Jack would watch its flickering reflections dance across the ceiling, while Harris read Sherlock Holmes stories aloud. It amused them both to attribute the traits of Holmes and Watson to each other, both thought themselves closer to Holmes and the other closer to Watson.

'You can't be Holmes, you like women too much,' Harris said, with a cheeky grin.

Jack, stung by Harris's insight, thought, *who's he been gossiping with?*

'Well, that also applies to you as well, I hope,' Jack said, with a knowing look. 'I wouldn't want anyone to think I lived in the same house as a man who didn't like women.'

'Touché!' Harris raised his hands in mock surrender. 'No need to worry on that score.'

'Pleased to hear it.'

'You're Watson, though. You're an army man, you carry a gun and you've been married. I rest my case.'

'Watson was a medical doctor, an officer, a gentleman and a crack shot with a revolver. Me, I was a private in the engineers and fired a rifle badly. I could never be accused of being a gentleman. I just don't see any similarity.'

'What is your surname, Jack?'

Surprised by the question and apparent change of subject, Jack answered evenly, 'Hailstone, why?'

'Well, assuming I'm Tweed, we would be Hailstone and Tweed or Tweed and Hailstone, not in the same league as Holmes and Watson.'

'Sounds like a firm of undertakers or solicitors.'

'Jack, you tell a good story. Ever considered writing them as short stories, like Watson?'

Jack looked perplexed. 'I don't read well, you know that, why would I want to write?'

'Fair point,' Harris nodded. 'It's just I hear that at the Institute, the WEA are offering weekly evening classes in creative writing.'

Jack stared impassively at Harris, determined not to show interest.

'Why not have a try?' Harris said, employing his best placatory body language.

'Can't afford it,' Jack said, dismissing the suggestion as he looked away.

'It's free from charge,' Harris said, to Jack's back. 'The WEA is a charity.'

Jack's intransigent look said he would not be persuaded. Harris, peeved at his resistance, stared him down, forcing him to respond.

'Look, I don't want to show myself up, alright and I don't need charity.'

'What if I attended with you?'

'But, you never leave the cottage.'

'True, though for this I'll make an exception.'

'Let it drop, will you?' Jack said, with a peevish glare. 'Is the paper near you?'

Harris picked it up and offered it, but Jack ignored the gesture.

'Anything on at the flicks?'

Harris opened the paper without enthusiasm, turning the pages languidly until he found the cinema times.

'There's "The Philadelphia Story" on at the Central at eight or there's "The Hound of the Baskervilles" at the Plaza at seven thirty.'

'No contest, "The Hound" it is. Come on, shake yourself, we'll just catch it if we get a move on.'

'I'll stay in, thank you.'

'Come on, don't be a spoilsport.'

67

'My leg is giving me jip, so I'll give it a miss, if you don't mind.'

Jack banged the front door rather harder than he expected to. *Good job the bluff worked, wouldn't want Harris to know what went on out here in the dark*, he thought, as he made for his kingdom. Taking to the track, he ambled towards the west and a falling sun shrouded in powdery clouds. Crossing the Albert, he glanced down at the rowing boats and smiled to himself. Scrambling down the embankment at Station Road, he cut through to Dale End where he joined the queue at the Plaza.

They paid separately but found each other in the dark. Disappointed by his lukewarm greeting, Vera squeezed his thigh. Jack put his arm around her shoulder and attempted to banish a strange feeling that he had been followed. *Had there been someone watching from the shadows across the street*? Jack thought with a tremor. *Did I imagine it, or was someone there?*

Chapter 11: The First, First Friday Club Meeting
Friday 3rd July 1942

'Come on George,' Bill said, steering him towards the bar. 'It's your round.'

George was not so sure, begrudgingly, he ordered three pints. Triangulating the brimming glasses, he gingerly lifted them from the sticky bar and dripped his way towards their quiet corner table. George placed the pints reverently in the centre of the table amongst the circular stains of pint glass and cigarette burns. Picking up the pints, they chinked glasses and chorused, 'Cheers.'

'Before we start, Bill has something to say.'

'A matter of urgency,' Bill said.

'What's the joke?' Jack said, his glass half way to his mouth. He sensed George had attempted to stifle a grin.

'No joke, it's serious. It could jeopardise our agreement.'

'"Jeopardise"? Never heard that word from you before, have you been practising? Come on, out with it.'

'We've heard from reliable sources that you may be batting for the other side.'

They both watched Jack's face intently over their pints. He gave nothing away, forcing them to elaborate.

'Have you gone queer?' George said, straining to avoid a chuckle, his eyes warning Bill not to give the game away.

'What makes you ask?'

'Well, you've got a live-in chap, from away, haven't you?' George said, looking pointedly at Jack.

'And you told Mrs Steele he's your nephew. Sounds fishy to us,' Bill said.

'He doesn't work, apparently. Is he your kept man?' George said.

'Or boy,' Bill added.

Jack kept his own council, [counsel] waiting for an opening to get his own back. Bill and George ploughed on.

'It's illegal even…' George said.

'More importantly, the good-looking women in the Bridge want confirmation before they look elsewhere,' Bill said, nearly messing up the punch line as he attempted to keep a straight face.

'And the not so good-looking women,' Jack said, joining the joke.

'Oh, them too,' Bill said.

Convulsions of laughter rocked the table; beer slopped from full glasses; other drinkers stared.

Sipping their pints in silence, they scanned the bar for nosey parkers. Having satisfied themselves there were no inquisitive ears tuning in, the meeting began in earnest. To everyone's disappointment, they soon realised that, even collectively, they had made little progress towards a solution. They eventually decided to search for information at the Reading Library in Madeley and the Institute in Ironbridge. George described the meeting as 'a bit of a damp squib' with a long face before nudging Bill.

'Go on then,' George said.

'Look Jack, me and George have been chatting ... we don't think your idea of a tontine is going to work.'

'Well ...'

Bill cut Jack off, saying, 'Good idea and all that, but we'll crack it soon, so we don't need a tontine.'

'Anyway, it's your round,' George said, studying Jack.

'Are you sure?' Jack said, with a questioning glance at the bar.

'Very sure. I got the last one and Bill got the first.'

Jack feigned incredulity as he moved towards the bar.

'Three pints of best and whatever you're having,' Jack said, smiling one of his special smiles at the barmaid.

'A bottle of Mackie then, thanks.'

'You're new in the Bridge, aren't you?'

'Second day.'

'Behind the bar?'

'No, second day in Ironbridge. I'm up from Ludlow, staying with my Uncle.'

'You working Saturday night?'

'Don't think so.'

'How about meeting me under the Albert at dusk.'

'You're a bit fresh.'

'Ask anyone, they'll tell you where it is. I'm Jack by the way. What's yours?'

'Jane, but ...'

Jack could see she had become flustered, but could not stop himself.

'See you Saturday then, Jane.'

'I'll bring your pints across when they've settled, shall I?' she said, avoiding eye contact, feeling embarrassed in front of the other drinkers. 'Where are you sitting?'

'Over there with those two old boys.' Jack said, smiling at her and pointing to Bill and George before sauntering back to his stool. She looked to be half his age, but Jack worked on the principle that if you did not ask, you did not get.

'Where's the beer then?' asked a thirsty voice.

'Give it a rest will you! The cracking new barmaid will bring them over when they've cleared and she's topped them off.'

A few impatient minutes later Jane appeared at the table with three clear brimming pints.

'You want to watch this one,' George said, with a knowing wink.

Jane coloured, staring pointedly at the empty tray, trying desperately to avoid eye contact with any of the men.

'You don't want to believe everything you hear about me,' Jack said, evenly.

'Just most of it,' Bill said, smirking to George.

Jane had turned and was halfway back to the bar when she gave Jack a coy smile over her shoulder.

'What about a story?' Bill said, beaming playfully at Jack. 'Go on, you know you want to.'

'Tell the one about the toff from London,' George said.

Jack maintained that his collection of yarns were all true accounts, though he didn't let the odd fact spoil a good story. He enjoyed the challenge of working himself into the story, usually in a cameo role in each of his stories. Taking a swig of beer to wet his whistle, Jack began.

'Well, he wasn't really a toff so to speak, more of an ex-military kind of a bloke. All waxed moustache, tweeds and carrying an umbrella in swagger stick style. Let's call him the "The Colonel". You know the sort, all self-important, present and correct, public school and all the trimmings.

'Apparently, he had come down from the main line on the Dodger. He got out at Coalport LNWR station. He's arrived for a business meeting at the China Works, which must be half a mile from the station.'

'Coalport is the terminus, he'd have to get out there,' George said sniggering.

Bill gave him a cautionary nod; they both knew Jack did not appreciate interruptions.

'Look, who's telling this story? Do you want to take over?'

'No, no. You carry on by all means. Don't mind him, Jack.'

George mimed closing an imaginary zip across his mouth and winked at Bill. Jack looked up at the ceiling with a resigned look, exhaling noisily. After a short disciplinary pause, he restarted the story.

'Well, as it happens, the Colonel is most put out at having to walk that far. He could be heard muttering, "Damn poor show".

73

Anyhow, after the meeting he planned to travel to Worcester from Coalport GWR, which as you know gentlemen, is across the river and a long walk via the Woodbridge. Anyway, he enquires what transport is available. Unfortunately, for him, he's askin' in a very high-handed manner, so of course no one wants to help.

Spotting an opportunity to have some fun, I bounced up and suggested that he could take the ferry across to the other side and catch a train from Jackfield halt, instead of walking all the way back to Coalport. "It's directly across the river sir," I tell him.

He doesn't know but I've entered him into a wild goose chase, as I know the ferry's out of the river being repaired. So our military man steps lively down to the ferry only to find it is out of service. By now he's bristling with indignation and his own self-importance, so not to be thwarted he hails this boatman who's floating passed in his coracle, minding his own business.

Well, as you can imagine, the boatman paddles alongside and asks what all the noise is about. The Colonel blusters a bit then offers him half a crown to take him across. You didn't see money like that often, especially in those days, so the boaty agrees and pockets the money.

Well, boaty soon begins to regret takin' his money, as the Colonel has no idea how to get aboard, spinning the coracle round and nearly tipping it up. Eventually, he's settled on the seat alongside the boaty, it's snug to say the very least. Anyway, at about the midpoint the Colonel starts waxing lyrical about the view and with an extravagant sigh, he leans his chin heavily on his hands, hands that are holding his brolly. You can see it happening can't you, gentlemen? The point of the brolly is resting on the bottom and what's the bottom made of?'

Jack looked to his audience for the answer.

'Cow hide,' they said in unison, nodding to each other.

'And how strong is cow hide?' Jack said, encouraging his audience with a wave of his hand.

74

'Not very,' chorused Bill and George with anticipatory grins.

'So where does the point of the brolly go?'

'Straight through,' they said, with pantomime timing.

'You've got it. The Colonel is about to make a tricky situation a whole lot worse. Without engaging his brain, he grips the brolly and makes to pull it out. At this point the boaty grabs him firmly by the arm and yells at him like he's never been yelled at before in his life. You know, like a Sergeant Major style to a raw recruit.

"Don't pull it out you silly bugger!" The Colonel has never been spoken to like that before and gets all flustered.

"Now listen here my man, there's no call for that kind of language."

Without releasing him, Boaty looks him square in the eyes and says, "You better be very sure of two things before you pull that out, sir. One, that you can swim in your clothes in fast flowing water, and two, if you survive that, that you can fight a very angry boatman."'

Jack waited for the smiles of appreciation to recede and then continued.

'Anyway, they press on towards the other bank with the Colonel looking rather sheepish. Then just out of reach of the bank, Boaty stops and extracts another half-crown from the Colonel for repairs. After paying up, the Colonel is now even more flustered and attempts a dismount, but stands far too rapidly for stability. Fortunately, the Boaty had anticipated him making an arse of the manoeuvre and has his paddle down steadying the craft. Unfortunately for the Colonel, he loses his balance and is forced to make a desperate lunge for the bank. With one foot on the bank and the other in the shallows, he turns to see Boaty pulling away effortlessly downstream with the brolly standing up like a mast. The Colonel was last seen shaking his fist and shouting that he would, "Report this to a higher authority!"

The short trip cost the Colonel five shillings, his umbrella and a wet leg into the bargain. To add insult to injury, the story goes that he arrived at Jackfield Halt just in time to sniff the drifting smoke left by his recently departed train.'

They had heard the story before but never tired of it as Jack embellished it at each retelling. Laughter and toothy grins broke out as they drained the dregs of their pints. Nipper lay under the table amongst the fag ash, cigarette butts, dried mud and wrappers. She watched Jack patiently for any sign that it may be time to go home to the fire. An exuberant voice called out, 'one for the ditch', as they swayed ever so slightly along their well-trodden path to the bar.

Chapter 12: The Horse and the Lady
Monday 7th July 1942

Jack stood stiffly, palms supporting the base of his spine, a grimace spread across his upturned face. Today he felt every one of his forty-two years. Feeling a little sorry for himself, he decided to take a break as an agitated voice rang out from the nearby lane.

'Hello, hello? You over there.'

Jack twisted towards the voice, a questioning look on his face.

'Yes you. Will you help, please?'

Jack could see a woman fighting to stay in control of a spooked stallion that appeared determined to unseat her. Forgetting his discomfort, Jack covered the ground swiftly. Taking the bridle commandingly, he calmed the animal. The rider dismounted in a flurry of boots and skirts. She flashed Jack a relieved, lop-sided smile. In that moment, it struck him how familiar she appeared. *Did he know this woman, surely, he did*? She smiled once more, this time at his puzzled look.

'Have you seen a ghost?' she said, as Jack's mind raced to catch up. His face betrayed his confusion: she obviously knew him.

Her face became tense as she picked her words. 'If I asked you, this time, would you stand me up again?'

Astonished, Jack rocked back onto his heels.

That smile is so distinctive. That's it yes, at the fete all those years ago, the same eyes.

'But, I was there.' Jack said, almost stuttering.

'You were where?'

'Yes, under the Albert.' Jack said, earnestly.

'I don't understand. Where exactly were you?' Her face relaxed gently as a germ of an explanation took root. 'Which side?'

'Moneyside,' Jack said, as if it were obvious.

'Sunnyside,' she said, as her shoulders sagged. Frustrated, she added, 'If I ask you this time, will you be there Jackson?'

'I'll be there.' Jack said, beaming his best smile.

'Yes, but which side?'

'Sunnyside then, if it suits you.'

She nodded.

'At dusk then,' he said, with a wink.

The stallion suddenly became restless jerking its halter from Jack's grip and abruptly ending their conversation.

'Saturday!' she shouted over her shoulder.

'Sunnyside!' he shouted back.

Within seconds they were gone, rider and horse galloping as one.

Jack squinted against the late afternoon sun as he trudged home. He began to recall how they first met. He remembered wondering if the church fete would be as rewarding as in previous years. Dressed in his best, he had cut quite a dash. To a stranger, he could have been a stationmaster or the goods manager, but definitely not a fitter.

He had felt the warmth of the sun on his back as he stepped from the shade of a Malthouse into the open fields. All around him people from the Bridge and surrounding villages were enjoying themselves.

His preference had been for married women, bored women, women with too much to lose. He liked good-looking women, though more importantly, he was drawn to women with danger in their eyes.

Losing interest in the tombola stall, he turned towards the bandstand, inadvertently blocking the path of a young woman. His eyes met their match. They stood face-to-face, toe-to-toe and far too close for comfort on such a public occasion. A quick glance told him she wore neither wedding nor engagement rings. Her eyes? Oh my lord, she possessed danger in those smouldering blue eyes. His usual self-assuredness deserted him. Hesitating, heart in mouth, he willed himself to speak.

Three unheard, unseen beats of a baton dismissed any thoughts of conversation as an enthusiastic brass band burst into life destroying any possibility of conversation. She smiled an apology and with a slight nod of her head turned away from his disoriented gaze. Dissolving easily into the throng gathered around the refreshment tent she disappeared from view. Longing to pursue her, but too embarrassed to follow, he remained rooted to the spot.

Desire gradually overcame his embarrassment, though by then she had merged with the crowd, becoming a single fish within a shoal. He thought rapidly, *how will I find her? Has she wandered towards the river,* he wondered. Or *maybe she would be promenading along the path amongst the throng of strollers.*

Reaching the river, he scanned the crowds for her, without success. Faced with the choice of turning left towards the Bridge or right towards the Boat Club and the Albert, he tossed a coin: heads for the Bridge, tails for the Albert. The coin chose incorrectly.

Nursing a pint in the Station hotel later that evening, he replayed their brief meeting over and over in his head. *Did she live somewhere in the Gorge? Why hadn't he spotted her before? Could she be a visitor? Had that been the local weekly paper in her basket? Worth a try*, he thought. An appeal in the personal column just might work. He began to compose a notice that he hoped she would recognise.

'To the bluest eyes at the summer fete, meet me, under the Albert at dusk on Saturday week. Tongue-tied Jackson.'

Why Jackson, he wondered, why not Jack, the name everyone knew in the Bridge? Maybe, he thought, he could be a different person with her.

He had hoped she would meet him under the Albert, but not ten years later.

Chapter 13: Under the Albert
Saturday 11th July 1942

Jack helped her aboard. She sat motionless, as if waiting for something, though Jack could not fathom what. From the moment he caught sight of her under the Albert he knew tonight would be different, it must be. She looked so different from the other women, radiating something intangible that he knew he had not experienced for many years.

He found difficulty, retaining eye contact, his eyes longing to explore her hourglass figure. Pulling himself together, he shivered with embarrassment as he recalled his original plan. Coney Island would not be in the script tonight; there had been an impromptu rewrite.

Rowing upstream, he encouraged her to talk about herself. For the first time for many years he wanted to listen and really understand. She spoke with gripping intensity. Her story enveloped him as they drifted on the current.

Something special started under the Albert on that evening. As she faded into the darkness, he felt both elated and troubled. He did not want to let this lady go or share her with anyone else. She talked to him as Jackson, tongue-tied Jackson. No one called him Jackson. Maybe Jackson could live a different life with her and leave Jack behind.

Christened Eleanor, she asked him to call her Ellie, though to him she would always be his Lady, the Lady Eleanor. Her father been killed in the first war. He died an inglorious, meaningless death, like millions of others from both sides. That he should be killed in the last week of the conflict took meaninglessness to a new level. She had been eight at the time of his death, one of five brothers and sisters. Their mother managed to cling on to the family home gallantly for nearly ten years before the bank eventually foreclosed on their outstanding loans.

Her mother's elder sister came to the family's rescue, offering them a roof over their heads at her home in Birmingham. Her sister and husband were childless; their house was large but too small to accommodate all of the children, especially an eighteen-year old, who longed for her own room. In truth, Eleanor wanted to stay near the Bridge, though she could not have explained why.

Her mother found the solution. Pragmatically, she persuaded the wife of a local industrialist to employ Eleanor as a stable girl. Her mother referred to the woman as her Ladyship, not a title, a nickname and very much tongue in cheek. Her mother and her Ladyship were well acquainted, though the relationship had not been common knowledge. They had boarded together at a Warwickshire finishing school. In reality, the arrangement came down to good old-fashioned blackmail. Her Ladyship's secret early life had been colourful and potentially embarrassing to both her Ladyship and her husband. Agreement had been easily reached.

Ellie had a comfortable room, in what had been the servants' quarters. She loved working with the horses; it had been a childhood dream come true. She missed her family, but gradually came to terms with her situation.

Her employers treated her with the consideration usually afforded to a distant member of the family. Over time, she became her Ladyship's confidante, aiding and abetting her many affairs. Despite her loyalty, she struggled to understand what drove her mistress to wander. Her husband appeared kind and possessed an elegance she had not experienced in a man before. She believed boredom lay behind her infidelities, as he habitually absented himself for long periods to deal with business in London.

Two years later, out of a clear blue sky, a chain of events was set in motion which would change Eleanor's life again. Her Ladyship frequently rode to hounds: as a prominent horsewoman, she received numerous invitations to join hunts throughout the county and beyond. On one such outing, she became separated from a trailing group as she rode across unfamiliar country. Her impetuosity drove her to jump the wrong fence in an attempt to catch up. The fence she jumped in ignorance guarded the vertical face of a disused quarry.

Little more than a year later, Ellie, now twenty-five, became the industrialist's wife.

Chapter 14: A Job for Harris
Wednesday 14th July 1942

'Fancy a job this summer?' Jack said, as he settled down opposite Harris.

'Not physical work, I hope.'

'Using your head, not your leg,' Jack said, attempting to gauge his interest. 'They need a schoolmaster type up at the big house.'

'Schoolmaster type?'

'To take lessons in the school summer holidays.'

'And how did you discover this opportunity?' Harris said, smelling a rat.

'Through a friend of a friend, you know how it goes?' Jack said, adopting a mischievous expression.

'Who says I could teach children?'

'You've been a kid and you went to a good school, end of story.'

'Just 'cos I can talk proper, don't mean I can do teachin'.' Harris said, theatrically wiping his nose with the back of his hand. 'How am I gonna do it, eh? Answer me that, mister clever clogs.'

Jack's face flushed with exasperation. 'Look, I don't want you to get all big headed but you were mustard at that WEA lesson last week. You're a natural.'

'Thank you for the compliment, though I believe your confidence is misplaced,' Harris said, with a stately bow.

'You'd be great,' Jack paused, as if picking his words. 'The job's yours, if you want it,' he said, with a serious nod of authority.

'When would I start?'

'A couple of weeks.'

'A fortnight,' Harris said, his voice reaching another key. 'Let me consider it, it's not much time to get organised.'

'Can't hold the job for long, make your mind up.'

'Shall we change the subject?' Harris suggested. 'What about your five-hundred-word short story?' He said, looking up from the newspaper.

'Haven't thought about it.' Jack said, a little too petulantly.

'It's me you're talking to, Jack. I'll bet you have been planning it since the last lesson.'

'I have thought about it, nothing written down though. How about you?'

'Need you ask?' Harris said, as he gave Jack a sideways glance as he folded the paper into his lap. 'How do I create a story based on a childhood memory, without a memory?'

85

'The key is creating. Just make something up.'

'Mister Thomas told the class most novice writers write about themselves, the people they know and the places and events they have experienced. Pray tell me how do I achieve that?' Harris said, spreading his arms in protest.

'But ...'

'But nothing. The only solution is for me to write about one of your childhood memories.'

'Okay.'

'A suggestion,' Harris said, becoming animated. 'Give me a headline for some of your memories and I'll pick one.'

'Come again?'

'"Chicken kills boy" or "girl, seven-foot-tall", that sort of thing.'

'Very well, Watson, I'm a storyteller, not a newspaper seller. But I'll have a go.' Jack said, theatrically scratching his head. 'How about: "homemade firework explodes in boy's face" or "pop bottles missing from pub yard" then there's "pig trips boy" and "boys make a ha'penny into a penny" or "cyclist falls from bike, frightened by leaves" ....?'

'Stop, stop, no more please.' Harris said, holding his hands in surrender.

'Which one takes your fancy?'

'The boy and the pig sounds interesting.'

'Are you sure?' Jack said, though nothing would stop him now. 'Well, before my twin brother, Robert, left to take up his scholarship, we got up to all sorts of mischief together. We both worked evening paper rounds in different parts of the town. We'd race to finish our rounds and meet up under the bridge and have a bit of fun before we went home.'

'Fun?'

'Kid's stuff, throwing stones at the faces, that sort of thing, just horsing about'

'Who's faces?'

'Just the faces in the bridge.'

'Help me.'

'Well if you look at a certain angle you can see the profile of two faces where the bridge ribs are bolted together in the middle. I'll show you.'

'If you say so?'

'Anyway, on this particular evening it's already gone dark, when we spot this cat coming towards us, carrying a dead mouse. The cat hasn't seen us. Anyway, we jump out to scare it and it drops the mouse and hops it. So, we're thinking what mischief can we get up to with this mouse. Then Robert comes up with this idea of sneaking up to a privy when there's a woman in there and chucking the mouse under the door to see how loud she screams.

'Down by the river there's some cottages where the privies are near the lane at the back. So, we hid in the lane and waited for someone to shuffle out to the thunder box. Anyway, we aren't waiting long before we see the reflections of a candle flickering in a jar and hear the privy door close. As we didn't hear any footsteps we assume it's a light-footed woman. So, Robert shimmies over the wall, tiptoes up to the privy, then fires the mouse under the door.

'We're surprised when there's no reaction, no scream, nothing. Next thing, this massive hobnail boot crushes the mouse and the door starts to open. Robert turns to run but in the dark, he hasn't noticed that the family's pig has come to see what the fuss is about. The pig has a sty but for some reason they let it have the run of the back at night as a guard pig or something. Anyway, the pig is mostly black and just about invisible against the darkness of the back yard. So, Robert spins to run away but falls headlong over the pig that's now standing right behind him. Anyway, over he goes, straight into the mud and slop. To make things worse, the old boy catches him a good one round the ear and sends him sprawling again. The only good thing is that his face is now covered in so much mud that the old boy couldn't have recognised him, even if he'd been his own son. By this time, I've loosed the gate, Robert makes his escape, but so does the pig.

'Picture the scene. The old boy is standing by the gate trying to decide who to chase, the pig or us: the pig is off in one direction and us the other. Lucky for us he chose the pig.

'We arrived back under the bridge unscathed. After we got our breath back and manage to stop laughing, we tried to clean Robert up a bit. But, it didn't do much good, he was still full of mud and ponged a bit too. He told Mum he fell over on his paper round and got a good ear bending for it, but that was the height of it, we got away with it by the skin of our teeth.

Well, what do you think? Any good?'

'How did the old boy get out of the privy so briskly?'

'Well, we think he had just gone out to read the paper or smoke. Whatever he was doing, he had his trousers on. That's how he was so quick out of the blocks.'

Harris nodded his head lazily, imagining the scene.

'Jack, that must be your short story. I can hear you now, reading it out to a spellbound audience. Assuming the old boy isn't one of them.'

They guffawed like school boys at the thought.

'Tell me the ha'penny story.'

'Okay, here we go. Robert and me used to get up early on Saturday and Sunday mornings and do a circuit of the pubs in the hope of finding coins dropped in the dark by the drunks. Quite often, we'd be lucky. We found a joey and a florin but mainly coppers. We had slim pickings for a couple of weeks; anyway, this time Robert finds a ha'penny. We were both set on buying aniseed balls but they were a penny, so we were stumped.

'I came up with the idea of putting the ha'penny on the railway line for a train to squeeze into a penny size. We gave it a try, but ended up being disappointed, the train made it bigger alright, but it didn't look anything like a coin anymore, so we lost out all ways round.'

Harris offered a polite smile. 'How about the one about the boy, the bicycle and the leaves? Any beer left? I'm parched, listening to you.'

'Not as parched as I am, telling stories,' Jack said, pouring beer into his glass. Refreshed after a couple of swallows, Jack handed the jug back to Harris and started.

'Well, one year we had a very dry summer. It was so dry the leaves withered on the trees, and as soon as autumn came they all fell at the same time. Strong winds then blew them into drifts. Robert and me, we were about twelve or thirteen I would think. We were out playing down by the goods yard in the early evening twilight. We decided to make the piles even bigger by pushing several smaller piles together. Eventually, we decided to push all the heaps together and make one massive pile. It was so big we could crawl inside; it covered both of us with ease.

But the leaves rustled with every move and got down our trousers and jumpers, it began to become uncomfortable and we were getting bored just lying there. Then I got this idea that we could jump up and scare people who were passing. Robert thought it would be magic, so we waited for the sounds of wheels or footsteps coming our way. We lay there silent as mice for ages. We were about to give up when we heard the sound of a horse clopping towards us. We peeped out and recognised the GWR delivery cart coming back to the yard for the night. The driver looked to be half asleep, all hunched up and his head lolling forward. The horse obviously knew the way back to the yard and its hay.

We waited until the horse was alongside, then we sprang up in a cloud of leaves. Our timing was spot on. The frightened horse jerked forward sending the driver onto his back, his legs and arms flailing like an upturned beetle. Anyway, the driver jumps from the cart swearing away, all set to chase us, but we legged it. Meanwhile, the horse hasn't broken stride clopping its way towards the yard, so the driver is forced to chase the cart.

When we got back under the bridge we decided it had been so much fun that we would do it again the following evening. This time we'd do it to this lad called Jimmy. We knew Jimmy from school, he used to go to choir practice and we thought he was a bit of a sissy, we bet he'd be an easy target. At school, he'd brag that his Dad let him borrow his bike on choir nights; it just had to be done.

We worked out that we wouldn't be able to hear the bike coming, unlike the horse, so we got in place under the leaves, taking cardboard tubes with us as peep holes so we could see Jimmy. More or less on time, we spotted Jimmy through the tubes. He was riding his Dad's adult-sized bike unsteadily. His legs were too short to sit on the saddle and reach the pedals so his body moved up and down and side to side with the motion of the pedals, a bit like a seesaw.

Like the evening before, we bided our time until Jimmy was ten feet or so away and then jumped up into the air screaming like banshees. We must have frightened Jimmy half to death. He lost control, and with an extravagant wobble, he veered towards us instead of away. His change of direction caught us out. Robert and me were frozen to the spot as Jimmy hurtled towards us. We all fell into the pile of leaves and ended up in a tangle. Fortunately, none of us lads were more than shaken up, but most importantly, Jimmy's Dad's bike survived unscathed.

'After the initial shock, Jimmy thought it was a real hoot, and asks if he could do it with us the following night. If I remember, a game of conkers got in the way of repeating the prank, thank goodness.'

'That's excellent material for a short story but I couldn't tell it.'

'Try imagining a story then. I just did with the leaf story.' Jack said, as he thought; *Talk your way out of that one, then.*

'Memory is the starting point for imagination, surely?'

Another excuse, Jack thought.

Chapter 15: Do Not Flush
Friday 17th July 1942

Half daydreaming, Jack glanced down the embankment towards the fence where he had found Harris. Fleetingly, he considered searching the undergrowth for anything Harris may have dropped. *Something to help identify him*, he thought. He suspected Harris had once worn glasses, *would he find them in the undergrowth? Probably not.* On balance, he wondered what would be gained.

He pressed on towards Lindley Station and his kingdom's eastern boundary. A little beyond the over bridge at Stockings Farm, a ball of toilet paper lying on the track bed took his attention. He had noticed it a couple of weeks ago. *Something to be avoided*, he had thought. He mused that he preferred newspaper to the square stuff the railway supplied, which felt like wiping your arse with greaseproof paper and about as effective.

Having reached the end of his length, he rewarded himself with a break and a cup of cold tea before turning back towards the Bridge. As he passed the toilet paper again, something caught his eye. The tightly wrapped ball had begun to unravel revealing a slight glint at its centre. Jack gave the ball a tentative prod with his boot. The ball bobbled over the uneven ballast, issuing a tiny tinkling note reminiscent of a dropped sixpence. Stooping, Jack discovered a ring lying amongst the ballast. Threading it with a pencil from behind his ear, he lifted and inspected it. In time-honoured fashion, he spat on it as a prelude to a vigorous polish.

Why flush a ring down the toilet? He pondered. *Maybe someone was trying to appear single? Second thoughts, surely, they'd just put their hand in a pocket and slip the ring into their coppers. Why flush an expensive ring away if you could avoid it? And anyway, it's doesn't look much like a wedding ring.*

Studying the ring through a lens from his grandfather's glasses he kept for such occasions, Jack made out the letters J and C engraved either side of a red stone set at the centre of engraved sunbeams. *Not my cup of tea,* he thought, *looks like a show-offs' ring. You wouldn't hear the last of it if you wore it down the pub.*

Closing his palm around the ring, he thrust his fist deep into his pocket and released it into his coins.

As he approached Coalport, he decided to check his beanpoles hidden at the top of the embankment toward the boundary fence. Nipper, nose to the ground, raced past him, following a compelling scent. Jack watched as she disappeared under the fence. He whistled for her to return, but without success.

A new rabbit run? Worth a try, Jack speculated, examining furrowed grass. Fishing inside his poacher's pocket, he produced a wire noose. *Where's Nipper?* He thought, *don't want to catch her*. Nipper appeared, bright eyed and full of vigour, looking pleased with herself. Jack strung the noose across the rabbit run and secured it to the fence wire. *Better check this tomorrow, just in case,* he thought.

'What are you up to?'

'Who's asking?' Jack said.

'Jenkins the farmer is asking why you are on my land.'

'Let me get this straight,' Jack said, with a tongue in cheek smile. 'Do you own the GWR as well as the farm?'

'No, but then again, neither do you, Jack.' They both chuckled.

'Here I am, saving your crops from my rabbits that live on the embankment.'

The farmer considered Jack with narrowing eyes.

'Whose rabbits? Those rabbits could be mine, living on the farm and eating the grass on the embankment. We should share.'

Jack thought for a moment.

'I'm not sure that's fair as I'm doing all the work.'

'Life's not fair, Jack.'

'How about this? If the head is through the noose facing the railway, it's yours. If its arse is facing the railway, it's mine. But either way, I've done you a favour stopping them eating your crops and as I do all the work: I should get the lion's share.'

'How much is the lion's share?'

'Well, it's a massive lion.'

'How about half each?'

'As it's you, fine,' Jack said, holding his hand out to shake. 'Look, I best get on, good luck with the harvest,' Jack winked, as they shook hands.

Rabbits were plentiful in Jack's kingdom. It was fortunately that Jack never tired of rabbit stew. He also loved a spot of pheasant, though bagging pheasants could be risky by comparison. Where rabbits were considered vermin and fair game, pheasants were owned. A brace hidden under his coat could be tricky, but he was yet to be caught for poaching.

Jack reckoned that pheasants were the least intelligent living things in his kingdom. He had witnessed half a dozen fledglings, flushed up and chased by a passing train. They had flown at least a quarter of a mile along a straight line with the train in hot pursuit, their alarm calls eventually subsiding as the train lost interest and followed the curving rails towards the river.

Their comical antics intrigued Jack. He enjoyed their manner of mimicking drunk old men resplendent in top and tails, as they ran stiff legged towards cover. Their ability to judge danger also appeared defective: they would attempt to hide in the open, when sneaking away would have been more effective; they would strut, when it would be more prudent to run, and run when they should fly. Having said all of that, he never actually caught one in the open; maybe they were not so stupid after all.

At four o'clock Jack's stomach began to growl. *Time to start back for the Bridge.* Two hours later, he pushed open the cottage door to find Harris stirring a pot on the range. To his surprise, plates and cutlery were set out and bread cut.

'You'll make someone a good little wife one day,' Jack said, dumping his bags. Harris thrust his hand on his hip and fixed Jack with a glare.

'Be careful what you wish for.'

Jack wondered what Harris meant, but decided to let it pass.

'Guess what I found on the track today!'

'I have no idea, but I'll wager you're going to tell me.'

Jack looked down at his boots; disappointed that Harris would not guess. Stung by the jibe, he remained silent until his desire to please Harris got the better of him. Producing his fist from his pocket, he unclenched it with a flourish, revealing the ring resplendent against his work-roughened palm. After a moment's reflection, he held it out for Harris to inspect. Harris looked in its general direction with studied indifference before turning away dismissively. Jack, peeved at Harris's lack of interest, tossed the ring in Harris's direction. Instinctively Harris caught it, as his reflexes overrode his indifference. Languidly he placed it in no man's land on a shelf above the range.

'I wouldn't wear a ring like that,' he said, with a disdainful glance at Jack.

Jack crumpled with disappointment. He had hoped Harris would be pleased with his find.

'Thought it might be yours, found it near where I found you,' Jack said, hoping he would take it.

'I certainly do not recall owning a ring,' Harris said, looking down at his hand dismissively.

'Try it.'

'No thank you, it belongs to someone with the initials JC.'

'Could still be yours?' Jack said. Harris ignored the remark and changed the subject.

'Today at work, I met the lady of the house. She visited the schoolroom to check on the estate children's progress. Wow, she's a real knockout!'

Jack summoned a disinterested poker face and grabbed his fishing gear.

Chapter 16: Her Ladyship
Tuesday 4th August 1942

Weeks on end passed when nothing out of the ordinary occurred along Jack's length. The perpetual routine of walking the line would have driven many men to distraction. Jack, though, welcomed the solitude that allowed him to confront his demons. He relived the blast that threw him through the air, miraculously he had survived, but his pals had not. He should have stayed with them.

On good days, he expertly observed his kingdom. He noted the first sightings of catkins, bluebells, primroses, orchids, swallows, martins and swifts, and had begun to compare them year on year. With greater difficulty, he plotted the last swallow of each year. The significance of their flight saddened him, not that he disliked the approaching winter months, just that it signalled the passage of yet another year.

Jack's stomach reminded him at eleven o'clock, time for a break. He enjoyed stopping at this particular spot, half a mile from anywhere, a no man's land of fields wedged between the railway and the river.

He cast around for a comfortable spot to sit when he noticed a slack wire in the fence above him. *Surely, it hadn't been like that yesterday,* he thought. Delving into his workbag he selected several tools and began to climb the steep embankment. Grabbing tufts of grass with one hand, while holding his tools in the other, he scrambled up to the fence line. Deftly, he slipped between the top two wires into a newly mown hayfield. Having located the problem, he began to tighten the loosened wire.

'I say, my man, would you mind doing whatever you're doing, from the other side of the fence, this is private land.'

Had Jack twisted to face the voice, he would have seen a woman seated at an easel some twenty yards away. The woman had obviously been lost in his blind side as he climbed through the fence.

'I'm not your man. I'm the GWR's man. I'll be out of your way in a jiffy,' Jack said, attempting to elevate his vocabulary.

'Don't be so insolent my man,' she said, standing from her work before striding purposefully in Jack's direction, riding crop in hand.

Her tethered horse watched with passing interest as she closed in on Jack. Her outfit of boots, skirt and waspish jacket accentuated her fine hourglass figure. Jet black hair released from a clasp cascaded over her shoulders and bounced as she strode towards him. Menace played at the corners of her full lips.

Engrossed in his work, Jack presented his back to her. Maybe if he had glimpsed the depth of determination reflected in her face, he would have taken avoiding action. The blow that landed across his backside, took him by surprise.

Straightening, he spun around in one powerful movement motivated by a mixture of pain, anger and surprise. Instinctively he grabbed her roughly by the shoulders and pulled her towards him as if she were a rag doll. His thunderous expression suddenly dissolved into a narrow-eyed look of lust as they kissed deeply and frantically. Hands searched for buttons and buckles as they sank towards the grass. The horse looked on, unmoved, contentedly cropping grass. Nipper hid.

Lying side by side, she languidly rolled herself up on one elbow to face him.

'You prefer it when I play the strident lady don't you?' Jack agreed with his breathless silence. 'But it's my turn now.'

Sitting up, she swung her leg over his chest to face him. Mesmerised, Jack lay back amongst the tufted grass as she teased him by seductively unbuttoning her blouse.

'No time for this,' he said, wriggling under her weight. She responded by tightening the grip of her knees against his chest.

'There's always time Jackson,' She said, pushing him back to the grass. 'There's a good man.'

Lying on top of him, she took his hand firmly and placed it on her thigh. He caressed her downy hair, moving his hand elliptically, elongating his stroke with each movement. She nibbled his ear. He shivered as the soft strokes of her fingers transformed to raking nails.

A shrill whistle echoed around the Gorge as the midday passenger train hissed its way in their direction. Sharing a resigned shrug, they parted. Jack stood on the track bed, the lady sat at her easel, as if nothing had happened. As the last coach disappeared around the bend Jack's head reappeared over the embankment.

'Can you wait an hour? I need to talk,' he said.

'I must leave by three.'

Jack waved an acknowledgment and turned towards the track. Nipper waited patiently under a bush as Jack rushed through his work.

*****

'Thanks for staying,' he said, kneeling to one side of the easel, 'I have something to ask.'

'Ask away, my man,' she said, reprising her lady character, while conveying her curiosity with a tilt of her head.

'Look, I'm serious,' he said, standing to add weight to his words. 'We know we haven't known each other long but I feel we understand each other so well,' Jack said, as he gathered himself. 'Leave him and live with me!'

There, he had said it. *How did I even think it, let alone say it?*

'What do you mean? Live with you and Harris, in your little cottage?' she said, turning her head back to her painting, laughing at what she took to be a joke.

Jack suddenly found himself well out of his depth, drowning in self-doubt. He saw a familiar schoolbook image of the doomed Matthew Webb fighting the Niagara whirlpool, though his own stricken face stared back from the picture. Stung by disappointment, physically hurt by the rejection and yet at the same time relieved that his world would remain intact, he swam for the shallows.

'Don't forget Nipper; maybe she would sleep in her own bed,' he said, hoping to strike the right note by adding to her joke.

Did I really mean that? Did it go that badly? Did I cover my tracks, he wondered? Questions flew around his head like wasps trapped in a jar. His plan had been derailed, he'd visualised a different ending, his leading lady had ad-libbed her lines, they were not in his script.

'Anyway, how is your husband these days?' he said, in an ill-considered attempt to change the subject and fill the gnawing silence. Paradoxically, it had been the last thing he had wanted to know.

'He is up in London, he goes most weeks, more often since the war,' she said, frowning as she wondered how the conversation had veered away at such a tangent.

'Business or pleasure?' he said, without thinking. *What am I saying?* Rising panic coursed through him as he realised he had no sense of what to say or do. Surprised by his implied insight, she unburdened herself.

'He subtly leaves correspondence around concerning meetings in London to justify his disappearances, but I suspect he goes for pleasure as well. Not that I can complain: when the cat's away the mouse will play,' she said, straightening her skirt with her palms.

'It's probably the war effort, most factories are making munitions now. I bet he's heavily involved,' he said, hoping to deflect the conversation yet again. Now light years from his original target, he felt deflated and worthless.

'Jack, I don't know what he does in London and it's probably just as well. It's top secret, I would imagine.'

'It's common knowledge, even the old Malthouse along the Wharfage is making stuff for the war effort,' he said, failing to stem the flow of ill-considered words.

'For goodness sake Jack, you're barking up the wrong tree.'

Her evident exasperation stunned Jack. He had been attempting to head for calmer waters, her face told him he had unwittingly asked the unthinkable question and charted a course back towards the eye of the storm.

'He is not interested in me, or any other woman, is that plain enough? Or do you want me to spell it out?' she said, as tears collected ready to fall. 'He doesn't like women the way you do Jack, do you understand?'

Jack desperately wanted to see her happy, to see her smile. A stunned silence threatened to envelop them both: Jack attempted to hug her but she broke free.

'He is very kind and thoughtful, in so many ways, but he is politely menacing when it comes to any thoughts I may have of leaving him. I am his token wife, just a smoke screen.'

What had he done? Jack thought, alarm in his eyes.

'I can't leave him and live with you. He would lose face and seek retribution. It would be subtle, but excruciating.'

'But ...' She silenced him with her hand. Heart in mouth, he helped her mount.

'I can't explain. I have said too much already. But if you truly want us to be together, we need to disappear without trace. There could be no going back,' she said, as panic picked at the edges of her determined expression.

A feeling of helplessness swept through him again as he watched her canter away. To his utter relief, she waved briefly as she disappeared from view. Disoriented, he found himself staring at the easel, stool and paints.

Chapter 17: Second First Friday Club Meeting
Friday 7th August 1942

Jack arrived late at the Station Hotel; Bill and George were already settled at a quiet table. Jack edged his way towards them through the forest of drinkers around the bar.

'Yours is in,' Bill mouthed over the hubbub, miming the pulling of a pint and then pointing at the landlord. Jack understood and pushed towards the bar. Jack smiled at the new barmaid as she looked up from the bar. She failed to return his smile, turning abruptly to serve another customer.

What's eating her? He wondered. *Looks like I've pissed on my chips there, what did I do?*

As Jack waited to be served, he became aware of the stranger standing next to him. It appeared to Jack that he had come from nowhere. Jack attempted to pick his accent as he listened in to his conversation with the other stranger at the bar. *He's certainly not from the Bridge,* Jack pondered. *Strange, he looks mean but smells like a tart's handbag. Still, it takes all sorts.*

Jack caught the landlord's eye.

'Bitter please. I think it's in.'

Bill better not be pulling my leg, he thought, as he glanced in Bill and George's direction. An affirmative nod from behind the bar came as a relief. The landlord cupped the glass under the nozzle and pulled the pump handle. Foaming beer squirted with a suppressed whoosh, until it filled the glass to its brim. Jack bent and took a sip, before raising it lovingly to the light checking its clarity. After exchanging knowing glances with the landlord, he moved thoughtfully towards the table.

'What do we know, then?' Jack said, with a raised eyebrow, hoping that either Bill or George had gleaned something since the last meeting.

'Well, I have learnt something,' Bill said, with a resigned look.

'What's that then?' Jack said, suspicious that he may unwittingly be setting up a joke at his own expense.

'It's bloody hard to find information without giving the game away,' Bill continued.

'Tell Jack your story then,' George said, grinning, as he leaned back heavily in his stool, which creaked in protest.

'Well, I was at the Institute and casually asked the librarian if there were any books about treasure. He takes me to the racks near the window and hands me this book, all ceremonial like, doing me a big favour.'

Bill paused for effect.

'What book?' Jack said, leaning forward, anticipating the finale.

'Guess,' Bill said, peering pointedly at Jack. 'You'll never get it in a month of Sundays.'

'Spit it out,' Jack said, showing his frustration.

Bill stalled for a few more seconds.

'Tell him, we haven't got all night,' George said.

'Sure you can't guess? You're going to kick yourself,' Bill said, leaning into his beer.

'This better be good mate,' Jack said, between sips.

Bill waited another couple of seconds before coming out with it through a broad mouthy grin.

'Treasure Island.'

'Jesus, Bill, you daft ha'porth,' Jack said, around his hand that suppressed a splutter of beer.

The sudden noise flushed Nipper from her customary spot under the table. Realising it had been a false alarm, she shrank back to her spot amongst the sawdust and fag ash.

'Long John bloody Silver, that's who you are,' Jack said, a half smile still lingering.

'Have some respect,' Bill said, with mock pomposity. 'Mister Silver to you, Jack.'

Bill scraped his stool backwards as he stood abruptly before moving towards the gents. He returned a few minutes later, smiling at the sight three fresh pints triangulated in his hands.

'Who are the outsiders?' Jack said, to neither of them in particular.

George decided he should answer. 'The new darts league Jack. Keep up will you. It's on the notice board.'

'Look what the cat's brought in,' Bill said in an undertone as he spotted a familiar face moving towards them through the crowd at the bar. Jack followed Bill's gaze.

'What's the secret then, you all look as thick as thieves.'

'Chas! Good to see you mate. When did you get back?' Jack said, with a surprised smile, as he stood and shook his hand.

'Very smart you look in that uniform, where did you pinch it?' George said, smirking quizzically.

'Hope you left him his underpants,' Bill said, nodding at George.

'Ha bloody ha. Here's me just off the train from camp, thinking I'll just pop in and see my old mates, they'll want to buy me a pint or two.'

'How long are you here for?' said Bill.

'Can't say.'

'Come back next week then, plenty of time.' George said, suppressing a smirk.

'Don't talk rot, plenty of time, my arse, there's a war on, haven't you heard?'

'Come on then, you're not a bad lot really, even if you're on the ear for a beer,' Jack said, getting up and taking Chas to the bar.

'Where's the tan from?' Jack said, nodding to Chas's face.

'Can't say.'

'Not Europe, I bet. You look like an American film star, I'm jealous,' Jack said, pulling money from his trouser pocket. 'Pint?'

Chas nodded.

'Are you going back out to wherever….

'No. I'll be reporting to a new unit when I've finished the training.'

'Stationed nearby then.'

'Near enough,' Chas said, as he moved away. 'Just off to water the horse back in mo.'

'Looks like Chas doesn't bear a grudge about his sister, Jack,' Bill said, as the loo door closed behind Chas.'

'Why should he, I didn't do anything.'

'That's not what the gossip says Jack,' George said, with a smirk.

'Look Grace went to London and copped it in the blitz, that's not my fault.'

'Yes, but the gossip said she went to London because of you, Jack.'

'It wasn't like that, I ….'

'Shh, he's coming back,' George warned.

'Come on Jack, time for a story,' Bill said.

'If you insist,' Jack said, enjoying the attention. 'I don't think you've heard this one,' Jack said, dryly.

'Pull the other one Jack, we must have heard all your stories by now,' said Bill, grinning at the thought that Jack could tell a new story.

'Well I still say you haven't heard this one,' Jack repeated.

'What makes you so sure?' George said. Everyone sensed a punch line and they were not disappointed.

'Well actually, I'm certain,' Jack said, before pausing for them to look up from their pints. 'Because I've just made it up.'

Bill and George cast disbelieving looks at Jack and each other. Chas remained impassive, not quite understanding the joke.

'All right then I haven't made it up,' Jack said, to vindicated nods. 'I've just remembered it.'

'Come on then,' said Bill, as George and Chas took a preparatory swallow and waited for Jack to begin.

'Well, it's about Captain Matthew Webb and my Grandpa. Grandpa must have been in his twenties, just married I think, don't think my father had been born by then.'

'You're going back a bit there, Jack,' George said, as he attempted to calculate how many years ago it would have been.

'Let me guess: they drank at the same pub,' Bill said, with a finger raised as if certain he'd been close to the truth.

'No, too simple,' George said, with a twinkle in his eye. 'I bet he taught the Captain how to swim, am I right.'

Avoiding an answer that could pre-empt the story Jack said, 'Do you want me to tell the story or not?'

They nodded tentatively, still unsure if they had been right, but happy enough to find out later.

'All right then. We all know that from time to time the great man would come down and practice in the river. Well, on this particular day, my Grandpa is sat on the bank minding his own business, watching the river closely, working out which peg to fish from. It's a stifling day so he's sat on the bank with his shirt off, when along comes the Captain, swimming upstream like a salmon. Grandpa waves, to his surprise the great man turns and swims towards him. The Captain tells him that the current is not strong enough, nothing like as strong as the tow of the sea tides he wants to practice for. Anyway, to cut a long story sideways, Grandpa suggests a way he can help.'

108

'Come on Jack, pull the other one, it's got bells on,' George said, with a practised look of disbelief.

'Yeah, play the white man, you've told us tall stories before, but this one sounds like a whopper,' Bill said.

'Well, Grandpa was never one for outright lying, but I suppose he could have embellished it a bit,' Jack said, with a wince of an apology.

'I bet you're going to try to tell us he helped the great man improve his stroke and is responsible for him being the first man to swim the channel,' said Bill.

'Well, do you want me to carry on or not?' Jack took a swallow, taking the silence to be agreement. 'The story goes that he did actually help improve his swimming, but not in the way you're expecting.'

'I bet he didn't,' said Bill, nodding his head incredulously.

'Anyway, he stripped down to his long johns and got into the water with the Captain.'

George, Bill and Chas frowned, wondering if they had missed something.

'Come on, get on with it. I'm getting thirsty,' said Bill, looking first at the wall clock and then the crowded bar.

'Anyway, the Captain floats into a swimming position and as agreed Grandpa grabs his ankles. The Captain sets off upstream against the current, using only his arms and towing Grandpa.' Jack paused for a mental picture to develop. 'Anyway, the Captain tows him up the river to Cressage, all of five miles, if not more.'

Jack took a swig of beer signalling the end of the yarn.

'What a let-down,' George said.

'Assuming we believe your story? The benefit to the Captain of your old Grandpa hanging onto his ankles would be much less coming back down stream wouldn't it, so, why do it?'

'Well, I'm sure you're right Bill, but we'll never know. You see by the time they got to Cressage, Grandpa's arms were so tired he couldn't hang on a moment longer. The Captain left him there and set off back to the Bridge without his dead weight.'

'Just say we buy your story for the moment, how did your Grandpa get back to the Bridge dressed in just his long johns then?' Bill asked.

Undaunted Jack pressed on, the beginnings of a grin playing at the corners of his mouth.

'Well, Grandpa was nothing but resourceful. He legged the quarter mile to Cressage train station and located the Station Master. He gave him some cock and bull story and persuaded him to lend him some overalls and give him a free passage back to the Bridge. The Station Master must have believed his story and anyway Grandpa had been a railwayman himself, so he was sort of duty bound to help.'

'You've got some brass neck expecting us to believe a story like that, as much as I like to believe it's true,' Bill said, as he nodded, knowing grins passing between him and George. But Jack had more to tell.

'As it happens, there is another version of the same story, one my father told. In his version, Grandpa invented the swimming story in an attempt to explain away how he got stuck in Cressage in broad daylight wearing just his long johns.'

'Come on then,' Chas said, none of them quite believing their ears.

'Well, Dad reckoned that it all started at the summer fair. Grandpa had been drinking since opening time with some of his pals. By mid-afternoon his mates were getting towards being tipsy, but he was absolutely legless.'

'How did they manage to get in that state by mid-afternoon then?' Bill said.

'Well, the story goes that some bright spark came up with the idea of having a pint in every pub down the High Street, Tontine Hill and the Wharfage. The old man thought he could handle his pop but, in truth, he was a bit of a lightweight. Lightweight is possibly a bit harsh on the old man, but some of those blokes could drink for England, he just wasn't in their league. They all worked up at the foundry and drank mild beer all day to replace the sweat. First division they were, when it came to drinking. Grandpa would have been at best in the central league reserves.

Well, by the time they got to Dale End they decided to have a break. They found a sunny spot on the bank near Station Road and lay down. Grandpa promptly fell asleep, dead to the world. Anyway, a couple of his so-called mates decide it would be great craic to strip him down to his long johns and put him gently into a nearby hay cart to finish his kip. After they've finished laughing they toddle off down the road to the Meadow Inn for another drink. It's not until they were on their way back to the Bridge that they remembered him. They go back to where the cart was standing, only to find it's gone. Apparently, they couldn't do anything for laughing. By which time Grandpa has slept his way to Cressage; from there the story's the same'

'So, which do you think is the real version Jack?'

'To be honest the second, but I'd love to believe the first were true, wouldn't you?'

Smiling faces reflected their thoughts until George swivelled in his chair focusing his attention pointedly at the bar. 'Whose round, is it?'

'Who cares,' said Bill.

'I do, I'm stony broke.' said Jack.

'Come on then lads, desperate measures and all that, coins on the table.'

'Look, there's enough for a half each to finish the night.'

'Lead the way Chas, with your looks we might get pints,' Jack said, passing Chas the collection. 'I certainly won't if the new barmaid serves us but you just might in that uniform. Especially if you try out your knock them dead smile on top of that tan.'

To everyone's disappointment, they ended the evening with halves.

George and Bill made mock salutes to Chas and swung untidily away in the direction of home, leaving Jack and Chas staring morosely into their empty glasses.

'Fancy a walk.' Chas asked, catching Jack's eye.

'What, in the blackout?' Jack said, in disbelief.

'There's some light from the moon, come on,' Chas said, as he spun on his heel.

'Where to?'

'The Dale.'

'The Toll House will be closed, let's give it a rest and hit the hay.' Jack said, with a hint of fatigue.

'Come on, don't be a spoil sport, we'll cross on the Albert.'

'What's wrong with some shut eye?'

'Nothing, if you can. It's stifling in that attic room at my parents. I can't sleep unless I'm pissed or knackered.'

'Why the Dale?'

'No reason, come on.'

Jack followed, begrudging each stride he took away from his bed.

'Come on keep up, we'll be at the Albert before you know it.'

'Bollocks.' Jack said, as he stumbled.

'You know June, don't you?'

'Bloody hell, Chas, have you been put up to this by the others?'

'No, just asking.'

'Yes, I know June, if you're talking about the June married to China.'

'Is there another June?'

'Stop rubbing it in. Yes, I know June, my Ellen and her were bosom pals, till…'

'And recently?'

'I pop in if I'm passing, for old time's sake. What's your interest?'

'Just curious.'

'You know China's missing?'

'No,' Chas said, quickly.

'Been missing for a while,' Jack reflected.

They followed the moonlight rails in silence, both immersed in thought.

'I used to think you were the Bee's knees: you and your gang would get up to all sorts. When I was at the Blue school, I heard lots of stories about when you were there. I was too young, only a nipper, couldn't join in with your gang, remember?' said Chas.

'Yeah, you were an arsey little squirt even then.'

'Less of the little.'

'Point taken.'

'Come on let's walk across on the outside along the girders, I dare you,' Chas said, with a challenging stare that Jack failed to glimpse in the dark. Chas vaulted the bridge rail landing stylishly on the outside girder. Extending his arms to aid his balance Chas began to step from girder to girder. 'Jesus, hold on, you stupid bastard.'

'Come on. It's like flying.'

'For Christ's sake Chas, come back.'

'Come on, you used to do it, surely you're not chicken?'

'No! Well, yes. Look, we never did it the bloody dark, or beered up.'

'This is nothing. In training, we do this stuff blindfolded.'

'You're bloody crazy, come back!'

'Not till I get across. You coming or not, you old fart?'

Jack ignored him and made for Sunnyside, stepping from sleeper to sleeper as quickly as the darkness would allow.

'You stupid, stupid bastard,' Jack said, as Chas climbed nonchalantly back over the rail. 'I'm off to my bed, if you're going to play silly buggers. Jack started back towards Moneyside. Chas continued towards the Dale feeling he had gained one up on Jack.

Chapter 18: Don't Touch
Monday 10th August 1942

Jack closed the garden gate and set off down the bank towards the station. He pitied people who hated early mornings. A low sun peered over distant hills, bathing south-facing Sunnyside in a warm glow. Sunlight reflected haphazardly from crooked windowpanes and cast deep shadows in the lee of shops and houses. Another new day had begun and Jack was glad of it. Had he been younger he might have skipped, if no one was looking that is.

Nipper waited in the yard while Jack stepped into the station office to sign in and check the notice board. He moved stealthily across the shining quarry tiles and opened the corridor window to dilute yesterday's stale tobacco stench. Unusually, the Station Master's office door stood open. Jack would habitually avoid Mr Barker first thing, as he could be relied upon to be grumpy. Seeing "little tin god" Barker and a new bobby in earnest conversation, Jack turned with the thought of beating a hasty retreat.

'Jack, meet Constable James. He's new, from Ludlow,' Barker said, by way of introduction. 'Constable James is charged with finding two evacuees. They went missing yesterday, about teatime. That's correct isn't it, Constable?' Barker said, as he swung towards the constable, transferring the burden of explanation. Jack noticed a look in James's eyes, which said, 'So you're Jack are you,' as clearly as if he had said the words aloud.

'Yes, brother and sister. The boy, Paul, is nine and the girl, Anne, is seven; they arrived from Manchester two months ago,' he said, referring to his notebook. 'We're asking anyone who is out and about to bring them to the Police Station if they find them.' His eyes squinted animosity at Jack. Constable James had rattled Jack's cage. Nodding his agreement, Jack hoped to disguise his discomfort.

'Why would I run across them?' he said, inclining his head, encouraging the constable to elaborate.

'It's a chance, apparently, Paul is interested in trains,' James said, with a non-committal shrug of his shoulders. 'They arrived by train, so they may think they can get home the same way,' he added, as something of an afterthought.

'So, they've run away?' Jack asked.

'Yes, it looks that way,' James said, as he scrutinised Jack.

'Let's hope we have more success finding them than we have finding China,' Jack said, laconically. The comment appeared to fire Constable James.

'You knew China, then.'

'Yes, everyone in the Bridge knows him.'

'Do you know his wife June?'

'Yes, she was a bosom pal of my wife's.'

'I didn't know you were married,' James said, but before Jack could respond he asked, 'Why did you say, "was"?'

'I'm a widower, that answers both of your questions doesn't it,' Jack said, as turned and stepped towards the door, 'Best be getting on, if you've finished,'

Jack trudged reflectively, into the low sun, his thoughts drifting to a game they played as children. They had called it hideaway. The game would be played on rainy days as they sheltered under the bridge or the viaduct. It involved imagining they were going to run away that night. The winners came up with the best hiding place and excuse if they were caught. A separate award was awarded for the best provisions list they imagined pinching from the Co-op.

Their bravado led them to try out the best places one summer's night. Fortunately, excuses were not required as they made it home before they were missed. The best hiding places included tree houses, barns, caves, railway huts, disused limekilns and a concrete pillbox. [handwritten annotation: Surely manned and in use in wartime? Maybe pre-war if Jack was then a child.]

They'll be hiding somewhere. It's warm enough to sleep outside but I'm sure they would feel safer inside, Jack speculated as he built up a mental picture based on his own childhood thoughts.

'Not so daggeldy today,' the voice said, interrupting Jack's thought pattern.

'Wow, didn't see you there,' Jack said, to the farmer leaning against a gate. 'Yes, it's certainly fresher today.'

'Miles away you were, been watchin' you cummin',' he said, raising his head to illustrate how far back it had been.

'You haven't seen any youngsters, a boy and girl? Runaway evacuees they are.'

'No, you're the first person I've clapped eyes on, 'cept the wife a'corse,' he said, his weather-beaten face betraying little concern.

'Going to be cracking day,' said Jack, looking up at the cloudless sky for confirmation, a hand shielding his eyes.

'Could do with some sun, might dry it out a bit,' the farmer said, prodding at a clump of clay with his boot.

'Best press on then,' Jack said, having no patience for small talk. Nodding goodbye, he turned and strode away. After a few paces, he turned back.

'If you find them, take them to the cop shop in the Bridge, will you?'

The farmer raised a lethargic finger to his cap in confirmation.

Jack's eyes swept the countryside as he searched for any signs of the children. Even in winter, the gorge could be claustrophobic but, in the height of summer, its abundant vegetation squeezed any view to a minimum. He needed to be on his mettle today.

Cattle gathered in the shade of a solitary tree, monotonously swishing their tails in a vain attempt to disperse a haze of flies. Rabbits ran for cover as his boots crunched across the stone ballast. A plump wood pigeon sat on the fence, apparently unconcerned by Jack's progress towards it, as if acting out a dare. Grass shoots had begun to reclaim a fire-scorched bank surrounding a charred, skeletal tree.

Jack's gut told him that the children would have slept in a trackside hut, if they had travelled in this direction. *It's what I would have done as a lad,* he thought. He speculated they would have made about three miles before feeling tired. If correct, *that would put them somewhere the other side of Coalport,* he thought. Sunday evenings are quiet along the line, they were unlikely to have been noticed. Overall, he considered the trackside would be the place to start looking; within fifteen minutes, he could put his theory to the test.

Shards of sunlight ricocheted randomly from the meagre, grimy window glass of the wayside hut. A hessian sack hung inside the window, preventing Jack from peering in. Sunlight streamed through the door as he opened it fully. Disappointed, Jack surveyed the stark interior. No children, but it looked like they had slept in the corner on a jumble of rags, sacks and old newspapers.

Bulls eye, they can't be far away. Best get a move on, the down passenger is due soon, he thought. Jack threw his tool bag into the shed and set off at a steady jog. Rounding the next curve, he caught sight of them about a quarter mile away. They were dawdling as only kids can, kicking stones as they went. *If they see me at this distance, they'll run for it,* he speculated. *But, if I take a loop round the fields, I could cut them off as they come out of bridge thirty-nine.*

Waiting out of sight behind the bridge parapet, Jack listened to their echoing footsteps as they approached. *Step out too soon and they could turn and run, too late and they would see him first and run past,* he thought. Judging the moment, he stepped out into their path: they were only a matter of feet away.

'Are you Paul and Annie?' he said, as he crouched down to their height, flashing them a welcoming smile. Carrying everything they owned wrapped in woollen jumpers, they looked tired, dirty and hungry. Gas masks in battered cardboard boxes hung around their necks by dirty, knotted string. Dishevelled versions of the children evacuated to the Bridge, just eight weeks ago.

'Going home?' Jack said, beaming a friendly smile. The crestfallen boy shrugged his shoulders noncommittally. Jack tried again.

'Where's home then?'

'Manchester, Mister.'

'You're heading the wrong way. The way you are going is to London.'

The dejected children sank forlornly amongst the tunnel entrance.

'See that sign post, it tells the miles to London, a hundred and fifty-five. That's a long, long way.'

Neither child replied or showed even a flicker of interest.

'Let's catch a train to Ironbridge.'

'We don't want to go back there, Mister.'

'Well, we should go and see the nice policeman and tell him you're safe.'

The boy's eyes widened a crack. 'We'll tell him we want to go home.'

'If you want too. Look there's a train coming soon,' Jack said, pulling a red flag from his trouser belt. 'I'll stop it with my flag.'

No answer.

'Got a handkerchief?' Jack said to the lad, snot running down his lip.

The boy looked puzzled.

'A hanky?' Jack said, pinching his nose by way of illustration.

No answer. A hanky corner poked invitingly from the boy's trouser pocket. Gently Jack bent down and pulled out a surprisingly clean handkerchief. Jack visualised the boy's mum saying, 'You make sure you wipe your nose, remember not on your sleeve, in the hanky, remember,' as she pushed it into his pocket while giving him a hug.

Jack wiped the boy's nose carefully, then folded the hanky back into squares and pushed it back into his pocket. Neither child appeared willing to speak but showed no inclination to escape. Glowering at Jack, they appeared to have accepted their fate, though not with good grace.

A distant whistle announced the departure of a train from Lindley Station.

'It'll be here soon.' Jack said, unconsciously swivelling towards the whistle.

No answer.

'I'll need to lift you high,' Jack said. The girl looked puzzled. 'To get you up to the carriage.' He demonstrated by holding his arms above his head. 'We're too low down here on the track.'

Jack looked for understanding in the girl's blank face.

'I'll need to lift you, all right?'

No answer.

The train slowed to a standstill in a cloud of steam alongside Jack's flag. Explaining briefly to the fireman as he herded the children towards the first coach. An obliging passenger opened the door and collected the children as Jack lifted them up. The guard belatedly caught up with the action, waving a green flag and blowing his whistle. The fireman acknowledged with a whistle, the engine groaned and lurched into motion.

The boy looked sheepishly at Jack, his hair flopping across his eyes making them difficult to read.

'How far is Manchester, Mister?' the boy said.

Jack imagined the distance on a map.

'About seventy miles, it's a long old way,' Jack watched for a reaction.

The boy's uncomprehending face looked away.

'You know how far you walked with your sister.'

The boy nodded.

'Well, Manchester is twenty times that far.'

The remainder of their short journey passed in silence as the children stared pointedly through the window, avoiding eye contact with Jack.

As Ironbridge platform appeared, the train slowed to a standstill. Jack slid the window down, leaned out and opened the door.

'Hold my hand.'

No answer. With their few possessions clamped tightly to their chests, protected by both arms, the sullen children stepped awkwardly down to the platform.

'Let's go and see the nice bobby, err policeman,' Jack said, correcting himself.

The children made an unhappy sight as they followed Jack unenthusiastically, heads bowed, shoes scuffing. Arriving at the Police Station railings, Jack attempted to smarten them a little before going in.

'See the blue light, that says it's a Police Station,' Jack said, pointing above the steep stone steps. 'Last one to the top is a sissy.' Jack came last.

Once inside they presented themselves at the high counter, which separated them from a fearsome looking desk sergeant. The children could only see his head from where they stood.

'Try to look a little more welcoming?' Jack said, with a wink, before looking down at the petrified youngsters.

The sergeant got Jack's drift and leant forward and beamed a big, laughing policeman's smile.

'And, what can I do for you children?'

'Send us home, Mister,' the boy said, with a defiant stare.

'And me,' she said, in a replica but smaller voice, accompanied by a pretty smile, which changed to a scowl as she copied her brother's expression.

'Why would you want to go there?'

'There's big buses in Mancky.' The boy said uncertainly.

'And trams. And proper ice cream. And the flicks,' added the girl.

'And it's safe, people don't touch you like here,' he said.

'What do you mean,' the Sergeant said, raising his shoulders and looking to Jack for an explanation.

'My Mum said for me to be careful and not let anyone touch.'

'And me,' the girl said.

'My Mum told me I must look out for me and her,' he said, looking towards his sister.

'Yes, you're older, I understand.' The Sergeant, agreed.

'And keep away from people like him,' he said, as he pointed venomously at Jack.

Jack's head rocked back in disbelief.

'Don't know what he's on about,' Jack said, looking truly puzzled.

'What do you mean?' The desk sergeant asked, his face becoming serious.

'He put his hand in my pocket. My Mum said, "Don't let anyone touch you".'

'And he touched my bum, too,' said Annie.

The desk sergeant looked to Jack for an explanation.

'I wiped his nose with his hanky and put it back in his pocket. He wouldn't do it himself. As for the girl, she couldn't reach the carriage door, so I moved my hands from her under her arms to the top of her legs, that's all.' Jack said, still visibly shaken by the accusation.

'That's fine Jack, I'll sort this out. You best get back to work. Thanks for your help,' the desk sergeant said, before turning his considerable bulk towards the children. 'Say, "Thank you" to Jack here, for bringing you back safe and sound.'

No answer. An awkward silence fell, broken only by Jack's footfalls resonating from the corridor tiles. Once outside, Jack took deep breaths and stared blankly at the pavement as he attempted to rationalise the children's accusation.

A shadow fell across his boots. Raising his head, he came face to face with Constable James. Jack felt James's eyes boring into him. James was an incomer and worse he appeared to be trying to make a name for himself, while showing little regard for the status quo or the natural order of the Gorge.

'Found the kids up the line, they're at the desk, if you want to see them,' Jack said, nodding his head towards the police station steps, inviting Constable James to follow his gaze. Taller and younger, Constable James ignored Jack's invitation and continued to stare menacingly at him.

'No need to thank me, anything for the police,' Jack said.

James made no reply and continued to block Jack's way. James stared at Jack as if waiting for an answer to a question he had not yet asked. Jack nodded his own silent question with an eyebrow raised, head tilted, inviting James to stand aside. Constable James eventually broke the silent standoff.

'This your dog, Jack?' he said, his intense stare never once straying from Jack's face. Jack fought to control his anger at being addressed by his Christian name, especially by James who had not earned the privilege, either by friendship or by being born in the Bridge.

Nipper sat at Jack's feet watching them intently, her head cocked. Jack considered his answer as he played for time. Constable James shifted his weight from one foot to the other and widened his stance, a move calculated to intimidate. The two men continued to stare into each other's eyes, neither looking away.

'I have nothing to HIDE, Constable,' Jack said, spreading his arms marginally and hoping James would hear his words as conciliatory, when they were not. 'Is there a problem?' he continued, raising an eyebrow and holding James's stare.

Nipper recognised the 'HIDE' sound and moved with as much stealth as an overweight Jack Russell could manage. Waddling down the alley, she disappeared around a corner.

'The problem is this dog of yours,' James said, pointing down at the non-existent Nipper. 'No collar. No nametag,' he continued, enjoying Jack's discomfort. 'That's a five-shilling fine, but then I doubt you have a licence either, which would be a further five shillings.'

Constable James appeared to be about to launch into further accusation, when Jack interrupted.

'What dog are you talking about?' He said, without looking down from the eyeball-to-eyeball stare.

'Don't play the wise man with me, Jack, the one at your feet.'

'A dog?' Jack said, looking down.

Constable James sensed he had been out-manoeuvred.

'The dog that follows you around, Jack,' James said, 'the Jack Russell cross, that answers to "Nipper".'

'Oh, Nipper! She's not my dog: she follows me around yes, but I don't own her, she's not my dog in that sense.'

Constable James's moustache twitched uncomfortably.

'Look, if you find her owners, I'd like to meet them,' Jack said, neutrally. Then with true venom in his voice he said, 'If that's all I'll be getting back to work.' Moving marginally to one side, Jack pushed past James, shoulder to shoulder, neither man backing down.

He's got my number, Jack thought, *I had best tread carefully around Constable James.*

Constable James's angry eyes bored into Jack's back as he sauntered away. Jack had won this confrontation, though he suspected it had been the first round of many. He anticipated that James would come back harder next time.

Nipper re-joined her master as he crossed the bridge. Jack stole a concerned glance towards the Police Station.

Chapter 19: Penny a Fish
Sunday 30th August 1942

'What's your Dad up to, with those willow whips?' Bill said, to Tom, knowing Jack could hear.

'He's gonna give you a good thrashing,' said Tom, grinning mischievously at Bill and George.

'Yes, you overgrown school kids could do with a lash,' Jack said, without looking up.

'I'll tell you what, he's going to mend that tackle basket at long last,' George said, gaining a nod of approval from Bill, as they both stared pointedly at the battered basket.

'Are you finished?' Jack said, sensing that, despite their leg pulling, they really wanted to know. He elected to play them along for a while and changed the subject.

'Looks good for fishing, river's slow and clear for once, what do you think?'

'Stop pissing about Jack, what are the canes for?' George said, nodding at them.

'Wouldn't you like to know?' Jack said, tying a length of gut to the thin end of a cane.

Bill and George made signs to each other, indicating that they thought Jack had lost his marbles. Studiously ignoring them, Jack rummaged in his basket eventually producing a couple of battered floats, a selection of hooks and some shot.

'Tom, tackle up this one for me.' Jack said, passing him a cane.

Jack tentatively cast in to check the weights and float were correct. Satisfied, he pulled out and leant the cane against the nearby wall. Turning, he could see out of the corner of his eye that Bill and George were still poking fun at him.

'Pretend rods,' Jack said.

'We can see that,' Bill said, smiling to George.

'Forgotten your rod, Jack?' George said, straight faced.

'They're for those evacuee kids I told you about.'

Blank faces stared back at him.

'The ones I found when they ran away.'

'I'm with you now,' said Bill.

'I bumped into them on Tontine Hill. Wanted to show them I'm okay. So, I asked them to come fishing. They'll be along soon.'

Bill, George and Tom chuckled; they had been playing dumb to get a rise out of Jack. Jack pretended he had not noticed.

'We could help them catch their first fish, like we did with Tom, when he was a lad,' Jack flashed an exaggerated wink to Bill and George, who nodded their understanding.

'Hello there, you two,' Jack said. 'Now, what do we call you?'

No answer.

'Well, you know me, I'm Jack, this is Bill and George, and this is my son, Tom.'

They all nodded and smiled reassuringly at the kids.

'Do the people you're billeted with know where you are?'

No answer.

'Okay, let's start.'

'We won't be fishing, Mister,' the boy said, peering up from under his cap.

'Why's that then?'

'At home my Dad say's I'm too young to take care of a fishing rod and she's even younger,' he said, staring at his sister.

'Well, you can't damage these rods. Your Dad would be fine with that, wouldn't he?' Jack said.

'Shall we catch some fish?' said Tom. 'I'll show you.'

'Yes, and Jack will give you a penny for each fish you catch,' George said, with his arm round Jack's shoulder. A sly wink passed between Bill and George.

'Honest? Will you Mister?' said the little girl looking up at Jack.

'Of course, he will,' agreed Bill.

Jack glared and mouthed swear words at them.

'You never gave me a penny a fish,' said Tom, joining in, winking at Bill and George, 'You must owe me a few bob,' he said to Jack. 'What do you think, George?'

Before George could agree, Jack brusquely changed the subject.

'Let's get going, I'll hook the maggots, you drop the lines in and Bob's your uncle. Let's catch some fish,' he said, as he knelt in front of the kids. 'Look, we need to call you something: why don't you tell us your favourite names?'

The girl wrinkled her nose and said shyly, in a little voice that Jack could hardly catch.

'Cinderella, Mister.'

'That's a lovely name, how about your brother?'

Jack looked towards the boy.

'Errol, like Errol Flynn. My mum says he's got cracking legs.'

George and Bill cast towards the far bank, short of Bower Brook. They planned to ledger for carp, but in truth, they were not fussy, any fish would do. Jack and Tom cast into the eddy and sat together on Jack's rickety basket alongside the kids. Happily, they watched their floats bob in the reflections of misshapen trees and a cloudless sky. Nipper sat in the shade of a nearby bush, stripping bark from a stick.

'What kind of a bird is that Jack?' Bill asked, pointing. 'It's got cracking colours.'

'A jay, or a corvidae.'

'You eaten a dictionary again,' Bill said. 'What the hell's a corvidae?'

'Its Latin I think.' Jack said, reflectively. 'One of the crow family. When the Romans were up at Wroxeter they probably called crows corvidae, or something like that.'

George nodded as something occurred to him.

'What, the Romans who buried our coins?' George said.

'Yes, but keep your voice down,' Jack said, looking around, gauging if anyone else could hear.

The children soon became bored and began to kick stones into the river.

We won't catch anything at this rate, Jack thought, looking disconsolately at the river.

'Now then you two, do me favour, take this tanner to the sweetshop and get some bull's eyes.' Jack said, taking a sixpenny piece from his pocket.

'Yes, Mister,' Errol said, holding out a grubby hand, expectantly.

'Know the way?' Jack said. 'It's by the Institute. Want Tom to go with you?'

'No Mister, we know the way,' Errol said, clutching the small gold coin tightly in his fist.

'If there's no bull's eyes get aniseed balls,' Jack said.

Errol gave a mock salute and skipped off, hand in hand with his sister.

'You'll be lucky,' George said. 'You won't see them again, or your tanner.'

'Come on lads, get a shift on, we need to catch some fish before they get back,' Jack said, looking mischievously towards Bill and George.

Errol and Cinderella reappeared twenty minutes later, all grins and bulging cheeks. Errol handed the bag of remaining sweets to Jack with a slightly apologetic look. Jack conjured a look of deep shock as he peered into the grubby white bag and showed Tom the remaining bull's eyes.

'Blimey, you don't get many sweets for a tanner these days.'

'Any for us?' said Bill, as he and George held their hands out like cheeky kids.

'Buy your own, there's only enough for us,' Jack said, smiling conspiratorially to the kids.

'You wait, we won't give you any of ours when we get them,' said Bill. 'Nah nah nu nah nah.'

'And anyway, ours will be bigger than yours, so there,' George added.

'HEY! Quick, Errol, your float's under, grab your rod!' Tom said.

'And, yours, little girl,' said Bill, pointing to her rod.

The children ran to their canes. Errol got to his first and pulled it out excitedly.

'I've got one, I've got one, you owe me a penny mister, look at that, it's a big un isn't' it?'

'Me too,' said Cinderella, 'I've caught one too.'

The three men shot satisfied smiles at each other. In truth, the fish were limp, but the children did not seem to notice. Bill and George unhooked the fish with great ceremony, passing size and weight comments to each other in stage whispers. Eventually the fish were returned to the keep net and allowed to recover before being slipped back into the river.

The day passed idyllically as they chatted and played the fool, whilst sharing sandwiches and drinks. Mysteriously, the children appeared to catch more fish than the grownups.

'We caught more than you. We caught more than you,' chanted Errol and Cinderella in unison as they ran in circles around the men.

Jack, Bill, George and Tom had perfected the fish trick; two would distract the children, whilst the other two secretly hooked fish onto the kid's makeshift rods. The men enjoyed the pantomime, especially the children's glow of excitement when they caught yet another fish. As a light evening breeze blew off the river, they packed up and sauntered happily back along the Wharfage.

'Thanks,' Errol said, rattling the pennies in his pocket as a combined thank you and taunt. 'You wait till I show the boys up at the big house school.'

'You don't want to give our secret away though do you,' Jack said, as he speculated, *all his classmates will be down here soon if we don't watch out.*

Cinderella shyly smiled goodbye. Jack gave them both a quick hug as they turned to go. The children skipped up Severn Bank, leaving the First Friday Boys and Tom to climb Tontine Hill.

At the bridge, Tom said 'TTFN,' and waved as he hurried up High Street towards Madeley and his adopted home.

If the men had been transported back to their childhoods, they would have draped their arms around each other's shoulders and shuffled across the bridge, kicking stones as they went. As grown men though, they sauntered and chatted happily, squinting into the sunset of a fabulous day.

'I'm gagging for a pint,' Bill said. 'It must be your round, Jack.'

'You must be bloody joking! I'm brassic thanks to you pair of bastards. That penny-a-fish lark cleaned me out.'

Bill and George looked at each other. Unable to help themselves as they burst out laughing.

'Don't worry mate, I'll get them in,' said George, putting a placatory arm around Jack's shoulder.

They were last seen squeezing into the back bar of the Railway Hotel, with thirsts to quench and banter to spare.

Chapter 20: The Third First Friday Club meeting
Friday 4th September 1942

Kicking mud from his boots, Jack casually glanced through the pub's window. A familiar scene greeted him. Men were gathered in groups around tables or by the bar. Spilt beer lay in puddles on the tiled floor, cigarette smoke hugged the discoloured ceiling, empty pint glasses littered the bar. He spotted Bill and George at their usual table, though something looked different, he could not tell what. It looked like they had been chatting to a bloke who just stepped away from the table. The stranger was saying something to Bill and George over his shoulder. Their heads were close together as if discussing a confidential matter. As the bloke moved away and pushed open the door to the gents, he half turned. *That face is familiar*, Jack thought. Then the penny dropped. *He's the bloke by the bar, the one who smelt strange.*

Jack nodded to Bill as they passed midway between the bar and their table. *They've been here a while*, Jack pondered, looking at their empty glasses. Playfully, George accused Jack of arriving late to avoid getting the first-round in. Bill returned to the table with three fresh pints.

'Been here long?' Jack said.

'Not long mate, just time to swat down a pint. Your first is "in" behind the bar,' George said, before taking the top off his pint.

'Heard anything of China,' Jack said, looking up from his pint at first Bill and then George.

'Nothing since you asked on Sunday, Jack,' Bill said, with a smirk to George.

'Not a dickie bird,' George said, before flashing a grin at Bill and asking, 'talking of China, have you seen June, Jack.'

Jack hesitated but sensed he could not ignore them.

'Well as it happens, I bumped into her on the footbridge on Monday.' Bill and George exchanged theatrical knowing glances, 'And how was she,' Bill said, caressing an hourglass shape with his hands.

'She looked fine.'

'Well we know that Jack, but how was she,' said George nudging Bill.

'She said she was managing fine.'

'With a little help from here and there, no doubt.'

Jack ignored their pointed grins as best he could.

'She's been working shifts since China went missing. I think China drank most of his wages. I got the impression she was better off since.'

'So, do we Jack, so do we.'

'Look, I know what you are thinking but I've met someone special and ….'

'Since when did that ever stop you,' Bill said, to laughter all round. The thunder in Jack's expression banished any thought of hilarity as an awkward silenced crossed the table.

'Didn't June have a glad eye for Chas going back a bit?' George said, attempting to change the subject.

Bill and George looked cautiously around the pub for eavesdroppers before starting the meeting. Jack stared at them sensing a slight distancing between them and him. It was nothing he could put his finger on though. *Maybe I'm over reacting. Mother always said I was over sensitive for a big lad,* he remembered.

The meeting progressed with little information gleaned which could help dispose of the coins. Jack began to think that Bill and George appeared less motivated than at previous meetings. As the meeting dissolved and their conversations drifted aimlessly away from the subject, Jack decided that a little of the usual comradeship had been missing. He felt a chill as he remembered a phrase his Mum had regularly used, "two's company, three's a crowd".

George raised the subject of the bombing raid, the one people referred to as 'the raid'. A Heinkel 111 had dropped three bombs between the bridge and the power station.

'I was chatting to Jimmy,' George said, looking to the others for confirmation. 'You know Jimmy? Based at Shrewsbury?' The others appeared to remember him, so he carried on. 'He has his theory that they were trying hit the petrol store at Farley. He reckons the siding at Farley could look the same as the limekiln siding, where the bombs landed, from the air.'

'But they're two miles apart,' Jack said.

'I still think they were trying to hit the power station,' Bill said. 'Or the bridge.'

'But the bombs fell between them,' George said.

'Just a bunch of frightened lads, got lost and dropped their bombs anywhere. They couldn't take them back now, could they?' Jack said.

Bill and George nodded at the possibility but then George's straight faced, announced.

'I think they were trying to break our resolve.'

'He's off his rocker,' Bill said, frowning at Jack before turning back to George. 'Break our resolve, how?'

George milked the silence and then with a flourish announced, 'By bombing the fishing club of course!'

The three erupted with convulsions of laughter. From this high point of frivolity, the evening drifted downhill until the towels were put up and the landlord called time.

Having said their goodbyes, Jack crossed the road and strolled along the footpath that hugged the goods yard wall. Jack knew the path like the back of his hand even in the blackout. He knew his position by the feel of the pavement under his boots and the echo of his footsteps against the high wall. Nearing the end of the wall, he looked for his next landmark, the footbridge, its lattice pattern girders silhouetted against the slightly lighter sky. Just feet from the bridge he caught a faint whiff of cloying aftershave on the breeze.

'Been waiting for you Jack,' a voice said, from somewhere near the base of the steps.

Jack held his tongue and coolly struck a match, illuminating the speaker's face. Fleetingly he glimpsed the man's menacing ferret-like eyes either side of an impressive nose. The face had few redeeming features. The match blew out.

'What do you want?' Jack said, conjuring a neutral tone.

'It's like this. You have something valuable and we're interested in valuables,' he said, pausing to see if Jack would bite, before continuing. 'Our organisation can help you convert your valuables into cash,' he said before stepping closer to Jack. 'For a consideration.'

'You know my name, what's yours?' Jack challenged.

'Best you don't know, Jack.'

'Well, shall I call you Spiv?'

'Don't push your luck, Jack.'

'I don't have anything of value,' Jack said, looking down at his feet. 'Unless you count Nipper, here. How much for the dog, Mister?'

'You're pushing your luck again Jack. The organisation don't take kindly to people who've got no proper respect. We provide a valuable service in these difficult times - don't knock it.'

'Does it look like I own anything of any value?' Jack said, spreading his palms.

'Who said owned?' he said, as he looked Jack up and down. 'And, no, you don't look flush, but looks can be deceiving,' he said, as he moved closer. They were now toe to toe. 'I look like a pleasant sort of a bloke, don't I? But, I can assure you I'm not,' he said, as he moved his coat gradually to one side, revealing the bulk of a gun butt in his waistband. 'Understand?'

Nervously eyeing the gun, Jack attempted an outward look of calm.

'Let me know when you want to deal with those valuables of yours,' he said, ending the meeting.

'Where can I find you?' Jack said, pausing for effect. 'Should I ever discover something valuable, that is?'

'Leave a message behind the bar at the Forrester's Arms. Do you know it?'

'Yes, in Madeley. Is that your local, then?'

'Don't try to be smart, Jack, it will backfire. A message left there will find me. Remember, I'll find you if I don't hear from you soon.' The spiv tipped his trilby as if auditioning for the silver screen, and melted into the blackness.

Jack stepped unsteadily up Bridge Bank, his head swirling with questions. *Had he been rumbled or had the spiv been flying a kite? How did he know his name? He could have been listening in at the bar. But, how did he know which way I would walk? He could have just been lucky, there's only two directions.* Jack began to feel comfortable. *Yes, he'd just been lucky.*

His heart sank as another thought struck him. *But, how did he know about the something valuable? Even someone with his brass neck wouldn't just go around randomly accusing people of having something valuable. He's been tipped off. Bill and George were talking to him, but what would they have to gain? Maybe they'd be happy to split it with the Spiv and cut me out. But, why would they do it, we've been mates for years?* Another of his Mum's sayings sprang into his head, "one in the hand being better than two in a bush" *Money could have turned their heads. What other explanation could there be?* He wondered.

Jack wished he could think of one.

Chapter 21: Under the Albert
Thursday 24th September 1942

Jack had left his note, in their usual place, she had confirmed. She was late, he fidgeted as he juggled the possible reasons. Had he been stood up? Fear and longing gripped him, as he prevaricated, should he stay or should he go. It could be a week before they could rearrange - no, he would stay.

*****

'Jackson, sorry I'm late.'

'You're here now, that's all that matters,' Jack said, as he pulled on the oars.

'I'm being watched,' she whispered, looking nervously around.

'We'll be fine, it's only nerves.'

'It's not so simple. I'm afraid of what my husband may do.'

'I can stand up for myself.'

'But not for me, Jackson, you can't stand up for me. He's ruthless and exceptionally subtle. I'm even beginning to believe he engineered his first wife's death.'

'But why?'

'I think he discovered her affairs and confronted her. Knowing her, she may not have backed down. She must have known their marriage was merely a pretence for respectability's sake.'

'Would he kill her for that?' Jack said, frowning.

'No, someone would do it for him.'

'You can't keep secrets in the Bridge, we would know if he had.'

'Jackson, he's a powerful man. You don't become so successful without knowing the right people. Look, he would pay someone from London probably. He wouldn't have trusted anyone around here.'

'What makes you think you're being watched?'

'Do you doubt me, Jackson?'

'No, but….'

'His gamekeeper is watching me while he's away. I'm sure of it.'

'Maybe your husband has asked him to make sure you don't come to any harm while he's away.'

'He's watching me, I tell you!'

'How did you get here tonight?'

'I sent him to the cottage hospital in the van with one of the estate children. The boy had fallen and damaged his arm. Fortunately, Beacher was the only man around with a driver's licence, so it didn't appear that I was getting rid of him. Why I'm late is another story.'

'Another story?'

'How well do you know Harris?'

'As well as anyone knows someone without a past.'

'Could he be a fake?'

'No, not a chance.'

'I spent time with him today. The boy who hurt himself had been in his care and so I asked him about the fall. He certainly knows how to turn on the charm. I happened to mention my family connections in Birmingham and a few places I know in the area. One of the places I mentioned was a nightclub, called Candles, do you know it?'

'Never been to Brum.'

'Well I'm sure he has, I swear he reacted to the name. His eyes widened slightly as I mentioned the club, I'm sure he knows the place. Think about it, he definitely reacted, if he has no memory why would he react.'

'That's hardly conclusive, is it?'

'I think he wants to be my friend, or that's what his eyes were telling me. He kept me talking, I think he was testing me, as if he knew of our meeting,' she said, before giving him a cheeky grin and asking 'you don't talk in your sleep do you, Jackson?'

'Ha bloody ha,' He said, before he coloured as a thought jumped into his head. 'You don't fancy him, do you?'

'Of course not,' she said slapping him on the shoulder playfully. 'Shouldn't I be more concerned about your reputation as Jack?'

'No, I haven't been with anyone since we met under the Albert.'

'Are you sure, Jackson?'

Chapter 22: Tom Gets Them In
Sunday 20th September 1942

'Harris, fancy a day out with Tom and me?'

'Thanks, but I should crack on with my studies for this teaching job,' Harris said, as he turned pointedly towards a pile of books stacked on the table. 'Another day, perhaps.'

'Well, if you change your mind I'll be out at the gate looking out for Tom.'

As he waited, Jack thought of interesting places they could visit. *We always go up to Benthall let's go somewhere different today, but where*, Jack wondered. Tom appeared at the bottom of Bridge Bank; Jack hurried down to meet him. Clamping his arm around Tom's shoulder Jack asked.

'Fancy a trip to Highley on the morning train?'

'What's down there?'

'You'll find out, won't you?' Jack said, with a mischievous grin. 'We'll be back on the evening train - will that be all right at home?'

'As long as I'm home before blackout.'

'Let's go then.'

'Is Harris coming?'

'No, too busy.'

*****

'Sit by the bank; I'll get the drinks. Back in two shakes of a lamb's tail.'

Tom lay on a grassy bank beneath the overhanging branches of a willow and gazed at the clouds drifting aimlessly by.

'Penny for them,' Jack said, handing Tom a drink in a half pint glass. 'Lemonade, all right?'

'Dad, can't I have a proper man's drink?' Tom said, frowning. 'I am a working bloke now,' he said, taking a begrudging sip. 'What's that you're drinking?'

'Best bitter, 'Jack said, savouring his first swig as if it were a fine wine, 'Cheers young Tom,' he said, taking a good swallow. 'The first pint's always the best, but the second, third and fourth aren't bad either.'

Tom grinned, but wondered what it would feel like to have so much beer in his belly. Remembering a saying Jack had often used to describe a prodigious drinker, "He's got hollow legs". *Maybe they were after all*, he thought.

'Dad, please stop calling me "Young Tom". I'm a working chap now you know.'

'You'll always be young Tom to me, even if you are all grown up.' Jack said, ruffling his hair. 'I'm off down the bank to see that fisherman, back in a bit.'

Tom followed his gaze and nodded.

'If I found my pint a little emptier, well I'd have to believe the sun evaporated it,' he said, with a hint of a wink. Tom guessed he would be a while, once he got chatting.

The glass of lemonade disappeared in short order. Staring at Jack's pint Tom became almost mesmerised by the bubbles rising through the golden beer. Surprised by the girth of the pint glass he slid his hand down the cool slippery surface until he gained a grip. He raised the glass unsteadily - its ungainliness surprised him, forcing him to grasp it in both hands. Steadying the glass, he raised it to his lips. Tom sipped. Surprised by its bitterness, he involuntarily gagged and went to spit it back into the glass but just stopped himself. His second sip had been no more palatable, but at least he controlled his gag reflex. There must be something wrong he thought, all the men at the pub took big mouthfuls and swallowed with satisfied smiles.

Maybe the pint was 'off', as Jack would say, but he'd said it wasn't half bad, which is good isn't it? Tom thought. He persevered, willing himself to enjoy it. *After all, I'm a bloke now, aren't I?*

Tom woke to find Jack looking down at him with a quizzical expression.

'Is there a hole in my glass?' Jack said, staring at the empty glass.

'Only at the top,' Tom said, pleased with his comeback, 'Sun must have vapourated it,' he added, before giggling and giving the game away.

'You could be right,' Jack said, throwing a pretend slow motion punch at Tom's ribs and ruffling his hair.

'Come on let's get on,' Jack announced over his shoulder, 'it'll be your round at the next pub.'

'But, I've no money.'

'As you're a bloke now, you need to buy your round, stand your corner,' Jack said, 'Anyway, I've got an idea, tell you later.'

They strolled upstream along the fishermen's path, occasionally stepping aside to allow heavily laden fishermen to keep to the path. Jack nattered happily to Tom about this and that.

'Let me show you how you can buy us both a pint.'

Without further explanation, Jack led them away from the station and towards Hampton Loade ferry. Tom hesitated but then followed. The river lay low and flowed sluggishly some distance from the banks. Ferry passengers were obliged to reach the ferry across an ever-lengthening plank walkway jutting out from either bank.

'Looks like business has been slow,' said Jack, surveying the scene with his arm around Tom's shoulder, 'I'd say the ferries finished for the evening.'

'Why are we here?'

'Well, have you ever seen the river so low and clear before?' Jack said, throwing a stone into the middle. 'You'll maybe find coins people have dropped from the ferry over the years.'

'Stop pulling my leg, you just want to get me soaked,' Tom said, as he searched Jack's face for any trace of a tell-tale grin.

'Have a look, you've nothing to lose,' Jack said, as he nodded towards the shallows.

Tom kicked off his boots unenthusiastically, still unsure if Jack had been yanking his chain.

*****

Water dripped from the bottom of Tom's trousers as they sat together at the pub bench. A fine day had slipped seamlessly into a warm gentle evening. 'Tom, best give me that florin. I'll buy the beer, they won't serve you.'

Tom begrudgingly handed him the coin. Jack returned with a pint for himself and a half for Tom and set them on the table. Tom impishly switched the glasses. Jack sat silently, his eyes saying everything. Tom bluffed it out for a while but then relented and swopped the glasses, before shrugging his shoulders and smiling.

'Cheers, to the first of many you buy me,' Jack said, with a wink.

Tom nodded, but then slid his upright palm across the table top towards Jack, who watched intrigued. 'Change,' he said, with one eyebrow raised.

'I thought it was my tip,' Jack said, poker faced.

'Hand it over.'

'What?'

'Hand it over. Please.'

'Anyway, how much did you find?' Jack said, dropping coppers into Tom's palm.

'A fair bit.'

'Well, how much is that then?'

'Six and a penny.'

'Show me.'

'Look, a half crown, three sixpences, a threepenny bit and a penny.'

'That's not six shillings.'

'It was before I paid for the beer. There was a florin as well, remember?'

'Damn good idea of mine, though. You have to admit your old dad knows a thing or two,' he said, preening himself.

'Tell me Dad, if you were so sure about the coins, why didn't you get some for yourself?' Tom said, with a smirk.

'Well, I didn't want to spoil it for you.' Jack said, before draining his glass. 'Come on, drink up, our train is due.'

They chatted happily between Jack's nods and hello's to workmates along the way back to the Bridge. Tom half-listened as he mustered the confidence to ask a question.

'Dad, can I live with you?'

The crucial few moments silence that followed told Tom the answer would be no. His chin met his chest as the rejection drove home.

'Tom, I don't know how to say this right, but I can't see how it would work.'

Tom became even more crestfallen now the words had been said.

'It would be great, but I can see loads of problems in the way,' Jack said, trying to look Tom in the eye, but he had turned away.

Jack explained to Tom's back, how with Harris there, there would be no room for him. How his adopted Dad would not hear of it. How his adopted Mom would be relying on his wage coming in. How impractical it would be for Tom to get to work from the cottage.

Tom listened as tears welled up, but instead of crying, he flew at Jack, windmilling punches at his chest. Jack held him at arm's length by the shoulders; gently restraining him as his whirlwind gradually subsided into limp sobs. Tom studied the ground disconsolately before lifting his head. He began to speak in faltering bursts:

'So you didn't want me ….. when I was a baby ….. you don't want me ….. now I'm sixteen ….. will you ever want me ….. as your son?'

'Tom, I wish it were different,' Jack said, through a grimace, 'and it will be one day.'

'One day, when?' Tom said, sticking his chin out as a challenge to Jack.

'Tom, I promise, when you make up twenty-one, you'll be your own man and you can decide your future and no one can stop you. If you decided then that you want to live with me, I will move heaven and earth to make it possible.'

They stood statue-still staring at the river, both of them wishing the question had not been asked. Twilight faded towards night, only goodbyes remained.

Chapter 23: Bill and George, no Jack
Friday 25th September 1942

Jack deliberated his life as he stepped metronomically from sleeper to sleeper checking the rails. The repetitive cadence created a state of mind that allowed him to debate the major themes he kept under lock and key at the back of his mind.

His thoughts drifted towards Harris; subconsciously he started to make a list. The gossips in the Bridge felt he had taken a massive risk when he offered his home to Harris, an outsider without a past, family or not. If he had family why not contact them, surely his home was where he should be? Jack knew he could not send him away, where would he go?

Jack liked Harris, he felt whole in his company. But, could the gossips be right? Jack did not think so, After all, Harris's injuries were visible for all to see and the blow to his head could easily have caused his amnesia.

Besides, Harris showed willing. He helped with digging the vegetable patch, cooking and washing dishes, all despite his damaged leg. Latterly though Harris had come up trumps as the tutor up at the big house. With two wage packets coming into the cottage, everyday life had become comfortable. They could pay Jessie, a neighbour, to keep the cottage clean and cook some evening meals. Not forgetting Harris's talent for bringing Sherlock Holmes stories to life; combined with a jug and a fire, they created a perfect evening.

On the downside, Jack felt frustrated that Harris had failed to remember any semblance of his past. Harris's presence also blocked Tom's wish to live with him. The situation had damaged his efforts to reconnect with Tom. And what about Ellie? She had been convinced of Harris's motives towards her and yet his reaction was to question her understanding. He had put Harris first ahead of people he loved, it was true and what sense did that make?

A quarter after five, Jack calculated, before glancing up at St Luke's clock for confirmation. *Damn I'm ahead of myself, it's only ten past.*

'All right, Jack?' Bill said, more by way of gaining his attention than asking about his health. 'Penny for them?'

Deep in his own private world, Jack would have strolled straight past Bill, sitting on the goods yard wall.

'All right, Jack?' Bill said, repeating his greeting, with a quizzical glance up into Jack's blank face.

'Sorry, miles away.'

'George and me are going fishing at our spot, you coming?'

'When?'

'Tomorrow on the morning train, coming back Sunday,' Bill said.

'I'm working the weekend,' Jack said.

'Shame. We'll catch some for you,' Bill said, with an exaggerated shrug.

Jack sensed Bill's reply lacked genuine disappointment. *Did they really want him to go or were they just going through the motions of asking?*

'Heard about China,' Bill said. 'The rumour is, they found his body today up at the works. Drowned in a sluice.'

'How?' Jack said.

'They say he must have fallen in during the night shift,' Bill said.

'But he knows the works like the back of his hand, he wouldn't just fall in,' Jack said.

'Not sober he wouldn't,' George said, with a knowing look.

'Best get off home,' Jack said. 'See you next week, then.'

They nodded goodbye and Jack trudged away. His aching feet forgotten as the pain transferred to his head, which throbbed with yet more questions.

The whole world and his dog know we were straightening the track this Sunday. It was on the notice board. Surely, it's common knowledge, he thought. *Maybe they just made a mistake.*

A few steps later he stopped.

No, it's not a mistake, first the spiv and now this. It all adds up: they're going to cut me out. I need to protect the coins for Tom's future.

'Come on, Nip, let's see if Harris has tea for us.'

Jack lifted the latch and pushed against the front door. Nipper shot through the opening ahead of Jack, timing her entrance to perfection. A familiar smell assaulted Jack's nostrils.

'Harris, smells like you've burnt the cabbage again,' Jack said, looking back and forth, between the steaming saucepans and Harris.

'Green beans actually, old boy,' Harris said, as his face appeared from behind the evening paper.

'Jesus, Harris, even Nipper won't eat this,' Jack said, burning his hand on the hot saucepan lid and dropping it onto the quarry tiles. Nipper dived for cover as the cast iron lid rebounded in her direction.

'Do you know how to cook, Harris?' Jack said, as he thrust his hand under the tap, running cold water over his burnt fingers.

Harris caught Jack's eye and beamed, then with a shrug of his shoulders delivered his killer line.

'Do you know, I just can't remember if I can cook or not.'

'Well, I can bloody well tell ....'

The penny dropped, Jack's peevish thought faded into a smile before fully forming, as he registered the funny side of Harris's comeback.

Jack and Harris shared the edible bits; Nipper got what looked like black concrete stuck firmly to the pot. Nipper fought ferociously to clean the pot, changing her angles of attack frequently, but eventually conceded defeat and sat down, whimpering lightly.

'Mmm, that was lovely,' Jack said, 'What's for pudding, Mummy?'

'Bread and jam, but only if you ask nicely,' Harris said, with his hands on his hips and a stern-mother-to-cheeky-son expression on his face.

'If you're going fishing tonight, can I come?'

'Why?'

'Just thought I'd give it a try tonight.'

'Sorry Harris, another time maybe.'

Chapter 24: Night Ride
Evening Friday 25th September 1942

Jack strode thoughtfully towards the Bridge carrying his rod and tackle bag, a halfpenny in hand and Nipper in close attendance. The toll keeper took Jack's coin.

'Trying Sunnyside tonight?'

'Been reports of a massive pike up by the Albert,' Jack said.

'I'd rather be in my bed.'

His real plan involved a difficult bike ride in the dark. Jack did not own a bike but he knew someone who did. The bank's head cashier owned one with a basket on the handlebars, ideal for Nipper. Jack's mind acted out possible problem situations as he crossed the road on Tontine Hill.

I'm riding out of the Bridge and Constable James or one of the other bobbies stops me, what do I say? Within a couple of strides, he had framed an answer and tried it out under his breath.

'I'm off up to Buildwas Bridge. One of the lads tells me there's a monster pike up there, thought I'd give it a shot.'

He believed in sticking as close to the truth as possible. Jack switched into the constable character and came back with.

'I've never seen you on a bike before? Whose is it and where's the lights?'

Switching back to his own persona, Jack imagined replying in a relaxed tone.

'It's Smoutie's. He said I could borrow it anytime. He's drinking in the Tontine if you want to check.'

The part about Smoutie's offer was true, though the offer had been made when they were both at school. Jack imagined trying to gauge the constable's reaction before answering the second part of the challenge. He thought he might say:

'I didn't think you were supposed to show lights in the blackout, so I didn't ask to borrow them.' He thought he might pause and then offer a solution: 'I could push it with no lights, couldn't I? It would take a little longer, but then I've got all night.'

Jack visualised the bobby reluctantly letting him go. He would then remount the second he was out of sight.

Jack strolled casually down Tontine Hill, cautiously checking for people watching him. Safely hidden beneath his cap his eyes darted into dark alleys and doorways as he checked for busybodies. No one paid him any attention as he sauntered along with Nipper just behind. With one last look around, he disappeared into Severn Bank, its front doors so close together one person could knock on two doors at the same time. Doubling back along Bath Road he reached the yard gates at the rear of the Tontine. Smoutie's bike stood safely inside.

His plan had been to climb the wall and release the gate bolts from the inside. Shouldering the gate just on the off chance, it swung open noisily as the loose bolts scraped against the paving slabs. Heart in mouth Jack stood stock still, his back pressed hard against the wall. Waiting to be discovered, he was rapidly inventing excuses, but no one came.

The quarter hour struck high in the church tower behind him. Light leaking from the Tontine's back door reflected faintly along the bike's handlebars. Grabbing the Humber, he swung it around and out of the yard and lifted Nipper into the basket before peddling away unsteadily. It had been decades since he last cycled; they said that "you never forget how to ride a bike", Jack was not convinced. The Humber proved difficult to ride, not helped by his fishing rod attached to the crossbar and Nipper moving about in the basket. He glimpsed Sunnysiders, but they paid him little attention as he rode towards Dale End.

A lorry growled in the blackness as it slogged up the steep bank towards him. As it came under the railway bridge, he saw its dim lights for the first time. Jack took advantage of the bank, freewheeling down the footpath towards the Meadow Inn. The lorry, now only yards away, suddenly swung across his path into the Meadow car park. Jack lost the lorry momentarily in his blind spot. Pulling hard on the brakes, he closed his eyes and hoped. Instinctively, he inhaled making himself smaller, narrowly avoiding the trucks tailgate as it crossed the footpath in front of him. Wobbling on jellied legs, Jack watched exuberant airmen leap down from under the lorry's canvas. They rushed towards the inn's back door laughing and shouting as they went, oblivious to Jack still shaking in the road.

Nipper nervously allowed herself to be lifted into the basket, having fallen out during Jack's erratic avoidance manoeuvres. Jack remounted, hoping the tremors that ran along his arms and legs would subside with activity. By Buildwas, his equilibrium returned just in time to dodge a series of potholes hiding in the gloom.

*****

Having slogged his way up the first half of the bank, he gratefully gave in. Even in low gear, the bank won hands down. He dismounted with a wobble as his trailing leg caught the fishing rod. He considered himself quite fit, though his burning lungs and aching legs disagreed. Confirmation of his lack of fitness came as he heaved into the hedge. Nipper took cover.

After spitting acidic bile forcefully into a ditch, he began to trudge grudgingly up the bank. Five minutes later, he reached level road. Recovering, Jack remounted. From his elevated position, he could see over the hedge and down to the curving 'S' shapes of the Severn dimly reflected in the flood plain below. Jack imagined a giant silvery slow worm slithering across a cricket pitch, its slippery skin illuminated by moonlight. The remainder of their journey passed in a blur of blackness, punctuated by occasional glimpses of the moon and stars.

Jack dismounted. Nipper gratefully hopped from the basket, landing untidily at Jack's feet. Wheeling the bike through the gate, he concealed it under a hedge. On reflection, he thought he may have been overly cautious, after all, *who would find a black bike miles from anywhere in the dead of night? Someone would literally have to fall over it and who would be out and about at this time of night?*

Taking a shielded work lamp from his shoulder bag, he set off in the direction of the river across the Eyton point-to-point course. As he reached the fisherman's path, tinkling notes of a pub piano drifted towards him. A glow leaked invitingly from around the blackout at the riverside inn just across the river. Oh, how he would have enjoyed sitting in the bar with a pint and singing along with the other drinkers. Choruses of 'Roll out the Barrel' faded away on the breeze. *Only a mile to go*, he told himself.

*****

Positioning the light, he began to dig out the soil with his hands. Locating the bag, he pulled it out by the strap allowing a coin to escape unnoticed. Having checked the coins, he refilled the void. Nipper considered this a fine game, digging out the loose earth, as swiftly as Jack could push it back. After much cajoling, Nipper finally accepted the void must be filled. Jack disguised the disturbed earth as best he could and started back.

'We'll Meet Again' floated across the river; he joined in under his breath. The pub could be only fifty yards away, but it may as well have been fifty miles. Jack stumbled as his boot found an unseen rabbit hole.

'Damn and blast it.'

He ripped the blackout shield from his light in temper.

As if a German bomber could see this little light, he chided himself. After a few paces, he had second thoughts. *But what if there's a keen as mustard gamekeeper out there somewhere, looking out for poachers. He'd want to know what was in the bag, wouldn't he? All these coins would be difficult to explain away.*

On balance, Jack preferred to see the path and take a chance. Resting by the bike, Jack had a feeling that the return hike had been more arduous; perhaps he had missed his way somewhere in the dark.

Hauling the bike upright against the twisted gatepost, Jack lifted Nipper back into the basket, mounted and made a wobbly exit through the gateway. Riding the bike after his trek proved challenging, as the repetitive circular motion confused his weary legs. Peering dimly into the blackness ahead, he concentrated on following the faint glimmer of moonlight reflecting back from the road's smooth surface. Nipper's nose twitched nervously.

Stopping at the junction of the lane and the main road, Jack rested for a few moments. The sound of a motorbike in the distance began to intrude upon the silence of the night. The thump of its single cylinder engine grew louder as it neared. Its shielded headlight appeared from his left, before it roared past, heading toward the Bridge. Astounded by its speed, Jack could only assume the rider had been familiar with the road ahead. *That bike's being ridden damn hard*, Jack thought, as the acrid stench of hot oil and exhaust fumes filled the air.

Having reached the top of what he hoped would be the last hill; Jack savoured the thought of a well-earned rest as he freewheeled down towards the Bridge. Nipper stood in the basket, sniffing the fields on either side. Gravity began to propel the bike, offering a welcome rest for his tired calves and thighs. Rushing air flapped Nipper's ear tips as she half looked back for reassurance. Fortunately, she could not see the detail of Jack's face, which had begun to show signs of concern.

Without warning, the hill suddenly steepened. Having previously gained momentum along the shallow slope, Jack elected to check their speed a little. His fingers squeezed the brake levers. To his horror, nothing happened. He pulled hard until the levers were clamped against the handlebars, still nothing. Panic set in as their speed increased unchecked. Gravity and the hill were winning. The handlebars began to shake. Jack struggled to control them as the increasingly unbalanced front wheel transmitted its warning. Blurred trees silhouetted against the night sky flashed by. The road took an unseen bend that swept away graciously to their left. They sped straight ahead.

An open gate invited the bike and its intrepid travellers into a newly mown hay meadow. Unseated at the first hay row, Jack slid down the now vertical crossbar, making agonising contact with the handlebars, as part of a slow-motion cartwheel which separated rider and ridden. The bike pirouetted and then collapsed, its handlebars and peddles gouging furrows in the sward. Jack landed heavily, shoulder first. The snap bag and coins smashed forcefully against his skull. He crumpled gracefully face first into the mown grass.

Nipper had been catapulted from the basket. She flew upright, paws ready to make contact. Her landing, though, occurred at a velocity well above her maximum running speed. After a number of involuntary roly-poly's, she came to rest in a row of drying grass, a little stunned but none the worse for wear.

A cold wet nose in the ear isn't what you would pray for, but given the circumstances it was certainly the lesser of many possible evils. At least Jack had no doubt that he was still in the land of the living. Groggily, the ex-trick cyclist wrestled Smoutie's bike upright and pushed it towards the gate. A cursory inspection revealed that except for clumps of grass adhering to the pedals and handlebars the stolen steed had fared better than its passengers.

Nipper kept her distance when invited to sit back in the basket, preferring to follow on foot. Jack, his body aching, remounted gingerly and set off at a sedate pace. Jack recalled no other hills between him and the Bridge, but he wasn't taking any chances.

They were soon at Marwood. Nipper by now regretted her decision and whimpered pathetically to be lifted back into the basket.

Not far now, Jack told himself, *at least we've not bumped into anyone.*

Bending to scoop Nipper into the basket, a dull red light caught Jack's eye. It shone faintly some distance off the road to his right. He propped the bike against a fence and made his way towards the glow. The smell of burnt oil and petrol grew stronger as he closed in. A motorbike lay on its side, just off the road. The pungent smell of petrol encouraged Jack to wrestle it onto its stand. The bike looked undamaged. Jack patted the engine cautiously. *I would have sworn this was the same bike that passed us but it couldn't be: the engine is cool, should be red hot,* he considered.

Nipper growled and then began to bark, low, elongated, insistent barks. Puzzled, Jack called her, but she ignored him. She continued to bark insistently. Leaving the bike, Jack moved towards Nipper down the shallow bank towards the river. Shining his light in her direction, he could only see dense undergrowth, no Nipper. She continued to bark from beneath thick bushes, which appeared impenetrable except at ground level. Jack lay on his stomach and crawled towards her, something he soon regretted as the ground became boggy. His suffused light found Nipper. Next to Nipper lay the rider. He appeared to be sleeping comfortably on his front, wrapped warmly in a flying jacket. Jack shook his shoulder without a response. Jack attempted to turn him onto his back. For the first-time Jack saw the horror of what had once been the rider's face. Jack had seen soldiers killed in battle, but somehow this had been different. Recoiling, he vomited into the undergrowth, then rolled away, spitting the evil taste from his mouth as he got unsteadily to his feet.

As far as he could tell, the man would have been about his own height and weight, but maybe a few years younger. Jack thought he must have misjudged the corner and been flung from the motorbike as it left the road and landed dead amongst the bushes. He doubted the body would have been found had it not been for Nipper, even in daylight.

Jack now faced a dilemma. How could he report the accident without opening himself up to scrutiny? He could imagine Constable James getting into his ribs with all sorts of difficult questions. He imagined him asking:

'Can you explain why you are riding a stolen bicycle with no lights at the dead of night? And don't say fishing.'

Or, 'That bag looks heavy, show me what's inside.'

Everyone in the Bridge would know the story by mid-morning. Bill and George would guess what he'd been up to. No, he definitely couldn't take the risk. It would be impossible to rebury the coins or hide them, even temporarily, as everyone would be watching him. As he saw it, there could be only one choice, to leave the body in the undergrowth and hope that someone else would find it.

With a heavy heart he lifted Nipper into the basket and swung his leg carefully over the crossbar. After making a sign of a cross in the direction of the body, he set off for home. Within ten minutes, they were back in the Bridge. He skirted the main roads taking the alleys back to the Tontine's yard. The Bridge felt unusually silent and extremely dark. He slid the bike back into the yard and made for home.

As he reached the crown of the Bridge he could see that the Tollhouse gate had been closed and locked, a sight he had seldom seen. Climbing the gate was his only option. Standing on the bottom hinge, he grabbed the pillar finial and swung his other leg onto the top rail between the throat high spikes. Gratefully he eased his battered, aching body over the spikes and back to the ground on Moneyside.

Peering back across the Bridge, he could just make out Nipper, leisurely scenting her way in his general direction. Unable to call or whistle for fear of waking the Tollhouse household he was forced to wait for her. She looked quizzically at the gate and sat down. Jack calculated that she should be able to wriggle under the gate, but Nipper did not concur. He bent and put his hand under the gate to show Nipper what she should do. She lowered her head but then stopped and gave him a 'you must be joking' look, her head inclined to one side.

Aching, tired and exasperated, Jack reached into his tackle bag and pulled out a piece of stale bread. Placing it on the ground on his side of the gate, he encouraged Nipper to come and get it. As he hoped, Nipper wriggled furiously under the gate and swallowed the bread whole.

The tired travellers shambled sluggishly up the bank towards the cottage. The penny dropped as he noticed the clock on the mantelpiece, both hands pointed to three. Their detour into the field had obviously taken longer than he thought. It also explained why the motorbike engine had been cool and why the Bridge had been so silent.

Jack carefully placed the bag and its precious contents inside his workbag and fastened it. Jack wearily climbed the narrow wooden hill to bed, hoping the creaking floorboards would not wake Harris. Nipper settled down on the rag rug in front of the range and soon began to snore and twitch.

Chapter 25: Reburying the Coins
Saturday 26th September 1942

Jack woke to the fuzzy realisation he had slept in his clothes. Movement proved challenging, he wondered fleetingly if rigor mortis felt like this. *Come on Jackson,* he chided, *pull yourself together, there's work to be done.*

Harris snored sonorously from the box room, which pleased Jack. *No need for explanations then,* he thought. Collecting his tool bag, he pushed stiffly through the front door into the new day. He attempted an air of jauntiness, despite his aching body as he arrived at the station. He planned to work down in the desolate countryside towards Lindley, allowing him plenty of opportunity to bury the coins.

Sod's law applied as he checked the office notices. A Wolverhampton based driver reported noisy rail joints across the Viaduct. The rails, must be inspected, it could not be avoided. A revision of his original plan would be required.

Experience told him that there would be no faults with the track. Jack had a theory that the confines of the Gorge and the shape of the viaduct conspired to create a slightly different sound from the rails. He checked each joint diligently but, as he had predicted, there were no faults and no cause for concern.

His thoughts turned to the job in hand, burying the coins. The brick and stone of the viaduct offered few opportunities, though it would be unwise to move closer to the station, now only half a mile away. *Somewhere near the old lime burners maybe,* he thought. *There must be plenty of hiding places at the disused powerhouse or even the burners themselves. But, knowing my luck they'd reopen the burners for the war effort, then I'd be sunk.*

Somewhere around here, he considered, *it's hidden by the bank of trees, it should be okay.* There were no buildings near the spot and no paths, just the railway. Jack decided upon a marker and sighted an imaginary line to the top of the embankment and a convenient fence. Jack scrambled up the embankment following the invisible line between the two points. He eventually decided to dig it as close to the fence post as possible. A hole dug here could conceivably be legitimate work for the GWR should he be seen. Using his posthole spade, he made short work of the excavation.

Distracted by the task in hand, he had overlooked the warning clunk of the distant signal. The regular gasps of a straining engine rounding the nearby curve registered with a jolt. Realising his mistake, he scrambled down the bank to the line side with just enough time to lean nonchalantly on his spade and wave to the fireman and driver. He waited impatiently to wave at the guard's van and watch the train disappear.

Scrambling back up the bank he stealthily buried the coins. *That was a close one*, he thought, as he filled in the hole and camouflaged the disturbed soil by dragging undergrowth across it. Jack took a last look around, satisfying himself he had covered his tracks. Striding out towards the station he worked hard at portraying a sense of nonchalance he did not feel.

The people of the Bridge considered gossiping a local pastime, railway gossips however, were even more mischievous and inaccurate. If he'd been seen, he could imagine the train crew telling the station staff, 'Oh, Jack's slacking along the Viaduct'. *Better that than a report of digging a hole halfway up the embankment,* thought Jack. At best, he'd have his leg pulled, at worst some nosy parker would have taken a look at what he'd been doing.

Chapter 26: Emergency Meeting of the First Friday Club
Sunday 28th September 1942

Bill waited for Jack at the bottom of Bridge Bank. There were no pleasantries.

'Jack, me and George are calling an emergency meeting tonight, be there.'

The last syllables were spat from Bill's mouth as he strode away. No reasons were offered but then Jack did not need to ask. Feeling sick at the pit of his stomach, he broke into a cold sweat. *They've rumbled me, or they think they have*, he thought, before it occurred to him, *Shit, I should have asked why they were back early.*

After the initial shock, Jack regained his poise. In his own mind, he had done little wrong. After all, he found the coins. His only mistake had been to involve Bill and George. He believed they were about to cut him out, by dealing the coins through the Spiv, what else could he do? Jack trudged towards Jackfield and the track straightening work that had been scheduled. He used the time to hone the lines he would use that evening.

*****

As Jack ambled towards the Railway Hotel, practising different expressions and reactions: he rehearsed looks of anguish, of incredulity and indignation. *In for a penny, in for a pound,* Jack speculated, as he straightened his back and pushed through the bar door. He joined Bill and George at their usual table; greetings were exchanged out of habit, though without the customary warmth. After checking for eavesdroppers, the meeting should have begun, but no one spoke. Bill and George stared pointedly at Jack, who stared back holding his nerve as best he could.

Bill, stone-faced, pushed his hand into his jacket pocket and pulled out a clenched fist. With great deliberation, he slid it slowly across the table towards Jack. Three pairs of eyes followed the fist's journey; two pairs knew what it held. As Bill's fingers opened theatrically, a coin rolled onto the table top. The coin rolled unaided towards Jack as if confirming the men's thoughts. It fell face up next to Jack's pint. Jack froze; the drama had caught him cold. His gut knotted. He almost caved in, but caught himself and conjured a convincing look of incredulity.

'Put that with the others, Jack,' Bill said, through gritted teeth, just audible over stools scraping back, as Bill and George stood in unison.

'Where did you get this,' Jack said, picking up the coin. 'Is this one of ours? What's this about, lads?'

'You know full well what it's about Jack. Be a man and admit it,' George said, stroking his comb over flat to his flushed scalp.

'My crystal ball is on the blink,' Jack said, hoping to lighten the mood.

'You've a bloody cheek Jack, I'll give you that,' Bill said, twisting and tightening his belt, while looking around for nosey parkers.

'You know exactly what this is about,' Bill continued, staring at Jack intently, his eyes burning behind the peak of his cap.

'Look, I'll get the beers and then you can tell me what's eating you,' Jack said.

Bill and George conferred in glances.

'We'll stay for one, but only as it's you Jack.'

Jack moved away to the bar and nonchalantly engaged the landlord in local gossip as he pulled the pints. He may have looked relaxed but inside his heart raced as he calculated and recalculated the myriad possible permutations of his story. Turning away from the bar towards Bill and George, he suddenly decided to take a chance and say nothing. He would bluff it out.

'You're spilling,' George said, watching Jack's wavering progress back to the table, 'Feeling guilty?'

'Why won't you just admit it?' Bill said, as he subliminally traced the shape of his moustache with his forefinger and thumb.

'Admit what?' Jack said, evenly.

'We hoped you'd be man enough to admit it,' Bill said, exasperation etched across his face. 'It's hard for us to accuse you as we've all been mates for so long.'

'But we will, Jack, we will,' George said.

Jack snapped and went on the offensive.

'Just spit it out,' he said. Taking a deep breath and looking from one to the other he continued: 'I'm fed up of this rot. Say what you've come to say.'

After a stunned silence, Jack saw his reward, as signs of doubt crept across Bill's face. He could do it; he could face them down, if he just managed to hold his nerve a little longer.

'The coins have gone!' George said, hesitating before accusing Jack, allowing him to jump in.

'When did you find out?' Jack said.

'When we went fishing on Saturday,' George said.

'We thought you would know....' Bill said.

'How the hell would I know, I've only just heard they're missing.' Jack said, cutting Bill off in mid-sentence.

Bill tried again: 'Jack, stop butting in,' he said, as his eyes nervously scanned the bar. 'Only the three of us knew. We know we didn't do it, so that leaves ....'

'Let me get this straight,' Jack said, cutting Bill off, his eyes narrowing with anger he actually felt; he was not enjoying being accused, guilty or not. 'You two supposed mates of mine are accusing me of taking the coins, are you? Is that what you're saying?'

'Look, Jack, we had to ask,' Bill said, mentally retreating. 'We thought you may have moved them for safe keeping or something.'

'And you think I wouldn't tell you,' Jack said, sensing that the wind had spilled from their sails. 'Right you've had your say, now let me have mine. Let's look at it from my side of the fence.'

Bill and George stared blankly back at Jack not knowing quite what to think.

'First of all, you arrange a fishing trip when everyone on the railway knows I've got to work,' Jack said, looking directly at Bill. 'And then you ask me at the last minute, so I've got no chance of organising cover. What do you expect me to think?' Jack then answered his own question: 'I'll tell you, I could think you planned it knowing that I couldn't go.'

'Jack, we didn't, honest,' George said, as he shook his head stridently.

Jack noticed Bill tearing his beer mat distractedly.

'The way I see it, you two could have arranged to be near the coins when I couldn't be there,' Jack said, as he spread his arms. 'What am I supposed to think, eh? I could think, you have them.'

'But ...' George said as he attempted to cut in, but Jack would not be deflected.

'And then there's your friend the Spiv,' he said, allowing his words to hang.

He watched Bill and George who, to Jack's surprise, gave nothing away. *Shit, maybe I've got this part wrong. No, hold your nerve. Give them both barrels. There's nothing to lose.*

'You know who I'm talking about, I saw you talking to him before the last meeting,' Jack said, with a questioning raised eyebrow. 'And at the second meeting, don't think I didn't notice.'

'Hang on Jack,' Bill said, raising his palm in an attempt to deflect him. 'I know who you're talking about now. He does look like a bit of a wide boy, now you mention it,' Bill said, looking pointedly a George. 'You know the one, with the big conk.'

'Oh him, he just asked the way to the bogs, that's all,' George said, helping Bill out.

'Why did he buttonhole me about the coins then? Don't suppose you know anything about that, either.'

'Don't know what you mean,' George said. Jack went back on the attack.

'You accuse me of taking the coins. From where I stand, you could easily be double bluffing me,' Jack said. 'You roll me a coin to prove something or other, it proves nothing to me. The coin could be one of our find, that you've taken!'

Bill and George shook their heads in unison at Jack.

'That's not what happened, Jack! You could see it that way, but you should trust us. We're your mates,' George said.

'That's rich coming from you pair. I should trust you, when you didn't trust me?' Jack leant into the table towards them and in a soft voice said: 'Look, don't you see we need to trust each other lads let's not fall out over a few coins.'

He leant back against his chair, confident now. He forced a resigned smile, which they returned.

'Anyway, whose round, is it? Let's have a pint and forget it; we're probably better off without the them. If it's ok I'll keep this one,' Jack said, spinning it in the air. Bill and George looked unsure.

'A reminder of being nearly rich,' Jack said, as he caught the coin 'heads'.

Making his way up Bridge Bank towards the cottage, Jack wondered if Bill and George would still believe him in the morning.

Chapter 27: The Spiv comes knocking
Monday 29th September 1942

Harris sat agreeably in Jack's scullery enjoying the pleasures of the warm sun on his back as gentle breeze whispering around the half open front door. Harris saw him first, only a fleeting glimpse but enough. The ferret eyes either side of his large nose had been sufficient. Harris's right hand felt for the shotgun beside the chair, as a large, unwelcome chunk of his previous life strode confidently towards the cottage, oblivious of his presence.

His knock rattled the door. Harris bided his time in silence. The door creaked as it opened fully. The Spiv stepped from shade into the low sunlight that warmed Harris's back. Initially blinded, he squinted at the figure sitting in the chair, his right-hand hovering over the gun in his waistband.

'Jack. I warned you I'd be back ....,' the Spiv said, faltering as his eyes adjusted. 'But you're dead, JC!'

'As you see Nobby, I'm very much alive,' Harris said, waving the shotgun menacingly. 'Put the gun on the table, use your left hand, barrel first.' Nobby complied. He stood motionless, gape mouthed, resolutely staring at a ghost.

'You didn't expect to run into me again, now did you Nobby?' Harris said, with a grin. 'You'd have come mob-handed had you known.'

'But the London boys rubbed you out. They told the boss, they'd thrown you off a train somewhere out in the sticks.'

'Nobby sit down, you're making the place look untidy,' Harris said, waving the shotgun in the direction of a stool by the door. 'Sit there, I don't want to miss if you try something stupid.'

Nobby perched reluctantly on the stool.

'What's the story?'

'Well ....'

'Nobby, don't bother lying. You're no good at it.'

'Would I ....?'

'Nobby, give it to me straight or I'll blast your knees one at a time.'

Nobby's confident body language collapsed into a cesspool of self-doubt.

'Well, I came here to put the wind up a bloke called Jack. The story is that he's got something we are interested in.'

'Something?'

'The script says valuables: coins, maybe gold coins.'

'How good is your info?'

'Well, him and his mates had been overheard in a pub talking about something valuable. My snitch didn't catch it all, but it didn't take much to connect the dots.'

'So, what's the plan?'

'I made him an offer, but he wouldn't play. I got a strong indication that his mates would, though.'

'Nobby, there's nobody here by the name of Jack. Do you hear me? There is no Jack here, get it?'

'If you say so, JC.'

'I do Nobby, I do,' said Harris. 'Before I let you go, you need to understand you have never seen me, get it?'

A silence settled between them.

'You wouldn't spill the beans to your psychopath of a boss, now would you?'

Nobby shrugged impassively, appearing to grow in confidence

'Just in case you're considering it, let me assure you it wouldn't be a wise move.'

Harris sensed Nobby was not buying his threat.

'Let's look at it this way Nobby old son. For starters, the London boys aren't going to be chuffed, if you let it be known I'm alive, now are they? They could get nasty if you embarrassed them.'

'I see what you're saying, but ....'

'If that doesn't convince you, then think about this. I could pay you back by subtly letting your new boss know you slept with that girl of his. Jenny that's the one isn't it?'

'But, I didn't, I didn't, you know I didn't, come on you wouldn't ...'

'I believe you Nobby, but he's not the trusting type, now is he? You were quite pally with her if I remember. You know how irrationally jealous he gets if someone even looks at her.'

'JC, you know I don't go for women. Okay, I give the impression I'm interested, but I'm not, you know I'm not. Come on, play the white man.'

'That would be your defence, would it? Think of the implications? Let's just assume that he believes you. That's when your problems would really start, he certainly isn't going to want a shirt lifter in his gang, now is he? And no one leaves the gang in one piece, do they?'

Nobby's colour paled into translucency.

'I'm glad you understand Nobby. Just don't cross me or the sky will fall in on you.'

'Your secret's safe with me, honest, JC.'

'Okay, I believe you.' Harris said. The Spiv relaxed a little but still looked perplexed.

'But, how are you still alive?'

'For old times' sake, I'll tell you. But don't even think …..'

Nobby nodded his agreement.

'Well it goes like this. Out of the blue a couple of weeks ago, I received a reverse charge call through the operator. The caller owed me a favour or two, no names, no pack drill. He warned me that two London boys had been paid to rub me out. I didn't need two guesses who would be behind the hit and it didn't take a brain surgeon to understand I should disappear.'

'Understood.'

'I attempted to change my appearance, but had little time. Someone tipped them off that I would be travelling by train to Liverpool. I had taken the country route as a precaution, but they knew my plan and were waiting at Bewdley Station.

'Fortunately, I saw them first. They weren't exactly wearing fedoras and carrying violin cases but anyone in the business would recognise them. They got into the carriage behind me, so I moved up one coach, which put us at each end of the three-coach corridor train. It left room to manoeuvre.

'I hid in the loo for a while. I ditched everything that identified me down the toilet, hoping the change of hair and no moustache would work. Unfortunately, the train carried few passengers. It took them no time at all to track me down. I sat next to a young woman. I figured they wouldn't attempt anything with a witness. The woman looked worried, she must have been thinking, 'why sit next to me, it's an empty carriage?' She got off at a request stop somewhere in the sticks. If I'd been smarter I should have got off with her and taken my chances, but I didn't.

'They had me trapped. My only option would be to jump and hope they didn't have the balls to follow. The train had been pulling up a bank, I could hear the engine straining. I found it difficult to tell how fast we were going in the dark, but I had no real choice but to jump, so I did. One of them caught my arm but couldn't hang on, I flew briefly before hitting the ground hard. As Luck would have it, I didn't hit any obstructions and my momentum rolled me down an embankment and under a bush. I gave my head a good wallop, and wrecked my knee and ankle but, importantly, I lived to tell the tale.

'I doubt they even saw me hit the ground. They must have reasoned that even if I survived, I wouldn't be back for more punishment. So, I guess they felt confident to tell your boss the problem had been dealt with. There you have it Nobby, warts and all.'

'You were bloody lucky. Living up to your nickname hey JC.'

'Correct. Now you stay lucky and keep your mouth shut,' Harris said, as he passed him the gun minus its bullets. Nobby needed no second invitation: dashing around the door he ran to the gate and down the bank.

Harris reflected that his choice to live without a past had been preferable to being a dead ex-gang leader.

*****

Jack, hidden by the trees bounding the woodland path watched mystified as the Spiv ran pal mal [pell mell] through the cottage gate and down the bank. *Why run, why so pale? Why does he looks like he's just seen a ghost?* Jack wondered. He watched with interest as the Spiv ran pell-mell down bridge bank until he reached the bottom. After walking for a few paces, he stood and collected himself. Jack sauntered thoughtfully towards the cottage.

'Have we just had a visitor?' Jack said, attempting a light tone as he piled his bags behind the door. *Why didn't I challenge him outright,* he thought.

'No,' Harris said, without looking up from his newspaper, 'No one ever calls here, you know that. Why, were you expecting someone?'

'Harris, are you sure?' Jack pressed

'I told you, no one.'

'That's strange, I saw the Spiv running through the gate? Why are you lying?'

'To be honest, I didn't want to worry you Jack. He was enquiring after you.'

'Okay, but why was he in such a hurry?'

'I put the wind up him with this,' Harris said, holding the shotgun aloft.

'Point it down man and put the safety on,' Jack said, as he motioned Harris to break open the gun, making it safe.

Now I know why he was running, Jack decided.

'Why did you need to scare him?'

'To help you, Jack.'

That doesn't add up? The Spiv would just come back with some thugs and I'd be on the receiving end. That's hardly helping me? Jack bridled.

Languidly, Harris waited for Jack to return from his thoughts, before he dropped the second bombshell, 'By the way, you've had another visitor,'

'I thought we hadn't any visitors,' Jack said, raising one eyebrow. 'Who?'

'A policeman,' Harris replied as if oblivious to Jack's jibe.

'His name?'

'Didn't say.'

Frustrated Jack attempted identification, 'Young chap, first uniform, no stripes, spick and span, full of himself, that sort?'

Harris nodded knowingly.

'Constable James,' Jack said, disconsolately. 'He's got it in for me; what did he want?'

'He didn't say much, something about those evacuees you found. Apparently, someone wants to press charges, didn't say who. He did say that you would know all about it.'

'Did you tell him, I had nothing to do with it,' Jack said, endeavouring to master his mounting turmoil. 'You know I took them fishing a few weeks ago and they were fine with me. You're their teacher you must know they're fine with me!'

'They've only been in my class for a few weeks, I didn't think that was relevant'

'Those kids were fine with me, James is just making the most of it.'

'Oh yes,' Harris said, as if just recalling, 'he also asked if you knew China or his wife June. I said I thought you did, after all you all know each other in the Bridge.'

'But he knows I knew her, I explained ages ago.'

'Anyway, then he asked if you owned gun. So I showed him the shotgun. He wasn't interested in that sort of a gun and asked if you had a pistol.'

'So you told him, NO!'

'Well, there was that gun in the drawer, so I showed it to him.'

'What gun in the drawer?'

'The one I told you about, the one Chas brought here for you. He said it was to remember him by, a sort of trophy.'

'I don't know anything about Chas coming to the cottage with a gun.'

'Yes, you do. Remember I told you about it, when you came back from the pub on that same evening.'

'No, you bloody well didn't.'

'Yes, I did Jack, it was a few weeks ago now.'

'Well I don't remember,' Jack said, distractedly. 'Anyway, what did James do.'

'He unwrapped the cloth from around it, studied it and then smelt the barrel. He said it had been fired recently and he was taking it as possible evidence.'

'You told him how it got here obviously and about Chas?'

'He didn't ask.'

Frustrated, Jack moved towards the front door. The low sun forced his eyelids to close. In that instant, Jack's mind kaleidoscoped its myriad fragments into a recognisable shape. Harris. Those suppressed gut feelings, those questions he'd never asked. The dismissal of Ellie's warning.

What a fool I've been. Harris was no friend; he's the enemy within.

'Harris, I'd like you to move out,' Jack said, abruptly. 'I need the box room, Tom wants to live here.'

'I thought I was your friend.'

'Yes, you were my friend, but you've been playing me for a fool from the very moment I found you, that's not friendship.'

'Are you sure you want to do this, Jack?'

'Why not, he's my son and it's about time I put him first.'

'I'll ask you again Jack, are you sure? You see, I don't want to leave, I like it here. I'll do anything to stay and I mean anything.'

'Is that a threat?'

'I'd prefer to be subtle, but then again… Yes, it is a threat.'

'You are no threat to me.'

'No? Try this out for size. If I move out of the cottage, I will be forced to take up an offer made to me by Montague Chubb. I'm sure you know who he is.'

'And why on earth would he help you?'

'He likes what I've achieved with the estate children. Montague has offered me the position of a live-in tutor. Imagine me living under the same roof as Ellie! And with him away so often, well anything might happen.'

'Go ahead then. It's not a problem for me.'

'Jack, I know about you and Ellie.'

'There's nothing to know.'

'Still bluffing, Jack.'

A silence fell as the two men weighed each up. Harris broke the silence.

'If you're still not convinced I have the upper hand look at this,' Harris said, holding a coin between his thumb and forefinger. 'It's Identical to the coin in your waistcoat pocket, I believe.'

'Where did you get it?'

'From your snap bag inside the tool bag. I hope you don't mind me taking one - there were hundreds of them.'

'So?'

'So, I could drop this information into the rumour mill. Bill and George should hear about it within a few hours. How much trouble do you want, Jack?'

'Why didn't you say something when you found the coins?'

'Jack, believe me I intend to have my share, but the timing was wrong, everything comes to those who wait.'

'You bastard.'

'That could be true of course, but then again I don't remember.'

'Don't give me that rot, you know exactly who you are.'

'Are you calling me a liar, Jack? That's the kettle calling the pot black, Jack. From what I've heard, you've been telling half-truths all your life.'

'Well, you heard wrong,' Jack said, leading with his chin belligerently.

'Am I?' Harris said, with the confidence of his convictions. 'You think you're a good man Jack, but you're a hypocrite, you're no better than me in lots of ways.'

Jack grew pensive realising Harris held all the cards.

'Jack I want to stay here until the war is over, then I'll start again. It can be as amicable or acrimonious as you like. I have no preference, but, remember I hold all the aces and I have nothing to lose which makes me a dangerous opponent,' Harris said, with the smug grin.

'You snake in the grass,' Jack said, slamming the door, narrowly missing Nipper at his heals. *heels*

'Stay and let's have a jug Jack.' Harris said, under his breath.

Chapter 28: Deep Water
Evening Monday 29th September 1942

Jack walked up and down Bridge Bank every day of his life, a walk that signalled either the beginning or the end of his day. This evening it felt different, as if the rules that governed his life had changed. Somewhere in Jack's mind, an alarm began to ring. For the first time, he felt, he was walking towards an ending, not a beginning.

As he and Nipper crossed the bridge bound for Sunnyside, Jack gazed up stream. The sun still hung high in the sky; he had time to kill.

Without thinking, he followed his childhood footsteps towards the underside of the bridge. Sitting with his back against the abutments, his eye traced the elegant cast iron ribs arcing across the river. His hands traced the smooth semi-circular slots worn into the ribs by the towropes of countless Trow's as they were hauled upstream. He looked wistfully up at the faces silhouetted against the sky. Good memories of Robert and their childhood gang flooded into his mind. He could see them all clearly in black and white. He could also see that Harris had taken Robert's place, a role he had not deserved. Not only that, he had then allowed Harris to come between him and Tom. To add insult to injury it was becoming clear to Jack that Harris had manipulated and betrayed him.

'A penny for them,' Bill said, as he sat down next to Jack. 'You look miles away, mate.'

'I wish I was.' Jack replied distractedly.

'Have you heard the news about China'?

'How can there be news, he's dead.'

'Well exactly, you know we all thought it was strange that he fell in the sluice even if he was drunk.'

'Yes, he knew the territory too well.'

'I heard the Police found too many holes in him.'

'Stop talking in riddles man.'

'The news is he was shot, small calibre apparently, a pistol they think.'

The colour drained from Jack's face as he stared at his boots in horror.

Christ, I'm being fitted up for China's killing. It would suit Harris to have me out of the way. And Constable James would be happy to see me take the blame and he would take credit for solving the case. The two of them may not be in league but they're both against me, how can I win, Jack panicked.

'Look, got to press on, meeting George for a swift one or two,' Bill said, as he sidled away not noticing Jack's ashen face.

Jack steadied himself and set off towards the Albert. The sun hung high over the power station chimneys. He gauged it would be another hour before Ellie could sneak away. He unlocked the boat, and rowed towards their rendezvous. Nipper, for once, followed Jack along the bank. He moored the boat and slumped untidily on the bank. Nipper sat down beside him, leaning contentedly against his leg.

Jack watched the boat's bobbing reflection. His reflective mood encouraged him to consider reshooting recent episodes of his life. *A good life*, he thought.

'But good to whom?' the Director in his head asked. He always felt his life and actions had been justifiable in black and white. But, within a few short weeks since his return to the Bridge the film in his head had changed genre to horror.

Finding the evacuee children would be treated as a heroic scene, but how would he portray the accusations, would they be seen as false?

Discovering the coins, would be a joyous scene, though casting would be difficult. There could be now no parts for Bill and George.

What about Harris, the man with no name, the man he had taken in and befriended? The man who fooled him completely, the friend who had become his enemy. How could he shoot this scene without appearing foolish?

The dead motorbike rider he could not help; someone's son, someone's husband, father or lover. Surely, the man deserved better from him.

Don't forget Tom. Tom could have lived with him, had it not been for Harris. No matter how Jack massaged the scene, he had deserted Tom for a second time.

What about Ellie, his Lady Eleanor, what had he done for her? He had offered her love and put her in danger. He could not protect her or let her go.

If he was linked to China's death by the rumours about June, the gun in the drawer could make the rumours facts.

The evening sun hovered as if determined never to set. She would not come. He knew that now. Not tonight, maybe never. A feeling of claustrophobia blew in from the river and enveloped him. Scrunching his eyelids shut, he tried to banish the feeling, only to see disapproving faces trapped behind his eyelids. Constable James, China, the Spiv, the evacuees and Harris, others were blurred but could have been Bill, George, Tom, Ellie and Montague Chubb. How many enemies could a good man have?

*****

The Director in his head began to coach. They had worked together for many years; though tonight Jack heard the Director speaking his own words, not Jack's. The voice gripped Jack's throat with an iron fist.

'You know your position is desperate, it's hopeless, you feel that don't you?

Listen to me, Jack, I need more. I need real intensity here.

Remember what we talked about, you are standing on the riverbank.

Forget the dog.

You're standing on the riverbank and your whole life is falling apart.

You've lost the sight in one eye fighting a war that will end in a defeat.

The same blast also battered your head and altered your moods.

Your friends see it, though you deny it. It's real though, Jack.

You're feeling desperate: you cheated your friends.

You're about to lose the only woman you've loved.

Okay, I know you loved your wife, but forget that for now.

The underworld, husbands, boyfriends and the police are closing in.

Do you feel the pressure mounting?

Are you ready to do this, in one take?

Look up to the heavens; give me resignation with a tinge of defiance.

More defiance, that's good.

Stare down at the river: don't look at the surface, look through it.

Now stare into the lens. Give me that determined look of yours.

Turn towards the river. Keep that look.

Give me that steely commitment again.

> Stare through your reflection: you're not in control
>
> Someone else is pulling your strings.
>
> Wade into the water slowly, deliberately, determinedly.
>
> Keep wading: let the water close over you. You're done.'

A comforting chill wrapped around him as the Director whispered:

> 'Why breathe when you can drink? Drink it all down, my friend.'

Moments passed before the Director announced.

> 'Cut, well done Jack, just one take.'

Part 2

2015 in Telford

Chapter 1: Meeting Joan

I pressed the keypad buttons, 1-9-3-7. The mechanism buzzed. Shouldering the door, I was enveloped by a dense, warm atmosphere associated with concentrated old people. That distinct odour always astounds me. The odour of stale school dinners, public toilets and damp carpets, partially masked by cheap air freshener. On a bad day, even the most battle-hardened visitors are temporarily incapacitated. The residents appear oblivious.

Moving towards the reception desk, I signed in, adding a few minutes to my visit by entering it an earlier time; I don't know why, there's no overtime here, only guilt. En route to the lift I pass a row of wing-backed chairs and the obligatory faded Constable print set amongst outdated dubious award certificates.

I found Mary, my mum, sitting upstairs in her room, aimlessly staring at the television. She's been at the home for just over a year, moving from South Wales after my father passed away.

Mum and Dad fooled the family completely, everything in their world looked fine and dandy. The real state of the nation only became clear when Dad found himself hospitalised following a fall.

'I tripped over fresh air,' He explained.

Mum's failing short-term memory and Dad's defective balance were challenging, but as a team they had managed. Even when things didn't go to plan he insisted with a resigned smile that his 'vertical hold' had been on the blink and that Mum was just having a bad day.

They survived by using Dad's memory for the 'to do list' and the 'where is it kept directory' and Mum's ability to fetch and do. The facade had been bound seamlessly together with rigid routines and a large square-a-day calendar: Monday washing; Tuesday library; Wednesday pensioners' lunch; Thursday Mum's hair; Friday Tesco; Saturday coffee in town; Sunday church. Impeccable teamwork allowed them to compensate and adjust to each other's frailties, presenting an untroubled picture to the outside world.

Dad recently reshaped the car against a lamppost and the gate pillars. At his subsequent court martial, he found himself demoted to co-pilot and navigator, which coincided with Mum's promotion to captain. By default, driving became a team pursuit. Mum specialised in steering and propulsion, whilst Dad aided with Sat Nav-like directions and gentle reminders of the target destination. As 'left' and 'right' could be easily misunderstood, they were discarded in favour of 'your side' and 'my side'. Dad's secondary duties included applying and releasing the handbrake at the appropriate moment and informing the captain of kerb or wall proximity during parking manoeuvres, but only on his side. Rashly, Dad would offer advice on lane changing and the finer points of roundabout etiquette. These interruptions were not part of his job description and definitely not well received.

Dad had been discharged from hospital on the strict condition that he and Mum move from their three-bedroom home into nursing care. Mum failed to come to terms with the modern nursing home complex, vowing: 'I'll never go on holiday with this firm again, half the people don't speak English.'

Sadly, their partnership dissolved irrevocably when Dad died, although their teamwork still functioned to an extent as mum made decisions based on what she felt Dad would have done in a similar situation.

Mum's short-term memory may be defective but her long-term still functions effectively. In fact, it appears to be gaining content, revealing many previously unheard family anecdotes. At the suggestion of the home, we started a scrapbook of Mum's life story, complete with photographs. It gave everyone a focus as Mum adjusted to her new surroundings.

Hearing the most interesting of Mum's anecdotes once or twice is manageable, but several times at each visit became tedious. Over time, Mum switched from endless repetition to silence as she retreated from conversation, favouring 'yes' or 'no' responses to my monologue. Filling the silences forced me to repeat myself but she didn't appear to mind.

Frustrated by our one-way conversations, I suggested we try a wheelchair ride outside. To my surprise, Mum agreed. We made it down the lift, along the main corridor and into the large open reception area, before I noticed she wore the wrong glasses.

'Mum, I'm just nipping back to your room to get your far-away's. I'll take your near-to's back with me. So, we don't lose them. Okay?'

I set off before Mum could reply and ran up the back stairs to her room. I helped Mum put the far-away's on. She said nothing, but I could tell by her quizzical look that focus had returned to her world. We toured the nearby cemetery and park. It had been a resounding success; our new routine had been established.

Mum happily goes out in the wheelchair no matter what the weather. If it rains, she wears a massive purple poncho. She remains snug and dry inside, only I get wet. She enjoys manipulating raindrops into a burgeoning pool in her lap. Having determined the pool has become sufficiently impressive, she gleefully cascades it over her knees and onto the path.

Our route passes through a sprawling cemetery with its myriad paths. Mum delights in the headstones, plastic flowers, squirrels and bird song. While discomforted by thoughts of my own mortality, I push and try not to think. The graveyard appears to have become an oasis within Mum's reduced world.

'That's a good one,' Mum said, nodding appreciation at a gleaming black headstone, resplendent with gold lettering. A small oval picture of the interred takes her special interest. I wonder if having your photograph snapped, now takes on a new significance. Do you suddenly think to yourself, *I hope it's good enough for my monument?*

We spot surnames derived from trades: Archer, Baker, Lamplighter, Shepherd, and Miller. We find lost soldiers, but most harrowing is the children's section, where bedraggled teddies guard small headstones. Rain, snow, sleet or sunshine the graveyard retains its colour, always a few shades either side of mid-grey. It offers a restful consistency in a constantly changing world: perhaps that's the attraction for Mum.

A creaking black iron gate separates the contrasting worlds of cemetery and park. I gratefully push through it into a world of children and play; a world of cricket, football, tennis, bowls, picnics, dogs, chickens and real flowers. Mum's favourite combination is to watch a few ends of bowls followed by scratching chickens.

Bowls offers her the serenity of the graveyard with the addition of graceful movement. Mum's interest in bowls extends to the groundsman's preparation of the green. Steady passes of mowers and rollers are keenly observed. We have been lucky to catch a couple of ladies' bowls tournaments, where four or five games are played at the same time, on the same green. Jack's and woods crisscross the green, in random patterns. Mum is captivated. She follows the ebb and flow intently, appearing to understand each nuance of play.

She reminds me of my Aunt Flo, who could follow snooker for hours on a tiny black and white telly. She studied each game with enormous concentration, knowing the table position of all the colours throughout the frame. As a boy, it mystified me: surely, the balls were black, white or grey; anyway, I wanted to watch "Doctor Who" on the other channel.

Leaving the bowls, we roll towards a diamond patterned wire fence separating the park and the chickens. Penned in, at the bottom of a garden are half a dozen plump chickens. Mum is amused by their jerky movements. She chuckles as they fling dust into the air and nods as they dig for freedom. Impossible to count, they hide under trees and bushes or inside their hutch and are seldom seen on parade together. Only four are visible out of five or six, I'm never sure. I crack the same pathetic joke each time.

'I bet its chicken for dinner, Mum.'

Mum graciously smiles even though she had heard the chicken joke many times before. It's almost as if she finds comfort in its repetition.

'Sarah?' she says, in the tone of a question.

'Sarah's busy, she has meetings after work Mum. Then there's the gym and she runs as well. She's fitter now than when we met,' I say, sensing that it's not been the answer Mum wanted.

'She'll visit soon. I'm sure.'

The park gate is wide and heavy. Mum loves to help our passage through it. The result is usually a tangle of Mum, the chair and me, as the gates' unbalanced weight ushers us untidily onto the footpath, where we wheel left towards the home and lunch. Romans marched this way along Watling Street nearly two thousand years ago. From Roman legions to wheelchairs: how the mighty have fallen.

I time our outings to arrive back at the home just before lunch or tea, as the process of eating provides a natural break and an opportunity to escape. Mum takes lunch at a table for four, tucked away at the edge of the dining room: the same table, the same seat. The trio of ladies who inhabit mum's table studiously observe the middle distance, avoiding eye contact and conversation with each other. However, they happily engage each other's visitors in rambling conversations whilst ignoring each other.

Mum informs me from behind her hand, in a confidential manner, that she is booked in at this particular hotel for Christmas. I nod conspiratorially, hoping I have struck the right tone. Making excuses, I begin the leaving phase. I wave breezily to Mum who has started to spoon her soup. Her companions offer fluttery waves of their own.

Mondays, Wednesdays, Fridays and either Saturday or Sunday, is my routine for visits. I had retreated from a daily schedule recently, the stress of which brought me close to joining their happy throng, permanently.

I met Joan on her first day at the home; she sat at the vacant chair on Mum's table, transforming the trio into a quartet. She regarded me intently through ageing bifocals, as Mum and I observed our ritual fastening of the bib and spreading of the napkin. No middle distance for Joan, she stared. Viewed me alternately through reading and distance lenses and finally over the top with unaided sight. Disturbingly, her eyes appeared to switch rapidly between a normal size, fish eyes and ferret eyes. Her head movements reminiscent of a chicken's jerky nods.

I guessed her to be in her seventies, maybe ten years younger than mum, but it was difficult to say as she possessed an ageless quality. A light shone in her eyes, signalling that she wanted more from life than waiting for death.

The goodbye phase progressed well, I raised my hand to wave, but the new inmate interrupted at this crucial moment, as she announced:

'Spare me a minute, Sonny Jim?'

Turning to face her, I smiled in an attempt to disguise my tetchiness at the interruption and made the somewhat oblique response:

'Hi, I'm John and this is my mum, Mary,' cracking a dutiful smile. 'I'm just about to go.'

'Next time, John?' she said, looking wistfully for agreement. 'It's important.'

I nodded, expecting she would have forgotten by the following day. Restarting the goodbye phase, I waved to Mum, her fellow diners responded, Mum spooned her soup apparently oblivious.

I half-heartedly wondered what could be so important. *She's probably batty, best give her a wide berth.* I added another five minutes as I signed out. A 'click' of the door release, allowed me through the solid, varnished doors and into cool sweet-tasting air.

Chapter 2: Secrets

I skilfully avoided Joan for a number of visits, before attending an evening residents and carers' meeting. I intended to raise the loss of Mum's hearing aid: the NHS would not replace for a third time. It had gone missing from Mum's room. A few days later pieces were found in the home's massive washing machine.

Okay, Mum became fed up with wearing it and put it in her cardigan pocket, but surely someone checks pockets before clothes are washed, don't they? Evidently not.

Having made my point, I excused myself before the meeting officially concluded. I found Joan waiting for me in reception. She looked every bit the Granny from next door, resplendent in a floral-patterned dress and fake pearls. She had positioned herself next to the door, blocking the exit. Armed with a steely smile, she had timed her intervention to perfection.

'Listen, Sonny Jim, this won't take long. Push me to my room will you, I've a secret to tell you.'

She crossed her hands in her lap firmly and waited to be pushed to the lift. Taking the handles, I set off for her room. Small talk broke out as the antiquated lift stuttered into life and made its jolting ascent.

'How's your Mum?'

'Same as ever.'

'She does enjoy her walks out, always a smile and a wave. I wish I had someone to push me out.'

'Second floor, menswear and haberdashery, going up,' I said, as part of my routine with Mum, though Joan didn't appear to approve. *I had always wanted to say 'Ladies underwear, going down,' but I somehow doubted that Joan would be impressed.*

The console pinged and after the requisite delay, the doors reluctantly juddered open. Having swung her chair around clumsily within the confines of the lift we headed along the corridor.

'This is my room, number thirty-six. It's open.'

As I stepped over the threshold, a pungent scent of lily of the valley and mothballs transported me back to my Granny's house. As a boy, in short trousers I'd considered it quite a pong. I wondered if you eventually reach an age when it smells okay.

Joan's room mirrored Mum's: the home's standard bed, wardrobe, sideboard, wing back chair and television. Personalised with ornaments, obscure pictures and faded photographs squeezed onto every surface. Her one piece of personal furniture, an old occasional table, held a collection of pictures of her and her husband. The pictures appeared to chart their marriage through a series of photographs taken at other people's weddings. The collection surrounded a circular glass bowl full of Foxes Glacier Mints, yet another reminder of my Granny. Joan triumphed in adversity by achieving a real sense of home. My resistance dissolved; maybe she wasn't such a mad old bat after all.

'Would you like a sweet?' she said, following my stare, 'please take one.'

'My Gran kept mints in a bowl like this, She would ask me if I wanted a "Foxes". I thought it funny as a lad,' I said, smiling in recollection.

Joan failed to return my smile: her face conveyed an altogether more serious expression. As if at the flick of a switch, Joan changed her persona from a dotty old granny to a confident, no-nonsense businesswoman, Margret Thatcher style.

'Here's the position,' she said, brushing an imaginary hair from her cardigan. 'People here think I've lost my marbles, I have no desire to disillusion them.'

I gave an involuntary jerk of my head and attempted not to appear gobsmacked; she certainly held the initiative and looked determined to keep it.

'Sit on the bed if you like,' she said, with an authoritarian cadence. Manoeuvring skilfully out of her wheelchair she stood behind her walker and released the brakes. Making a wide unsteady turn, she crossed the room towards her chair.

'Pass the Bible, please,' she said, pointing to a battered book on a shelf, surrounded by a clutter of ornaments.

'It's a long time since a young man sat on my bed,' she added, with a wink.

I placed the heavy Bible into her waiting hands. Joan opened it to the back pages and produced an ancient, homemade envelope, which she placed ceremonially in her lap. As she closed the Bible, I fleetingly recognised that the envelope had left its imprint on the flyleaf.

'Sit on the chair if you prefer,' she said, gesturing towards her visitor's chair. 'Do you believe in buried treasure John?'

'Like Treasure Island.'

'No, real treasure.'

'If you say so,' I blustered

'This holds the clues to hidden treasure,' she said, waving the envelope. 'Will you help an old lady find it?'

I hesitated 'Well, I ... err,' I said, wondering what I had got myself into.

'Don't worry. I'll find someone else,' she said, as she judged me. 'There'll be others I can trust, others happy to help.' With a look of resignation in her eyes, she said, 'Don't worry, I'll manage.'

'No ... that's not what I meant at all. I'll be happy to help,' I said, stretching out my hand towards the envelope, in an attempt to show interest. She looked unconvinced and moved the envelope back into the haven of her lap.

'Are you sure? Once you're in, there's no backing out,' she said.

Her chin set prominently, as if delivering a line from a gangster movie.

'Take a minute or two,' she said, watching me intently, 'because once you've seen this, there's no going back.'

Obviously, my earnest nod placated Joan as she passed me the envelope with a severe stare.

'How did you come by the clues?'

'They fell out of the family bible during the move from my old house to the home. All the bashing about must have dislodged it. I bet it's been in there for decades.

The envelope had been roughly folded from a GWR flyer promoting a seaside special to Barmouth. A second flyer lay folded inside; on its reverse were five lines of spidery writing in pencil, set out as a poem but with neither rhythm nor rhyme.

'Go to the Trowman's broken anchors near the Lion's head

Look above the eye that watches the time

You have seen it before

Find it in the book

It hides the second part'

'What do you think it means Joan?'

'I don't know exactly? But I think it's all based around Ironbridge.'

I nodded and asked, 'Can I take it with me?'

'I'll keep the original, you can take this photocopy,' she said, passing the copy while squinting sideways at the wall calendar. 'Shall we schedule our next meeting? How long do you need?' Without waiting for my reply, she carried on. 'Let's chat again on Saturday, meet in the lounge about tea time. It's the Marie Celeste here at weekends, we won't be disturbed.'

'Why me, Joan.'

'Let's see, you live in Ironbridge, you can use these computer things and your [you're] happy to help old ladies.'

'And how do you know that?'

'Listening to your Mum.'

And I was the only choice, I thought.

'Have you seen anyone lurking about outside?' She said, as she gazes distractedly through the window.

'No.'

'You'd tell me if you did, wouldn't you.?'

'Yes, I'll check next time, if you like.'

*****

I felt good as I drove home, though I wasn't sure why. A batty old lady had involved me in a madcap scheme and I felt good. I had few interests since being made redundant. The truth is I felt sorry for myself, though I shouldn't have been, how many people get to retire early with a full pension plus redundancy money? Unfortunately, the rejection I felt drove me into an Internet franchise business to prove myself. It proved that I hated working for myself and especially from home.

I actually missed the IT department would you believe? They always pressed my button at work, but try fixing your own PC for the first time and you suddenly understand their value. I'd love the opportunity to rant at the coffee machine again, even monthly meetings sounded appealing in my darker moments.

Maybe I had been presented with an opportunity to use my brain again, solving Joan's puzzle. Could it conjure the thrills of my youth, like riding bicycles at full pelt at night through country lanes, without lights? Moonlighting, our gang called it. Well, maybe not. I somehow hoped that Joan's mystery might just put a spring back in my step.

Chapter 3: Short Trousers

My daily dog walk with Lucy is when I think. 'Think' is perhaps an overstatement, anyway, it is when my mind slides into neutral and thoughts and memories flood in. Meeting Joan had metaphorically put me back in short trousers, which conjured memories of my school days.

I had not regarded myself as a troublemaker at school, I thought of myself as being full of fun in an understated way. Though my achievements were few and none of them were academic, I'd had my moments. Luckily, I transferred to a brand-new school when it opened halfway through my first year at senior school. It saved me from certain destruction at the hands of the teachers and pupils at the rougher school I had attended.

My old school had been housed in a two storey, red brick Victorian building with 1881 proudly inscribed high up on the gables. The teaching staff's role appeared to be to keep order at all costs, education came a poor second. I witnessed at least two fights between teachers and pupils. It had been shocking enough that fights took place at all, but inside the school building. These fights were played out along the main corridor for some to witness and everyone to hear, "Fight, fight, fight".

Thankfully, the new school differed greatly. The vast majority of teachers were young, enthusiastic and great to be taught by. I even got to stay and take 'O' levels, all three of them.

At sixteen, I entered the workforce as a mechanical apprentice whilst the brighter of my classmates went on to study 'A' levels at grammar schools. Most of my achievements if you can call them that, occurred when someone pressed a button deep inside me. There would be no particular warning, it just happened and I just reacted.

The graveyard lesson after lunch in a classroom facing a blazing sun witnessed one of my button pressing moments. Even with the windows open, the room's humidity reached jungle proportions. Seated towards the back, I had an excellent view of the playing fields and the trees beyond. The sweet warm smell of my Granddad's ripening tomatoes invaded my memory. Textbook pages blurred as my eyelids gradually slid closed. The desktop drew my head into its orbit. Miss Copse's voice faded.

An air of anticipation gripped my classmates as a chalk bullet flew in a shallow arc over their heads and found its target: me, and pressed my button. I expertly grabbed the rolling chalk and without a moment's thought hurled it back in the direction it came. During the split second between release and contact, a slow-motion dread gripped [gripped] the audience. Horror struck I watched as the chalk arrowed towards Miss's bosom.

Time suspended within a vacuum of silence, as the class held its collective breath. All eyes were wide and directed at Miss, but their thoughts were on me. Would he get the cane? Would he get expelled? Would he go to jail? The tension grew towards breaking point. Miss looked down and gently brushed the chalk mark from her top. Then with studied deliberation, she raised her eyes until they bored into my skull.

The beginnings of a smile played tantalisingly at the corners of her mouth. The broad smile that followed triggered an outburst of relieved laughter, some of the class applauded.

It wasn't much of an achievement but I bet there aren't many lads in this world that could strike a female teacher on the bosom with a piece of chalk from the back of the classroom and avoid both jail and cane.

The boy, if boy applied to him, was massive, which was something of an understatement in under fifteen rugby vocabulary. Being both tall and rotund he proved impossible to tackle, any normal lad just bounced off. His teammates chanted, 'Tank, Tank, Tank', whenever he had the ball. The game had been lost before half time. Tank had made or scored about ten tries, the referee had stopped counting. Our only tactic had been to hope that Tank got the ball in his own half and ran out of puff, before he got to our line.

Midway through the second half, the referee, our PE teacher, awarded them a penalty near our line. Our team stood dutifully ten yards away, all jockeying for a safe position to avoid Tank as he charged for the line. Instead of employing the studied concentration appropriate with the proceedings, his teammates lounged haphazardly, waiting for the formality of Tank scoring another try. Their kicker even mimed kicking the conversion.

I stood respectfully in our thin red line, a little to the Tank's left, when, inconveniently, something pressed my button. Tank tapped the ball and started to rumble towards our line. I set off at an angle towards him. My teammates watched in horror. No one on either side moved, stunned by the David and Goliath moment. Unfortunately, I had been badly miscast as David.

The Tank's eyes were trained straight ahead at the try line. He had not seen my approach. I think I tripped. The trip changed what would have been a tackle around his chest into a torpedo like head butt, which connected forcibly with his groin. The Tank dropped the ball as if shot and sank to the floor like a poleaxed ox, narrowly missing me on his way down.

The Tank lay torpid, clutching his crown jewels. His teammates gathered around discussing the best method of lifting him towards the side line. Their uncoordinated attempts to raise all of him at the same time failed. They eventually resorted to dragging him away. The referee found immense difficulty in disguising his convulsions of laughter, and drew the game to a respectful close. We lost the game by a cricket score, but we had finally stopped the Tank.

Chapter 4: Falling Down

Mum had fallen during the night and grazed her head, but despite the upset, she still wanted to go out in her wheelchair. I had discovered a new route to the park, through a neatly laid out housing estate. It had the benefit of truncating the morbid graveyard section. As we passed a couple of for sale boards, Mum surprised me by speaking. She had been having a good day.

'I should buy one of these, it'll be cheaper than the home.' Mum said, gazing up at the for-sale sign.

'But, how would you look after yourself Mum?' I said, in my best reasonable voice.

'I'd manage, don't you worry.'

'The doctor said you needed nursing care.'

'I don't remember that!'

'Remember, you ended up in A & E three times in the same week.' I said, exasperation taking over.

No answer.

'Remember you broke your arm; you were in hospital for a couple of months. Remember?'

'I don't remember that.'

'It's why you're in Shropshire, near the rest of the family.'

'If you say so.'

It's unbelievable. She can't dress herself; can't prepare meals; won't ask for help; falls regularly and still believes she can live on her own.

Through the gate we rolled, past empty tennis courts captured by high fences, down the ramp shrouded by trees and, around a corner to the oasis of beautifully manicured bowling greens.

'No bowls today, Mum.'

Her shoulders slumped. Fortunately, the grounds man appeared. He is second best to a game of bowls, but beggars can't be choosers, as she would have said. He followed a shiny new machine, which appeared to be running a little too quickly for his short legs. Back and forth they went, cutting laser-straight lines across the green. The new thing looked like a lawnmower but instead of leaving a beautifully manicured surface the rotating blades chopped the smooth surface leaving thousands of cuts. Unimpressed, Mum dismissed his efforts with a petulant flick of her wrist.

'He's ruined it.'

'He's let air in,' I guessed.

Unconvinced, she looked away petulantly. We withdrew our patronage, slipping away along another ramp before negotiating the cycle gate and rounding the deserted play area. Next stop, chickens, they could not escape. Ejected from their greenhouse home, now full of new plants, they strutted, huddled and fussed under the dense Leylandii hedge.

'It looks like they're all here today, no chicken for lunch today then,' I said.

Mum grimaced slightly. We moved on towards the litter bin that once marked the start of Mum's routine shuffle up the hill towards the road. In better days, Mum routinely wriggled forward in anticipation of her walk behind her chair. The bin's significance had been forgotten, relegated once more to merely holding litter.

A distorted metal bench seat, half way between the bin and the road, served as our next landmark, its plastic skin melted and peeled, disfigured by a fire started for fun. Rust crept across its twisted frame, discouraging all but the youngsters who sat on its rounded back, feet on the seat, all 'so what' and 'whatever'.

Mum named it 'the drinking seat' in honour of its other guests, the cider drinking men, who sit and shared their hazy world, nodding blindly as we pass.

'The drinking seat's empty today, Mum.'

'Too windy.'

We passed through the fine Victorian gate guarding the park from the road and started the last leg of our outing, along the Roman straight pavement and back to the home. Trucks passed within inches, buffeting us with disturbed air, covering us in diesel fumes and cigarette smoke.

On a good day men dig holes in the road; resigned motorists' sit silently waiting for a green light, only to be overtaken by Mum in her chariot. She passes magnanimously bestowing them with a queenly wave.

We were late to the table, catching up with proceedings as the soup arrived, tomato again. Fortunately, Mum likes 'that one'. Glancing at Joan, I noticed she was in gracious old lady mode. With a sly wink, she suggested we meet in the garden in ten minutes.

'Hi Joan. You were quick.'

'Soup and bread is enough for me,' she said, pointedly staring at my paunch.

'I'm having no luck with the puzzle, Joan, can you give me some background? It might help.'

'Shall we start with the envelope?'

'Fine.'

'Well as you know I found it in the family Bible.'

'Yes, I noticed its outline imprinted in the page.'

'The Bible is inscribed to my late husband Tom's father, Jack,' she said, opening the front cover. The printed inscription had faded, but 'Prize' and '1913' were still legible above 'Jack Hailstone' printed in copper plate capitals.

'What about the clues?'

'I assumed that the clues were created by Jack for Tom. He must have hidden them in his Bible to be found by Tom as it would be passed down to him, just as it passed to me, after my Tom's death.'

'That sounds logical. What do you know of Jack's family history?'

'I've heard some third-hand tales and I did some genealogy research at the library last year.'

'I wouldn't know what's important, so if it's okay try telling me everything.'

'I'll start with Jack. He was born in 1904. I had understood that he had been an only child, but the 1911 census listed two boys of the same age, Jack and Robert, they were presumably twins. By the 1921 census, only Jack was listed. Jack married Ellen Churm. She died tragically in 1926 giving birth to her first child, my Tom. After Ellen died, Jack stayed a widower. According to the gossip he preferred to play the field, and very successfully by all accounts.

Tom was brought up by one of Ellen's sisters and her husband in Madeley. Tom didn't really know his own father until he was eight or nine. Somehow, Tom got to know about his real Dad and would sneak off and visit him on Sundays. They would do all sorts of exciting things together. Jack drowned in 1942. Accidental death according to hearsay, but my Tom never believed it.'

'Surely they knew how he died? From an inquest or something?'

'From what I was told it was put down as an accident, but it could have been an open verdict or something like that, I haven't seen anything written down. There were so many theories that fitted the facts. Apparently, it could easily have been an accident, or Jack could have committed suicide, or had a heart attack. Then again, some people thought he could have been murdered. Take your pick.'

'Murdered?' I had not been expecting that.

'Yes, a jealous husband or boyfriend, maybe,' she said, with relish.

'What was the popular opinion then?'

'There wasn't one really. I know my Tom felt he had been murdered. Jack knew the river too well to have an accident.'

'Have you seen any newspaper cuttings about his death?'

'No, I've only heard the stories by word of mouth.'

'What was the local paper at the time?'

'I remember the Wellington Journal, that was the popular one, came out on a Saturday I think.'

'When did Jack die, again?'

'The end of September 1942, but it could have been October.'

'I might see if there's any archived copies. How old was Tom when Jack died?'

'About fifteen or sixteen I think. I know Jack left him the cottage but stipulated that he must be twenty-one for some reason. A friend of Jack's stayed there until Tom took possession.'

'What about you and Tom, how did you meet?'

'I met Tom in 1959. It was a bit of a whirlwind romance, we got married later the same year and I became Mrs Hailstone. Tom had changed his surname back to Jack's by then, you see. He was fifteen years older than me but it made no difference to us. He'd been living in Jack's old place for a good few years by then. Everyone had him down as a confirmed bachelor. I suppose his life ran along similar lines to Jack's. They both worked on the railway, they were both single and both lived at the cottage. The only difference being that Tom appeared to have no luck with the ladies, until he met me, that is. Tom thought I was chocolate. He just wouldn't leave me alone, but I didn't mind, he was a good man. We were never blessed with children mores' the pity, so this line of Hailstones died out with Tom.'

'Chocolate?' I said, with a questioning grin.

'If someone said you were chocolate, it meant they thought you were the best. I think it was a hangover from the war: chocolate was rationed and highly prized. Makes me sound like I was a prize cow, doesn't it?' she said, smiling in recollection. 'But you know what I mean, don't you?' Joan blushed a little as she explained.

'So, you never actually met Jack then?'

'No, I was only just born when he died but I knew him through my Tom.'

'Tom and Jack got on well, then?'

'Oh yes, Tom loved his dad. They were cut from the same cloth. Tom's adopted dad was in the army even before the war and was away, so Tom would slide off and go to Jack's cottage.'

'How did Tom find out that Jack was his real Dad?'

'You know Tom never said, I assumed he found out from his school mates.'

'Any other links, other than family? How about work, have you any idea what work Jack did?'

'I told you he worked on the railway.'

'Yes, sorry.'

'Tom told me, Jack went straight from school to the GWR. He was still working for them when he died, twenty odd years later. Jack and, later my Tom worked in the Gorge for the GWR. The line closed in the sixties so my Tom transferred to the main line in Wellington. Work was never the same for Tom after moving out of the Gorge, but he stuck it out until he retired in the nineteen nineties. As he said at the time, he didn't know anything else.'

'Wow, look at the time, I promised to be back home by now. I'll be visiting Mum on Monday, shall we catch up then?'

'Anytime will do, I'm not going anywhere,' she said looking down at her walker.

'See you then.'

*****

A cold shiver ran down my back, as I realised I had no recollection of the journey home. I must have engaged auto-pilot as I processed Joan's information. Hang on, yes, there was that car that overtook me. It blew its horn and the lads inside gave me two fingered salutes in time to their deafening music. Why were they so pissed off with me? That's it, I'd been dithering, distracted by the sky blue Mini, in the Brew House pub car park. It looked like Sarah's.

So, anyway, back to the day job. What were the facts? Well, Joan had found the note in a Bible inscribed to Jack. It would presumably pass to Tom after Jack's death. Though the Bible would probably be part of the contents of his cottage so Tom wouldn't have got it until sometime later, being only sixteen at the time. The flyers were printed in 1938, so the clues were probably written by Jack, between 1938 and his death.

Chapter 5: Archived Newspapers

Archive copies of the Wellington Journal were available on microfilm at the central library. I requested the second half of 1942 and sat down at a film reader to trawl through the articles. Once I became familiar with the quirky way the reader worked, I started to work my way forward from June. The Journal filled its pages with classified adverts, reports from police courts, quarter sessions, church events, farming, thrift, motoring fatalities, claims of bigamy, tragic children's accidents, petrol ration dodgers, black marketers, home guard absentees, government advice and some local news.

The letter columns were full of furious readers who let rip at the use of army and air force lorries for the conveyance of personnel to local dances and pubs. Which part of 'no petrol for joyriding' did they not understand? Also, huge lorries being used to carry one man to work, when bicycles could be used: 'are we out for economy or not?'

Disquiet was also expressed about the 'torrent of black market trophy weapons' being offered for sale 'this must be checked before they fall into the wrong hands.'

The first issue in October eventually paid dividends:

*****

Local Ironbridge man missing

Saturday October 3rd 1942

A missing Ironbridge man is presumed to have drowned whilst fishing. His dog, fishing tackle and a stolen boat were located at the riverbank near Marwood up stream of Ironbridge. Jack Hailstone was last seen on the evening of Wednesday 30th of September 1942 at 7pm setting out to go night fishing. The boat was identified as having been taken from the rowing club close to the Albert Edward Bridge. If anyone has any further information please present themselves to the desk sergeant, Ironbridge Police Station.

I trawled through the next four editions expecting to find an article confirming that Jack's body had been recovered. I checked three times without success and then moved on to November, restricting my search to the headline pages only. On my second pass I spotted the story halfway down an inside page, just one column wide, the story had obviously lost significance by November.

Body recovered from Severn at Ironbridge

Saturday, November 21st 1942

The body of a man believed to be that of Jack Hailstone, aged 38, whose home address was given as Bridge Bank, Benthall, was taken from the River Severn downstream of the Iron Bridge on Thursday the 19th of November. Mr. Hailstone had been missing since 30th September. His body was observed floating past the Wharfage in Ironbridge. Local river men recovered the body by use of coracles. The body will be formally identified and a Coroners Court convened during the week, probably on Tuesday. The Journal understands that identification has been delayed due to the length of submersion.

Followed by: -

Ironbridge Coroners Court Findings

Saturday November 28th 1942

An enquiry was conducted on Wednesday November 25th, by Ironbridge deputy coroner Mr. J. J. Jackson, who recorded a verdict of 'Found Drowned', saying that there was insufficient evidence to show how Mr. Hailstone got into the water.

The Coroner also concluded that the heavy fishing bag and the probability that the body had been caught on an obstruction caused the body to remain submerged for longer than the expected three days to one week. These circumstances had led to the body's advanced state of decomposition.

Mr Hailstone's son identified the body by his pocket watch. The funeral took place at St Luke's Church, Ironbridge on Thursday, where the service was given by Rev. W. T. Baker

Found drowned, the verdict, but how did he die? Accident, suicide or it could have been murder. No one appeared to know.

Chapter 6: The Specialist

On the day of Mum's appointment with her Geriatric specialist, at our local hospital, I arrived early, anticipating problems. To my surprise, I found Mum in her chair, coat on and ready to go. After several laps of the hospital car park, I eventually found a space.

Two pounds fifty pence to park at a hospital, it's outrageous. No change given, correct money only. I didn't have the correct change. Eventually I changed a note into coins with the help of a shifty looking man with bulging pockets full of coins. Maybe he had just disembowelled a parking ticket machine. Offering him grateful thanks, I re-joined the queue. The queue progressed slowly, I realised why when it became my turn and the machine demanded my registration plate details before it would issue a ticket. I could not remember it to save my life and I could not see the plate from the machine. I headed back towards the van until I could read the registration plate. I returned but now the queue had lengthened. Would I remember the registration until my go came around? It had been touch and go, but I managed, just.

Hospital waiting rooms appear to engender a strange soporific quality that is so powerful people succumb to dozing fits within seconds of sitting down. Eventually, a lady volunteer, clip board in hand, announced Mum's name and ushered us into a small office. Behind the desk sat Mum's specialist. We sat uncomfortably in the cramped space between the door and the desk. I guessed her to be a tad younger than me and surprisingly unafraid of showing a little too much wrinkly cleavage. She introduced herself and asked what family relationship I had to Mum. Having satisfied herself, she started the customary pleasantries, addressing them to Mum.

As Mum failed to respond within some sort of prescribed timescale, the same questions were redirected to me. The questions appeared to assume that as Mum failed to respond, she could neither hear nor think. She discussed Mum's condition in front of her but without reference to her. Eventually, a decision emerged to tinker with the timing of mum's cocktail of drugs. The decision appeared to have been made on a 'suck it and see' basis; with little science involved.

'Thank you, we will see you again in three months. The office will send an appointment through,' she said, dismissing us with a wave of her hand which appeared to encompass the office and the door. Mum continued to stare into the middle distance even though we had been dismissed. I found the whole experience deeply unsatisfactory. Back in the car park, I eventually got Mum and her chair back into the van. I started the engine, only to find that there were two cars waiting for our space. I now had the opportunity to play God. Scrutinising both cars and occupants I attempted to decide who deserved our space. I decided to turn to the left, blocking one car and allowing the other to take our place, such power. Suddenly the dynamics changed as an unseen driver pulled away, vacating a space. I didn't even receive a 'thank you' wave.

*****

I wheeled Mum to the lunch table, where only a duo sat waiting, no Joan. I excused myself with smiles and waves and moved towards the lounge, where I found Joan waiting none too patiently.

'You took your time, young man. I have been waiting for you for at least ten minutes,' she said, with a steely glint in her eye.

'Have you missed lunch?' I said, turning towards the familiar aroma of school dinners permeating from the dining room.

'I took lunch earlier in my room, if you must know,' she said. 'Anyway, what did you make of it?'

'Nothing. Can't make any sense of it.'

Her eyes narrowed, she looked distinctly unimpressed. Wishing to avoid her bad books, I decided to run through my thinking to show I had been doing something.

'I think the cryptic clues were designed to be decipherable by only the person they were written for, which is common sense I suppose,' I said, playing for time as I ordered my thoughts.

'Obviously,' said Joan, as she impatiently gesticulated. 'What is your point?'

'I thought if we knew who the clues were written for, it might help decipher them.'

'There's no doubt in my mind that Jack wrote them for Tom,' she said, positively. 'What difference could it make who they were written for?'

'Well, if the clues refer to things that Jack and Tom talked about or places they had been or things they had done together. The clues would be based around things that no one else could guess. A bit like us I suppose.'

She paused and glanced through the window. 'So, how do we proceed?'

'I guess we need to understand what they had in common. If you tell me everything you remember, we may spot a link.'

'All right, here goes,' she said, wriggling into the back of her chair in preparation. 'Tom would tell me stories about his dad over a glass of beer around the fire. Apparently, when Tom visited Jack, Jack would find interesting things for them to do together. Tom loved spending time with him.'

Joan beamed in remembrance as she produced an old Turkish delight box from her bedside table. Delving inside she finally withdrew her lightly clenched fist and slid it towards me across the table top, before opening her palm with a flourish. Out rolled a tiny silver sixpence. I picked it up admiringly.

'Jack told Tom to keep it for a rainy day,' she said, wistfully cocking her head. 'Tom gave it to me when we first met, as a sort of keepsake.'

The sixpence, with its worn but recognisable head of a young Queen Victoria, stared up at me.

'I bet this coin could tell some stories,' I said, looking at its date. 'What is the other coin in your hand?'

'Oh, it's a Roman one Jack gave to my Tom, not long before he died.'

'Did Tom ever know how Jack came by it?'

'Believe it or not Jack told him he won it in a pub game. I think…'

A reminder tone rang out from my phone cutting Joan off, as she looked set to elaborate at length.

'Look, I've got to go, can we chat again on Wednesday?'

'But I haven't told you any stories yet.'

'Sorry, I've got to go. Tell me on Wednesday, okay?'

'I'm going nowhere,' she said.

Arriving home, I looked in the post box hoping to find a creative writing book I had ordered. Disappointed, I pulled out a solitary card inviting me to re-join a gym, first three months free. Confused, I turned it over and found Sarah's name in the address line. *Strange, she goes to the gym three or four times a week, maybe she's changed gyms?*

Chapter 7: A Walk to Benthall

Mum's clacker had been causing concern at the nursing home, apparently, she had begun to cough and splutter more regularly, recently. Mum had spluttered on and off when she drank for the last twenty years without a problem. The clacker is our family name for the thing in your throat that sends air into your lungs and hopefully everything else into your stomach. Our family clackers can be troublesome, causing fits of choking when something 'went down the wrong way', as Mum would say.

Unimpressed by my non-medical assurances, the home's procedures kicked in. The home's G.P. examined her and referred her to a speech therapist. The speech therapist visited and determined that Mum should have her drinks thickened to reduce the chance of choking.

The problem then became one of dehydration, as Mum hated the thickened drinks. The thickened drinks were ok if you drank them straight away but if you left it, as Mum habitually did, it congealed. To be honest I couldn't blame her for not drinking the thickened drinks, how refreshing is solid water, tea, coffee or orange juice, all drinks she previously enjoyed? I attempted to explain my logic to the staff but encountered the, 'what if she chokes on our watch' brigade. Blame culture and procedures were getting in the way of common sense. I rolled my eyes and carried on.

*****

'Hi Joan, I'm sorry but I'm no further forward with the puzzle. Have you remembered anything about Jack and Tom?'

'Only that, when I thought about it, many of Tom's stories involved Benthall in some way.'

'That's a coincidence, Benthall Edge is a regular dog walking area of mine.'

'I understand it's lovely up there.'

Attempting to avoid further small talk, I tried to move the conversation along 'Let's hope there's a clue in one of Tom's stories.'

'I've remembered lots,' she said. 'I remembered Tom telling me about an oak tree they would sit under; it was their den I think. It was a special tree apparently, it ....'

'Don't tell me, its branches touched the ground all the way round.'

'How did you know that?'

'Because one of our regular dog walks passes below a magnificent oak, its branches touch the ground. It's half way up the hill above The Mines.'

'Is it the same one, I wonder? It's seventy years ago,' she said, with doubt in her voice.

'That's nothing for an oak, they live for hundreds of years. There's an oak in Sherwood Forest called Major Oak which is over eight hundred years old. They say Robin Hood sheltered in it.' I said, feeling that I had justified my assertion.

'I remember Tom saying it was a magical place. I think he said that if you stood with your back against its trunk you couldn't see out. You were in your own private world.'

'It's the same one,' I said, beaming at her. We were making progress. 'Anything else?'

'An avenue of horse chestnut trees, they collected bags of massive conkers. Tom would swap them at school for cigarette cards and marbles.'

'I know the conker trees too, they are up near Benthall Hall.'

'Tom also talked about fishing pools, sledging, ancient battles and all sorts. I think they sledged on the sloping fields up near that funny little road, The Mines. Must be near that oak tree,' she said, making the connection. 'Jack made a sledge out of bits and pieces he cadged from the railway. It got so heavy it took two of them to tow it uphill. Tom said it made up for it downhill, apparently, it went like a rocket.'

'Any more about the pools and the battles?'

'I think the pools were private, they had worked out a way to get in round the back, through a reed bed I think. They would take a line each and bait, but no rods in case they had to make a run for it. As for the battles, I think Tom said they would look for musket balls, somewhere up at the Hall.'

'I'll take Lucy that way tomorrow, you never know.'

'It could be a wild goose chase. Won't your wife be getting upset with all the time you're spending on this?'

'Sarah's my partner. She doesn't seem to notice to be honest. She's so involved with inputting addresses, phone numbers and bank details into her new laptop, I think her whole world sits behind that screen,' I said.

'You be mindful,' she said, holding my eyes with a stare and a theatrically raised eyebrow.

'See you in a couple of days.'

*****

Surprised, I found Sarah at home, hunched over her laptop and surrounded by haphazard piles of CDs, as she saved her favourite music tracks to iTunes. She appeared tired or stressed and definitely unwilling to chat.

I sloped off to the office to check my emails. While I had the laptop open, I speculatively keyed 'Benthall Battle' into Google. A local history society site came up first in the search. It confirmed there had been a skirmish around the church in 1645 during the Civil War. The action had been in defence of the Hall, held by the Royalists. It appeared that Benthall Church had been largely destroyed in the action. *A step in the right direction, maybe?* I speculated.

I planned to walk Lucy to Benthall but Murphy's Law applied and I ran out of time. I took her to the local park instead, she loves it there, not for the walk, it's too short, but for the food she forages. Off the lead, her route includes every picnic bench and associated shrubbery plus all of the waste bins. Without fail she finds discarded food, the older the better. I don't think I've ever seen a slim beagle, Lucy certainly could do with losing a kilo or two.

The following day started with more disruptions, but eventually Lucy and I got out for our walk up to Benthall. We took our usual route over the bridge, up Bridge Bank, along Spout Lane to The Mines. I squeezed through a ragged gap in a hedge that had been a gateway once. The gate's rusted remains lay to one side, half-buried in the undergrowth, its posts now dissolved into the straggling hedge. The oak tree Joan had spoken of looked down on us from the top of the field. It resembled a galleon in full sail cresting a giant wave, a magnificent sight. Its lower branches hung down so low that its leaves swept the earth as the branches swayed in the wind. *It must have been Jack and Tom's tree, just three short generations ago, nothing in an oak tree's life*, I thought.

Thinking about the story Joan had told, I could easily imagine that the field surrounding the oak would have been the place they tobogganed. Shaped like a lopsided bowl with the longer side running into a flat base and shorter side being much steeper. It looked perfect for a rapid run, with the short steep slope preventing over enthusiastic sledge riders crashing into the surrounding hedgerow. The field had been part of a dairy farm years ago, its farmhouse and outbuildings now derelict, the pasture rough and brambly. Much had changed in sixty years.

From the hill brow, a view opened out across more neglected fields, crossed by three lines of pylons. We walked below the buzzing cables and through the stile into the avenue of horse chestnut trees Joan had recalled. Planted along a shallow rise they pointed the way towards Benthall Hall. They had the feel of a grand entrance abandoned in favour of a more convenient route.

As I strolled up the avenue towards Benthall Hall it occurred to me that most of the stories Joan had told about Jack and Tom were set nearby. The oak tree lay behind me. The church stood to my right at the side of the Hall. The pools surrounded by reeds were to my left. I should start to look for clues. I could recall individual words but little context. Time, an eye, some anchors and a Lion's head came to mind.

Turning left out of the avenue, we routinely followed the bridleway along the stonewalls bounding Benthall church. We would usually walk straight past the church but today Lucy had scented her way through the lych-gate and into the graveyard. I followed.

Gravestones lined the outer walls, sheltering from winter winds. Grander tombs gathered around the church itself. An even sward carpeted the churchyard and served to accentuate random leaning headstones. Crumbling white paint coated the body of the church, creating an illusion of lightness. It could almost have floated away had it not been anchored by its brick and stone additions at either end. The path led to the base of a small tower and stopped at what could have been the original entrance, its arch bricked up, abandoned in favour of an entrance in the new addition. My eyes were drawn to the multi-paned window above the bricked-up entrance, Between the brickwork and the window lay an oblong mosaic, a sundial and a gargoyle of a lion's head. The penny dropped: had I found the lion? The sundial would be telling the time? If so where were the anchors and the eye? *They must be around somewhere.*

Framed in stonework, the mosaic mirrored the width of the sundial's face. A shadow fell between 10 and 11, as sunlight intensified the mosaic's colours and illuminated the shape of an eye. "Above the eye that watches the time", I recalled. Above the mosaic, I could just make out a curve of words, an inscription of some kind. The algae encrusted words were frustratingly difficult to decipher.

'Out of the ... strong came ... forth sweet ... ness'.

Could the inscription be the answer, if so where were the anchors? Idly I gazed across the graveyard. Two impressive stone family tombs stood alongside the entrance. Beyond them, surrounded by tufted grasses, lay two unobtrusive but large cast iron grave markers. Intrigued, I bent to read the weather worn inscriptions and noticed symbols at each corner of the second marker, they represented broken anchors. The inscription included, 'Trowman of this parish'. I had found all of the clues, if not in the correct order. But what did the inscription mean in terms of the treasure?

I took photographs of the inscription to show Joan. Elated, I set off taking the short way home along the route of an old inclined plane through Benthall Edge wood along the Shropshire Way. Lucy happily took excursions from the path following deer tracks with nose down, tail up, enthusiasm. The power station soon loomed large to our left. The rain of condensing steam splashed loudly inside the imposing cooling towers. Once down onto the old railway path, I began to jog toward home.

*****

Sarah had written 'Meeting tonight' on the whiteboard. She would be late. I jumped in the van to visit Mum, and, hopefully, Joan. Finally, I had something worth talking about.

Chapter 8: Above the Sundial

I slowed and stopped at the crown of the road waiting for an opportunity to turn into the home's gateway. Two men sat on a bench staring towards the home. I thought of Joan and took a sneaky picture with my phone. I received a two-fingered salute from the one with the bottle, as the one with the can laughed. *Not so sneaky*, I conceded.

Mum appeared to have retreated further into her own private world since my last visit. Conversation dwindled to the odd word, not even 'hello'. Thankfully, she still smiled. I hoped that somewhere deep inside her, she lived in a world that I failed to understand, a world where she could be happy.

Fortunately, Mum still enjoyed her trips out in her wheelchair and today would be special as Lucy came too. Mum enjoyed holding the extending lead and watching Lucy's antics. Lucy loved visiting Mum. She had perfected her 'lovely little dog' routine as cover for her number one priority, finding food. Wagging her tail enthusiastically, she moved stealthily around the inmate's chairs, hunting down broken biscuits and pieces of cake.

*****

Passing through the graveyard, Mum showed interest in a sport's bottle of water I had brought, I helped her to drink from it. To my surprise, something in its design allowed Mum to drink easily and without help. She gripped it proprietarily, until she had drunk every drop. So much for thickeners, I thought. If I had any doubts, they were dispelled when, during a clacker spluttering attack, I attempted to remove the bottle from Mum's mouth, only to see her tighten her teeth around the end. She refused to let go and continued to drink throughout her spluttering. Eventually, we persuaded the staff to allow her to keep water bottles in her room, though I believe they were hidden when the speech therapist visited.

After settling Mum at the lunch table and observing the usual rituals and pleasantries, I said my goodbyes.

'I'll see you on Friday Mum, then I'll be away for a couple of days but I'll be back soon.'

Mum nodded.

'See you the day after tomorrow,' I said, in my best dutiful son voice.

She answered with a fluttery wave and moved swiftly to spooning soup, tomato again, no problem.

*****

I climbed the back stairs to Joan's room. Finding the door ajar, I knocked and sauntered in. I must have given Joan quite a start as she grabbed her walker looking quite shocked.

'Have you had lunch?' I said.

'Yes, soup and a sandwich,' she replied, while pointing to the empty dish and plate abandoned on her over bed table. 'I was hoping you'd drop in once you'd visited your Mum. Any news?'

'I think we're getting somewhere.'

'Come along young man, don't keep me in suspenders. Spill the beans.'

'Well, I think I have found an answer to Jack's clue. I went up to Benthall Church with Lucy yesterday and found the time.'

Joan furrowed her brow. 'Sorry, you've lost me.'

'The clue said, "Above the eye that watches the time" or something like that. Well, the time is a sundial and the eye is a mosaic and above the eye is ......'

'Are you sure you have the right place?' Joan said, cutting across me. 'Surely you should have found the Anchor and the Trowman first, wasn't that the order of the clues?'

'But, I have found them. The Trowman and Anchors were on a cast iron grave marker.'

'I think you will find that what you're describing as a "Marker" is known as a "Ledger",' she said, school teacher cadence. 'What about the lion's head? You haven't mentioned that. I do hope you were in the right place.'

'Sorry, the lion's head is under the sundial. I don't think the lion and anchors are that relevant, just Jack's way of saying to Tom, "Start at Benthall Church". If you see what I mean?'

'That makes sense. If he had included Benthall Church as part of the clue, then anyone could have found it,' she said, nodding.

'I bet Jack would have shown Tom the broken anchors on the grave marker, sorry, ledger. If you think about it, a broken anchor on a grave would interest a young lad.'

'What did you find above the eye?'

'I'll show you now, just give me a moment while I sort through these photos on my phone, I'm trying to find the best one. Look, here's the picture of the sundial, the mosaic eye, and above the eye is the inscription. I'm afraid the inscription isn't too clear at the moment: I'll zoom ....'

'There's obviously not enough pixels in the camera for a shot like that.'

I zoomed in, until we could read the inscription. *Not enough pixels my arse,* I thought. I zoomed it to readable size. Joan read it aloud.

'"Out of the strong came forth sweetness." I know it, I know those words. I can visualise them in my head from my childhood. That's it! They're on a tin of Golden Syrup. I can picture them. As a little girl, I would stare at the picture of the lion lying down in the sand with bees flying around. It was on the side of the tin and above it or below it, those were the exact words.' Joan's eye's sparkled, after an instant of recollection she continued: 'When I was a youngster we were allowed a dribbly teaspoon of syrup on our porridge. Only if we were good mind you, times were hard, not like today.'

'My problem is that I can't see how we use the inscription, to work out the clue,' I said.

Joan appeared not to hear me and continued her recollections.

'You know, thinking about it, I remember Tom saying that Jack always made them syrup sandwiches to take with them and how it ran everywhere on a hot day.'

'Brilliant, well remembered, but I still don't get it.'

'Neither do I young man. Unless the treasure is hidden in a Golden Syrup tin somewhere?' She said, with an ironic narrowing of her gaze.

'What were the next lines in the clue?'

'Something like; "You will have seen it before, find it in the book, it hides the second part." Any thoughts?'

'None.' She said, somewhat crestfallen.

'By the way, I have another photo for you,' I said, as I found it on my phone and turned the screen towards her. 'Are these the men you asked me to look out for?'

Joan took the phone and glanced at the screen before handing it back while offering me a withering stare.

'You're not taking this seriously young man. They look like wino's to me and not too keen to be photographed by the look of that gesture. They don't represent any sort of threat, but I think you know that, you're just taking the Michael.'

'Let's catch up when I come to see Mum next,' I said, feeling a cold draught of disapproval blowing across my knees. *Short trousers time again,* I thought.

'I'll be here, don't you worry.'

*****

Back at the house, I switched on my ancient laptop and made a cup of coffee while it booted up begrudgingly. I started to key the inscription into a search engine. By the time, I had inputted 'out of the strong' the full phrase came up as the first option:

Out of the strong came forth sweetness.

The old bat had been right. A BBC News article from January 2008, celebrated 125 years of Golden Syrup. Recognised as the oldest brand in the world, bla, bla, bla. Its trade mark of a dead lion and swarm of bees bla, bla, bla, from the Bible bla, bla bla.

236

Further down the list, a Wiki page referenced that the text had been taken from Judges 14.14. The penny dropped with a pronounced clang. Find it in the book. *Could the book be Jack's Bible?*

Chapter 9: Second Clue

Mum had suddenly lost the ability to sit up straight and lolled to her left in her chair. Even more disturbingly, she appeared unwilling to open her eyes. The nursing staff thought her condition could have been caused by the recent change in her medication. Alternatively, she may have had a minor stroke during the night.

Mum made something of a recovery during the following weeks and even attempted to use her walker. Unfortunately, she leaned severely to one side while keeping her eyes firmly closed, which made plotting a straight course difficult.

Despite her problems, her appetite for a spin in the wheelchair remained undiminished. With Mum wedged upright with pillows, we set off through the doors into the outside world. She barely opened her eyes during her ride. Feeling a little disconsolate, I pushed on offering a running commentary of what I thought might be of interest.

Mum spoke, her words escaping weakly from her mouth. I bent down beside her and with a little encouragement, she repeated her words.

'That robin's following us.'

I had been about to dismiss her words as irrational ramblings when I realised that I could hear a robin singing nearby. With my dismissive bubble pricked, I remembered that we had passed several robins, stridently proclaiming their territories along our route. For someone without sight 'that robin's following us' had been spot on. I chuckled to myself as I patted Mum on the shoulder. I had underestimated her yet again.

*****

'Joan, I think I've made some progress. The answer to the clue may be in your family Bible. Can we look in Judges 14.14?'

'I'm sorry, I don't understand.'

'You know the inscription, the one on the Golden Syrup tin?'

'Yes.' She said, nodding slowly as if wondering what the connection would be.

'Well, I checked it out on the Internet and it originally came from the Bible. Apparently, it's from Judges 14.14. Maybe the solution is somewhere hidden within the text?'

'I'm with you now. If you put the Bible on the table, I'll look it up.'

Joan flicked through the surprisingly pristine pages of the battered Bible, eventually locating the text, about a third of the way in from the front.

'I can't see anything out of the ordinary, can you?'

Looking over her shoulder, I had to agree. I did not know what I expected to see but there appeared to be nothing visible. Surrounded by a decorative border, the text had few spaces for clues. There were no tell-tale imprints of an enclosed message, no writing between the lines.

'Is the answer in the text do you think?'

'Hardly,' she said, 'though it is part of Samson's Riddle: maybe it's a play on words?'

'Read it out, let's see if we can spot anything.'

'Judges 14.14 says, "And he said unto them, Out of the eater came forth meat, and out of the strong came forth sweetness. And they could not in three days declare the riddle". It makes no particular sense to me.'

'Me neither,' I agreed. 'We must be missing something.'

'I didn't know Jack, but from what I understood from my Tom, I wouldn't say he would be one for riddles or tricks with words. He was cunning maybe but not sophisticated.'

'It could be worth finding out about the church, just in case we've misinterpreted the clues, but beyond that, as I say, I'm stumped.'

'Let's sleep on it, something might just occur to us.'

'Ok, I'll look on the net for a local history society, maybe they could help.'

'Give me an update when you visit your mum next, I should be easily found, without clues.'

*****

The local history society gave me Don Foot's name and telephone number: he agreed to chat to me if I would kindly go to his cottage. Before I could ask any questions, Don insisted that I first tell him where I lived and how long I had lived there and who I knew. I soon realised that my twenty-five years' residency did not qualify me as a local.

'Did you know your home housed the telephone exchange in the front room?' He said, establishing his credentials.

'No. How long ago?'

'Well, I can tell you it was still the exchange in 1947 because I was sweet on one of the girl operators, can't remember her name. Anyway, I was in the house when the flood water came up under the fire grate and we had to leave on account of the electricity. Yes it was 1947 or maybe 1946; both bad years for flooding.'

'Did you go out with her?'

'No, didn't get any luck there, even after I gave her a piggyback through the flood. She married a chap from away and left the Gorge.'

'Did you know a man called Jack or Jackson Hailstone? He worked on the railway.'

'The one that drowned in the war?' He said, as if there were many.

'That's the one.'

'Why are you asking?'

'Well I'm helping his daughter-in-law with her life story, I lied; she's a friend of my mother's, they're in a nursing home in Wellington together.'

'Remind me, what's her name,'

'Joan.'

He nodded as a smile played across his features.

'Did you know her?' I guessed by his reaction.

'I should say so,' he said, with a momentary glint in his eye. 'I knew Jack by reputation of course, he was reckoned to be a bit of a lad, but I was only a youngster when he drowned so I didn't know him to speak to.'

'Do you remember anything about his drowning?'

'Not really, it wasn't that noteworthy, there was so much going on. The Bridge was a dangerous place in the early part of the war, during the black out and all that. The rationing encouraged poaching and the black market, run by gangs, some from as far away as Brum.'

'Sounds exciting.'

'There was all sorts going on. It wasn't unusual for people to be killed in accidents, you see. There were several munitions accidents and deaths in the area, none of them recorded of course. I remember there were three killed in the sand quarry when the face gave way and buried them. Then there were countless accidents in the blackout, people being run over, or falling into things, yes they were dangerous times. You know, if you were out at night, the lads would leave their white shirt tails hung out to help to be seen.'

'What sort of munitions did they make, Don?'

'All sorts; they assembled shells and bombs; they even made bomber wings up at the works. Everyone was working shifts and overtime.'

Don looked into his fire lost in memories of his childhood.

'Do you know anything about Benthall Church up by the Hall?'

Looking up from the fire he stared at me steadily as if considering my question. 'St Bartholomew's?'

'Yes, I think so. I only know it as Benthall church.'

'That's the one. Well, the current church is quite old, built on the site of an older church that burned down in the civil war. What is your interest?'

'I'm working on a ramblers' treasure hunt and looking for interesting objects to create questions and clues about. Things like the sundial, the mosaic eye, the Lions head or the broken anchors on the Trowman's grave. Do you know anything about them that might help?'

'Not really, though I do remember reading somewhere that there was a beehive built into the tower. If I remember correctly the bees got in and out through a pipe inside the Lions mouth.'

'How long ago?'

'Not sure. I think I read it in a pamphlet written about the church; I've probably got a copy somewhere,' he said, waving his arm towards a snug. Through the half open door I could see many random piles of books, papers and photographs.

'It's ok, another day maybe. Did you know Jack's son Tom at all?'

'That's a strange one. I only realized he was Jack's son when he took over Jack's cottage at the end of the war. After that chap Harris left. I think his adopted parents lived in Madeley. Welsh name Jones or Evans, something like that.'

'What was he like?'

'Tom was quite a bit older than me, worked on the railway, didn't know much about him. I knew his wife before they got married. I knew her as Joan Finch, she was younger than me and quite a looker. I fancied my chances there, but she went off with Tom in the end: baby snatching it was.'

'Would she know you, if I mentioned your name?'

'I doubt it. Anyway it's time for the Archers, can't miss that I'm afraid, watch your step on the way out. Come back anytime, bring Joan with you.'

*****

'Hi Joan.'

'What are you smiling at?'

'Know a chap called Don Foot?'

Cautiously she raised her head, 'Should I?'

'He knows you, led me to believe you were close at one time.' I busked.

'I'm sure I don't know what you mean, there's only ever been my Tom,' she said. Her penetrating, no nonsense stare drew my line of questioning to an abrupt halt.

'Have you made any progress with the clues, or are you here to waste my time?'

Wow, I hit a nerve there.

'No, I mean yes, in a way.' I blustered.

'Stop talking gibberish, spit it out.'

I somehow expected her to finish her sentence with "child"; I paused for her to say it. Recovering, I said, 'I don't see how it helps, but apparently a beehive had been built somewhere in the tower, the bees would fly into the hive along a pipe from the lion's mouth.'

'I can see a connection between the lion, the bees, the honey and the inscription, but I don't see how it helps us.'

'Neither do I. Maybe it's a red herring and Jack just wanted Tom to look in the book and we've missed the significance, somehow.'

'I suggest we concentrate on the Bible; it looks to be our only lead. Pass me my magnifying glass; it's on the top of the wardrobe.'

Joan crouched over the Bible and peered through the lens studying each word. Leaning over her shoulder, I attempted to help before being encouraged to sit on the bed and wait my turn.

'What's that down there?' Joan said, looking up in my direction. 'I think there's something down there,' pointing with her forefinger towards the spine. Can you open it as far as it will go,' she asked, miming the required action, 'and don't break it, it's been in the family for years.'

I lifted the Bible and bent the covers back towards each other as far as I dared. A line of small but legible writing appeared from its hiding place against the binding.

'159 and 1, 2 up at 53½ mph, when your head is level with the top, look under your feet.'

'What do you make of it?' said Joan, as she copied the words in a notepad, arranging them in the style of a poem as the first clue had been set out.

159 and 1

2 up at 53½ mph

When your head is level with the top

Look under your feet.

'The first clue was written in such a way that only Tom would understand, I wonder if this one is similar? Having said that I can't understand why Jack created the puzzle. Why go to the trouble, why not just tell Tom the secret?' I said, thinking aloud.

'Could we be missing something?' Joan said, shrugging. 'Hang on, Jack may have written it down for Tom to find when he was older. Tom was only sixteen when Jack died, he could have been much younger when it was written, couldn't he.?'

'That's right, the clues were written after the flyer excursion date and before Jack died, obviously. Tom would have been about twelve at the time of the excursion and maybe sixteen when Jack drowned, so that fits,' I said, believing we were making progress, maybe.

'The clues are still as clear as mud to me,' she said, frowning. 'Maybe that Google thing will come up trumps?'

'Good idea,' I said, trying to sound enthusiastic. 'Joan, I need to go, I've a train to catch. I'm in London for a few days. I'll come and see you and Mum when I'm back. I'll work on the clues while I'm away, okay?'

*****

Settling into my hotel room, I hooked up to the Wi-Fi and started to search the web. There would be no pubs, shows or sightseeing for me, until I made some progress with the clues.

I searched '159 and 1.'

Answers, '=160', this from a web calculator, followed by plenty of products with 159 model numbers. A 159 Alfa Romeo car, a 159 Electric locomotive and a 159 Gulfstream aircraft. 159 appeared to be popular model number, but none of the products were manufactured in Jack's day.

Next I tried '2 up at 53½ mph.' It threw up all sorts of bizarre references as diverse as losing weight, strange speed limits and slope drilling, whatever that is.

As a last resort, I deleted all but '53½ mph' and searched again. The search threw up the calculator again, plus strange references to anything with 53 in the text. I stared at the search bar with one hand on the laptop lid ready to give up. Then, 'railway' popped into my head, as a common theme between Tom and Jack. I searched 'Railway 53½ mph.' nothing much came up in the first few results but further down I found a reference to Sherlock Holmes, something else they had in common. A message board question, dated way back in 2003, asked how Holmes had estimated the speed of a train. The question concerned a story called 'Silver Blaze', and the text they quoted read:

'We are going well' said he, looking out of the window and glancing at his watch, 'our rate at present is fifty-three and a half miles per hour.'

'I have not observed the quarter-mile posts,' said I.

'Nor have I, but the telegraph posts on this line are sixty yards apart, and the calculation is a simple one.'

Chapter 10: Sarah and Precious

It had been an intense seminar that had inspired me to start writing seriously. As I swung into the drive, I noticed Lucy sitting on the back of the settee, watching me through the front window. She's not usually allowed in the lounge, I thought.

During the confusion of zapping the alarm, patting Lucy and pulling the case through the door, I missed something small but extremely significant lying on the kitchen table. Dragging my case upstairs, I sensed a strange feel to the house. If Lucy had not been bouncing around demanding attention, it would have probably occurred to me. Dumping the case unopened I returned to the kitchen, Lucy in hot pursuit.

This time I saw it, lying in the middle of the table, transmitting its crushing message. My stomach rolled, my legs buckled and my heart pounded as I stared, through eyes welling with tears, at the ring I had given Sarah when we first got together.

After some time, I started to wander around the house making a haphazard inventory. Her house keys lay under the letterbox. All her clothes were gone, except those, I had bought for her as presents. Her laptop, favourite pillow, house plants, what little furniture she brought with her, her passport and files, toiletries and her family pictures, all gone. Not much really, but enough to create the feel of an empty house.

'This is the last time.' Yes, that's what she'd said as we had made love. Yes, and it had been the last time too. I thought at the time that I had misheard her, but no.

*****

'Hello. Hello. Is anybody there? HELLO.'

OH SHIT, it must be Thursday, I remembered. Precious, our cleaner had let herself in.

'Good morning,' I said, as I hurried downstairs to meet her in the kitchen.

'Is there a note for me?' she said, raising one eyebrow as she glanced quizzically in my direction.

'Sorry, Sarah's out.' I said, hesitantly.

'I gathered that, did she leave a note and my wages.'

'No actually she, didn't. Look I'll go to the cashpoint.' I said grabbing my wallet hoping to cover my embarrassment. 'Back in ten.'

'Okay. I'll get on, see you in a bit.'

Returning fifteen minutes later, I found Precious sitting at the kitchen table behind two freshly brewed coffees.

'Coffee,' she said, gesturing for me to sit. 'You want to tell me something?'

'Sorry, Sarah didn't leave any instructions. Just clean what you think needs doing,' I said, attempting to avoid eye contact.

'She gone, hasn't she?'

'What makes you say that?'

'You been digging in the garden again? She's not out there, is she?' she said, barely suppressing a grin at her own joke.

'No, she's gone away for a couple of days.'

'Are you gonna play games with me. I can tell she gone. You don't fool me. All her special stuff's gone. So tell me.'

'Well, err ...'

'Stop shilly-shallying, tell me.'

'Well, she's left me, a couple of days ago.'

'Why?'

'Don't know, we didn't have a row or anything, though things haven't been wonderful recently, you know how it is?'

'She say anything, you know, a warning or something?'

'No, though the last time we had a row, she said I wasn't the person she thought I was. But that was months ago.'

'Where she go?'

'No idea.'

'You don't know or you don't care?'

'It's not like that. She didn't leave anything to say where she's gone, I mean nothing.'

'You may not want to know, but man, I do. You rang her mobile?'

'Her number doesn't ring out.'

'You rang her mobile company, her work, her son?'

'No.'

'I can understand maybe you don't care, but I need to know she okay,' she said, reaching for the cordless phone. 'Ring her work,' she said, pointedly passing me the handset, with a don't-fuck-with-me look.

'But…'

'None of that shilly-shallying, just call the number,' she said, with her hands on her hips.

'Hello, can I speak to Sarah Hunt, please?…Her partner…Can I leave a message?…She doesn't work there anymore, is that what you said?…When did she leave?…But, I'm her partner…Did anyone else leave at the same time?…I'm sorry, too.'

'Well, what they say?'

'They just said that she doesn't work there anymore and, no, they couldn't help. Something to do with their privacy policy, gobbledygook, etc., etc. You know, the usual BS.'

'This is too bad. You need to be more forceful! What about her mobile? Second thoughts, I'll call. Pass me the phone and drink some of that coffee.

'No, it's not the number I'm talking from…No I've lost it and I'm calling to cancel the number…No, I don't know my memorable name…What do you mean, can you speak to the account holder?…Okay. Thanks for nothing!' She put the phone down looking crestfallen.

'The number was cancelled on Sunday; he smelt a rat and wouldn't tell me anymore. You ring her son,' she said, passing the phone.

'Are you sure you don't want to do it?'

'Don't you be funny now, just get on and do it.'

'Hello, Steve…Yes, it's been a long time…I'm fine and you?…Listen, have you heard from your mum recently?…No reason, really…Okay, yes…No, I don't know where she is either…Thanks, bye.'

'What he say?'

'Hello.'

'I told you before, don't mess, this is serious.'

'Well, he didn't appear to be surprised, he just said it wasn't the first time, whatever that meant.'

'Still waters,' she said, staring blankly at her coffee. 'What about her old house? You ring the rental company. Second thoughts I'd better do it, what's the address again?'

I handed her the phone, fearing what she would do next.

'I'll come at this a different way, like through the back door maybe…Good morning, I'm interested in a particular property to rent, it's been recommended by a friend of mine…Yes. It's 30 Lakeside Crescent…Oh what a shame, my friend must be behind the times…Out of interest how long ago was that?…No thank you I'm only interested in that particular property…Thank you, bye.'

'They're not the rental agent for the house anymore, their client sold it a month ago,' she said, before pausing deep in thought. 'Wow, she's been planning this for some time. Let's see, three months' notice for the renters, then at least a couple of months to sell, that would be a minimum of six months, surely.'

'Look, this isn't an initiative test. She doesn't want to be found, maybe we should leave her to her new life,' I said, hoping to end the conversation.

'Don't you start getting sorry for yourself, now. Get onto one of those computer dating sites. There should be a woman in this house.'

'Precious, we need to have a little chat, I don't think ...'

'Later, later I need to get on. See you next week,' she said, over her shoulder as she bustled through the back door.

I can't afford a cleaner anymore. I thought.

Chapter 11: That Robin

Another TIA had struck Mum. For some inexplicable reason, they usually struck at lunchtimes and resulted in symptoms serious enough for an ambulance to be called. On the first two occasions procedures determined that Mum be bounced from the ambulance into A & E then MAU, and finally into a medical ward and then back to the home. The process took five days. Mum lost weight, became dehydrated and we learnt little more about her condition.

As a result of these experiences, the senior nurse at the home decided that in the event of another TIA, they would want to take responsibility and nurse Mum at the home. It took great courage on their part to keep her at the home, but they were repaid with smiles and Mum's swift recovery. The staff at the home knew her as a person, knew what she would eat and understood her toileting challenges. In hospital, she had become a name on a whiteboard and, in the worst case, she'd had been left unfed and soaked in urine.

Her recovery took longer after each succeeding event but one constant remained, she always wanted to go out in her wheelchair. Mum waved her way past her sedentary housemates on her way to the front door. She would not leave through the back door at night this time.

'Mum, Sarah has left me.'

'You liked her, didn't you?'

'Yes of course I did.'

'She never loved you.'

'What do you mean?'

'That robin's following us again.'

*****

With our jaunt in the wheelchair and our mealtime rituals completed, goodbyes waved and promises of a swift return offered, I set off to find Joan.

'John, you look like you've lost a pound and found a penny, what's the matter.' So, I told her about Sarah, Joan listened intently, without interrupting for once. Had she contracted laryngitis? I wondered as I scrabbled to change the subject.

'I think you may have hit on something with the Sherlock Holmes story, you know. I remember my Tom telling me he and his dad would sit round the fire on dark evenings while Harris read Sherlock Holmes stories. Jack and Tom loved them.'

'Well, that fits, doesn't it? Both clues were written for Tom.'

'Let's think of it in a railway context then.'

'Okay. What's the first line again?'

'I would have thought you could have remembered it by now. I can, it's 159 and 1.'

'Just testing.'

'The first line makes no sense to either of us, does it?' she said, with a shrug, 'so let's try the next one.'

'Then up 2 at 53½ mph. Could it mean, two up on a bicycle or something like that?'

Joan dismissed my attempt at humour with a withering glance.

'Have you ever heard someone say, "I'm going UP to London to a visit my sister" or "she went UP to London to see the Queen"? It's an old saying you don't hear much these days.'

'I think so.'

'It could mean towards London?'

'If you're right and the Sherlock Holmes bit is also correct, the second line could mean two telegraph poles towards London,' I said, dismissing the theory as being too far-fetched.

'Exactly, two telegraph poles towards London, from 159 and 1.'

'Just find out what 159 and 1 means, that should be easy.' *Not*! I thought.

'If it's easy, it won't take long,' she said, as she moved away behind her walker.

No pressure then, I thought.

Another oblivious drive home beckoned as I puzzled the meaning of 159 and 1. In desperation, I drove to the library in the hope that rereading the newspaper articles about Jack's death, might throw up something I'd missed. I began trawling through the 1942 summer editions, when an article caught my eye in an issue dated before the story of Jack's disappearance.

Police appeal for information

Saturday September 31st 1942

Local police and military police are asking the public for any information concerning a stolen Velocette motorbike found on Saturday 24th last, near Marwood where it appears to have run out of petrol. The authorities wish to interview Private Charles Adams, also known a Chas, who is believed to have absconded from a Herefordshire military base with the vehicle late on the 23rd August …

    Ploughing through back copies I thought how easy it could be to miss something relevant. In the issue after the one reporting Jack's disappearance, another story appeared also concerning a missing person from the Ironbridge area.

Prominent Ironbridge Industrialist's Wife Missing

Saturday October 10th 1942

Eleanor Chubb, wife of local industrialist Montague Chubb, last seen leaving the stables at her family home on the morning of October 3rd, has not been seen since. She had indicated that she planned to exercise a recently purchased stallion. The alarm was raised when she failed to return by 5pm. A search party was organised. Sometime later her mount was found in close proximity to an area known for ancient bell pits, mine shafts and air ducts. Mr. Chubb returned from business meetings in London to organise an enlarged search. The search proved unsuccessful and was scaled down after the third day. Tragically, Mr. Chubb lost his first wife in a hunting accident five years ago.

I then scrolled back towards the beginning of the year looking for any other accidents or missing persons. I soon found an accident that bore out what Don Foot had been saying about the dangers of the blackout.

Missing man found in culvert

Saturday 26th September 1942.

The body of James Mitchell, locally known as China, was recovered last Sunday, from an overgrown culvert at the Coalbrookdale Works. Mr Mitchell had been missing, since he failed to clock off from his nightshift on morning of Tuesday the 18th of August 1942.

I then searched through later editions in the hope of finding the stories conclusion :

Unlawful killing

Saturday 3rd October 1942.

The corners inquest held on Monday 28th September found that James Mitchell had been killed by a single gunshot through his heart. A verdict of unlawful killing by person or person's unknown was recorded. Local police officers are pursuing enquiries. It had originally been thought that Mr Mitchell had accidently fallen into the culvert during his night shift at the Coalbrookdale works.

Chapter 12: Trainspotting

As a lad in the early 1960s, I'd been a keen train spotter. TV programmes were in black and white and a second channel had only just been launched. We were practically living in the dark ages, and yes, train spotting could have been described as "cool" if the meaning existed then. Sixties pop music had not been invented, no Beatles or Stones. We were subjected to Mogadon music from Perry Como, Frank Sinatra and Peggy Lee, 'proper singing' as my father would have said.

Today, time spent with a camera and a pint of beer on Bridgnorth station, watching preserved steam engines from platform 1, is about as good as it gets. No, I don't take pictures of the engines, I go more for street photography: passengers, firemen, drivers, porters and guards. Yes, I can justify a couple of pints, I've earned them riding my mountain bike down the old railway line from Ironbridge. Getting back can be tricky, though. However, none of my railway knowledge had helped crack the clues. If the clue had a railway link, I must have been on the wrong track.

"Excuse the pun!"

Entering the booking hall at Bridgnorth station part of the Severn Valley Railway, I joined the queue. Only the British can queue round corners and take turns at two windows with the required precision and self-righteousness. As my turn approached, I caught sight of the lad at the booking office window. He looked so young he might have been selling tickets as part of his Duke of Edinburgh bronze award, doing good deeds in the community or something.

'One and a dog, please.'

'Would that be for the whole line, sir?'

What did he take me for? Of course, I wanted the whole line.

'Yes, please,' I said, forcing a smile.

'That will be £18 which includes £2 for the dog. I take it you're a senior, sir?'

I would have loved to have confounded the cocky little chap by saying no, full fare please. But, that would cost me another £2 for the privilege of possibly being considered younger. I found it disturbing that I obviously looked well over the line between adult and senior and suspected my recent loss of Sarah had taken its toll. I mean, who would take a chance if it were marginal? Only a cocky little chap, I thought. However, in his defence, at his age I would have monitored anyone over forty in case they dropped dead on the spot.

'If you put your card in now, sir, chip end upright and in first.'

He mimed the expected procedure to aid my understanding.

Of course, it's bloody well the right way up and round. Okay, so I may be entitled to a senior ticket, but that doesn't mean I can't use a chip and pin machine.

'If you wait for the prompt sir, then enter your pin.'

He watched me with a resigned look, in the expectation that I would screw up the pin number entry.

I never get my pin wrong, Sonny, I thought. Well, it's true, I do use the same pin number for all my cards. So, shoot me!

'That seems to have gone through okay, sir. Please take your card and have a pleasant journey on our railway today,' he said, as he smiled the sickly sort of smile normally reserved for your granny.

But, before I could gather the tickets and card, he struck again, scoring even more points for his D of E.

'Would you like a copy of our booklet sir? It's called "Through the Window".'

He must have caught some sort of hint from my body language.

'It's free,' he said, as he pushed a copy towards me through the window aperture.

I attempted take it casually as I didn't wish to appear too keen. My delay probably served to confirm the lad's suspicion that I had insufficient RAM, causing the processing delays he had witnessed. I caught a reflection of his head shaking piteously as I shuffled away.

Fuck you, too, I thought.

'Have a nice day,' he said.

Game, set and match to the young lad.

I settled into an empty compartment. My own private bubble of 1950s style complete with massive box sprung bench seats, netting luggage racks and faded black and white photographs of even more faded resorts. The compartment is truly wonderful. Wonderful, that is, until another passenger invades it; possibly an ardent conversationalist, a railway buff or worse a single parent with three unruly children. Lucy earns every penny of her £2 ticket as she deters other passengers from joining us. Railways suffer from the wrong kind of snow, leaves on the line and the wrong type of passenger.

262

Lucy's talent for deterring other passengers was not required though, as my demeanour shrieked 'loser'. And who wants to sit with a loser? I must have looked infectious. Maybe 'loser' was not printed on my t-shirt, but it oozed from every pore. I had tossed coins into the Trevi Fountain with three different women and now had no chance of returning with any of them. Loser.

Nothing beats the view from the last window in the last carriage, the old-style windows you can open by sliding them down. Treat yourself one day to the mesmeric blur of wooden sleepers and shining rails. Poppies catch your eye, their brilliant redness peppered across vivid green crops. Long grasses sway and bow in deference to the train as she sweeps majestically passed at a stately twenty-five miles per hour.

I absent-mindedly thumbed through my free guide. The pages were packed with text blocks, arrows and drawings. There appeared to be a double page spread for every two miles. My eyes rested on a string of familiar looking numbers,144/11 in the midst of dense text. The gist was that the numbers denoted the distance from Paddington and that this quarter milepost denoted the boundary of the first section of the line purchased from British Railways.

Eureka so 159 and 1 could be another way of saying 159/1. So just fifteen miles from 144/11, it must be somewhere in the Gorge?

*****

At home I dug out a couple of old local OS maps and laid them out on the floor. Grabbing string from the junk drawer I marked out the miles from the map scale and placed it along the course of the old line. Though rough and ready, it indicated that the treasure should be somewhere between Ironbridge Station and Buildwas Junction. The viaduct appeared to be the midpoint and possibly the place to start looking.

Chapter 13: Knock First

Arriving unusually early for my visit, I found Mum still in her pyjamas. Her carers offered to get her ready if I would not mind losing myself for ten minutes. I agreed happily and went to reception with the idea of reading a newspaper, but halfway there I changed my mind and went off to find Joan to tell her my news.

An accomplished singing voice leaked around her door and into the corridor. I knocked, waited for a moment and pushed the door. My first sight was of Joan standing unaided in the centre of her room, singing along to Glenn Miller. At first, I thought I had made an error. Shit, I'm in the wrong room? As if by magic, she dissolved into the Joan that I knew.

'Don't you believe in knocking before you enter, young man?' she said, appearing to rediscover her composure.

'I did knock, honest - maybe you didn't hear me over the music. Anyway, you were singing from the middle of the room?'

'You've got it wrong as usual, I was stuck in the middle of the room, just out of reach from my walker. I was panicking trying to reach it, not singing. But as you see I managed without falling, no thanks to you.'

My eyes must have been deceiving me, I thought.

'Anyway, let's forget about this misunderstanding, how are you feeling John.'

Time to change the subject, I thought.

'I made a discovery yesterday. I think I know what 159 and 1 means. It's a quarter mile marker, like the ones that weren't there in the Sherlock story.'

'You've lost me. Stop talking in riddles.'

'Well, in the old days, railway companies marked out each railway line with posts every quarter of a mile, showing the distance from their head office. Here in the GWR's case, the number of miles from Paddington.'

'I hope this is relevant, it sounds a little nerdy for my taste, can't you cut to the chase.'

'No, not really; let me explain. The marker we are looking for is one-hundred and fifty-nine and a one quarter miles away from Paddington.'

'Obviously, but where is that precisely?'

'Well, the Severn Valley Railway preservation is part of the same line that Jack worked on. Based on the position of the markers in the preserved section, our quarter mile post should be somewhere here in the Gorge.'

'Whereabouts?'

'Not sure.'

'Are we getting warm then, do you think?'

'Yes, but we'll need to be red hot, to find it.'

'What's next then?'

'We need to find a map indicating the original position of the posts.'

'I'll leave that for you to sort out. Will it take long?'

'I hope not,' I said, before going off at a complete tangent as I remembered something. 'Joan, you remember those two men I took a photo of, the ones you said were wino's.?'

'Vaguely.'

'Well, there some different ones today, sat in a parked car in the lay-by. Come to think about it, they were there last time I came too.'

*****

I had hoped to see Mum before tea but it was now already after seven. Still it's worth another entry in the visitor's book. Mum enjoyed going to bed straight after tea. She appeared to spend more time in bed than out these days.

She opened one eye and acknowledged my presence with a weak nod and fell back into a deep sleep. Drained by a day where nothing had gone to plan, I slumped into her comfortable wingback chair and picked up the local paper from her occasional table. I thought about opening a window, but decided against it, preferring to swelter in silence. After all, I would feel the cold one-day myself, wouldn't I?

The head and shoulders of Thandile, the tall night sister, appeared around the half open door.

'Before you go tonight I would like to speak with you, I'm here on my own at the moment, so if you don't mind coming to the desk on your way out, that would be good?'

I started to read the paper again, the words began to swim. I said my goodbyes to Mum, promising to return the following day. Standing at the nurse's station, I looked towards the sister but she raised her palm and continued her telephone conversation. She possessed a unique blend of caring, composure, athleticism and brooding menace. The Victorians would have referred to her as handsome. Her cheeky grin or warm smile negated her challenging presence to a point, although a man would be unsure how to feel if he met her in a dark alley having slighted her.

'Please wait in the visitor's room, I will be with you shortly,' she said, with her hand clamped over the mouthpiece.

I did as requested and settled at the end of the settee furthest from the door. I scanned the fading pictures as I resigned myself to the probability of being asked to complete the latest customer satisfaction survey. Moments later she entered the room carrying an iPod player, which she placed on the coffee table and tapped the screen.

A raunchy nightclub style saxophone burst through the silence. Stooping low she adjusted the volume, once satisfied, she stood and fixed my eyes with hers. Satisfied she had gained my undivided attention, she began to shimmy her hips in time to the music.

Staring deeply into my startled eyes, she teasingly opened the top button of her blue uniform. She turned, never losing eye contact, miming the lyrics over her shoulder while smoothly rotating her backside in my direction. Casually she turned back towards me, opening her uniform slowly, one delicious button at a time, before stepping out of it as it fell to the floor.

Swaying her torso in time to the beat she leant forward, her breasts close to popping out of her low-cut bra. Pouting, she slid her index fingers sensuously through the elastic of her knickers, shimmying closer and closer. Her perfume enveloped me.

Abruptly she raised herself to her full height and spun around, coquettishly retaining eye contact over her shoulder.

'I'm glad I haven't lost my touch' she said, lowering her eyes towards my crotch for confirmation. She gathered up her uniform and iPod and swept through the door.

The insistent beep, beep, beep of the corridor call service commanded my attention.

Woozily I realised SHIT. Only a dream.

Collecting myself, I mumbled my goodbyes and rushed past the nurse's station. Beam me up Scotty, I thought, as I clocked out, still red-faced, embarrassment leaking from every pore.

*****

Looking up the road to the lay-by, I could see that the brown nondescript car had not moved. I decided to take a closer look. Standing in the car's blind spot I studied its occupants: two men roughly my own age, one maybe younger, both wearing raincoats and caps, both reading newspapers, fast food wrappers on the back seat. Moving up to the passenger door window I attempted to make eye contact.

Ignoring me he stared studiously straight ahead at the windscreen, and said something to the other man out of the corner of his mouth, before reaching into his inside pocket and pressing an ID card against the side window next to me. Police.

Chapter 14: York by Train

Having searched the Internet, the National Railway Museum appeared to be the best organisation to help locate the quarter mileposts. It felt right to travel there by train. I enjoy the way the train sets the agenda: it won't go anywhere other than where it's going, it won't go any faster and there are no Sat Nav instructions to listen to. There are downsides, however.

'I'm on a train. Yes, a train. You might lose me any minute. No, on a train … a train. I think I've lost you. Are you there?'

Quiet carriage? Stickers only. Empty lager cans and lipstick marked coffee cups abandoned on tables or floors mark the visit of the 'what's-a-waste bin' tribe. Then there's laptop man who dominates a whole table and four seats, single-handedly, his body language screaming:

'Don't sit near me, go and stand at the end of the coach. Can't you see I'm working!?'

How is it that this species appears to think that it's perfectly acceptable for others to stand whilst they cover the table with laptops, plug-in drives, two mobile phones, all plugged into a socket on the other side of the table with leads trailing everywhere?

I longed for a little old lady to challenge laptop man.

'Have you got another ticket for your bag and coat, sonny?' she would say, staring at the aisle seat. Having sat down next to laptop man, she would bump him pulling down the centre armrest, audibly suck her teeth repeatedly and stealthily release deadly farts in his direction.

I ask you, what is wrong with aimlessly staring through the window. These days, people appear to go to extreme lengths to be in their own bubble. No one offers eye contact. If they are not watching catch-up TV on a tablet, their heads are in eBooks. Failing that, they hide under beanies in ostrich mode, back to the wall, feet on the seat, distorted drum and bass escaping from their skulls, or maybe that is how it's supposed to sound.

Jesus, I must be old. I remember when…

But, I do remember when I made a hell of a racket in Queen Street, Cardiff during my mod teens, playing my brand-new Phillips cassette player with chart toppers recorded from the radio. Talk about distortion, those were the days!

York Station's wonderful curved roof stood above the signs for the NRM. I joined a half term crocodile of grandparents and restless grandkids as they gradually dissolved into the swarming masses around the exhibits. A young woman looked from her screen as I approached the research desk.

'Can I help?' she asked, with an almost genuine smile.

I'm so glad she didn't ask 'how may I assist you today?' Yes, I'm touchy.

'Yes, please, I live in Ironbridge.' No reaction. 'It's in Telford, in Shropshire.'

'Oh, I know, it's over near Wales isn't it?'

'Yes, that's the one.'

I hope she knows more about railways, I thought.

'How can I help?'

'Well, across the river from my house is the old track bed of the Severn Valley Railway. I wanted to know where the quarter mile posts would have been placed.'

I don't know what sort of reaction I expected, but I didn't get one. Perhaps she usually dealt with a better class of railway nut.

'I would suggest you start with our Colonel Cobb Atlases,' she said, as she swung round in her chair and pointed to the top of a line of filing cabinets against the wall.

'They are over there, the index is in volume 1. If you don't find what you are looking for, then come back to me.'

The maps were comprehensive and from the correct era but did not include quarter mileposts.

'Unfortunately, the maps don't appear to include quarter mile posts,' I said, with an apologetic look for disturbing her important work again.

She looked unfazed, as if she'd known. *I wondered if I'd been sent on a wild goose chase, to teach me the value of the information, when and if I found it.* Looking up from her screen she asked evenly, 'Would there have been a station in close proximity to your quarter mile post?'

'Well, yes, Ironbridge Station or to be exact Ironbridge and Broseley Station.'

'I'll look in my station map index. Do you have something to write with? I'm going to give you a six-digit number.'

I must have looked pathetic. Assessing correctly how ill prepared I was, she looked up her index and wrote it down on her pad. Ushering me to drawers of microfiche, she selected three from the "I" section and led me to a vacant microfiche reader.

'Do you know how to use one of these?' she asked, as she switched it on deftly, without looking.

Feeling on firmer ground I said, 'Yes, I used one of these back in the early nineteen seventies, when they were cutting edge technology.'

'Oh, I'm sorry, I wasn't born then.'

I could see she was not interested. I couldn't blame her. I attempted to read the fiche and began to realise how much I had forgotten. Backwards, upside down, arse about face, you name it, I tried it. My frustration proved worthwhile however when I found on the last fiche a milepost denoted as 158/111 standing at the east end of the station platform. The fiche reader reflected my blurred but very satisfied smile. Picking up my phone, I took a photo to show Joan.

*****

Spreading out the Ironbridge map I had marked up, I attempted to explain.

'Look, 158/111 would have been about here, give or take 50 yards or so,' I said, pointing to a pencilled star.

'Shouldn't we be talking in metres? Yards are old hat these days.'

'Yes, but when the quarter mile posts were laid out and the telegraph poles erected, they would have been measured out in yards. This map has the same scale.'

'So how far is a quarter of a mile in metres, then?'

'Well, I'm not a hundred percent sure, but the old 440-yard athletics race is now 400 metres, I think.'

272

'That doesn't make much sense does it, because if I remember correctly the old mile race is now the 1500 metre race, but based on what you've just said it should be the 1600 metre race?'

'Can't tell you,' I said, spreading my palms. 'Look, let's look at the map. This is where the sidings were, it's where the car park is now. The post stood here by the boundary wall. Although the station has been demolished, the wall survived and should give us a good reference point.'

I looked up from the map to check that Joan understood but need not have been concerned, she had already begun to calculate its position.

'This piece of string represents half a mile on the map scale, so if I hold one end on the mark by the station and then bend it around the curve of the line we get to ....'

'The viaduct!'

'If it's on the viaduct I'm hoping there will be something marking the spot.'

'What makes you think that, then?'

'Well, when they abandoned the line they just ripped up the tracks, signals, telegraph poles, huts, everything. But if it was built into the viaduct, it may have been too difficult to pull up and may have survived.'

'Without pinpointing the quarter mile post, we could be as much as 100 yards out, couldn't we?'

'I'm afraid it's worse than that, Joan.' I took a deep breath. 'This is where the if's start.'

'How do you mean?'

'Well, the treasure could be 100 yards give or take from the centre of the viaduct. And that estimate relies on the telegraph poles being 60 yards apart and that "up" is towards London.'

Joan looked pensive.

'Potentially another problem: what if we can't work out where the telegraph poles were in relation to the quarter mile post. There could be up to sixty yards to the first pole, which increases our margin for error to one hundred and sixty yards.'

'A bit like looking for a needle in a haystack,' Joan said, sounding deflated.

I stared at the map vacantly.

'At least we know which haystack to look in; before, we didn't even know which field,' I said, trying to be positive. 'Look, tomorrow I'll walk Lucy that way and look for any evidence of quarter mile markers and telegraph poles. It's got to be worth a try.'

'Makes sense,' Joan said, 'By the way, did you know I have a hospital appointment tomorrow?'

'What's it for?'

'Never you mind, but if you picked me up afterwards, you could show me what you've found.'

'Won't the home be worried?'

'No, they won't have a clue. I've booked a ride on the disabled bus and told them I'm meeting my sister there and that she will be bringing me back. You see it's all organised.'

'But, you haven't got a sister?'

'No, but they don't know that, do they?' she said, with a sly wink.

Chapter 15: 440 Yards

Imitating a 1950s-style robot I attempted to pace out 440 yards from where I guessed the original marker would have been. Unfortunately, my legs were too short to produce a comfortable yard stride. This forced me to adopt an elongated stride reminiscent of a schoolboy hop, skip and jump, or, in new money, the triple jump.

My metronomic series of strides denied Lucy the opportunity to sniff or take toilet stops without being yanked forward in mid-sniff or worse. The manic sight of a dog being dragged by a trainee goose stepper mumbling in time to jerky movements should surely have prompted calls to the RSPCA.

'Four-hundred and thirty-seven, four-hundred and thirty-eight, four-hundred and thirty-nine ...'

At the end of my four-hundred and fortieth stride, I scraped the path with my heel to denote the quarter mile mark. I could see no obvious signs of the 159-mile post. Lucy had resigned herself to participating in an inferior walk. She gave me a piteous look and sat down, then lay down to emphasise her displeasure. As we were now well away from the hustle and bustle of dangerous traffic, I did as bid and let her off the lead.

My search discovered many items, most of which should have been in a bin. Lager cans, sweet wrappers, punctured dog's balls, bags of dog poo, single gloves and drink cartons. Most of the items I could understand being thrown or dropped in the undergrowth, but bags of dog poo defeated me. Why go to the trouble of fiddling it into a bag, a tricky operation at the best of times, and then throwing it, bag and all, into the undergrowth? Why not kick or flick it somewhere safe to biodegrade and save the world from another plastic bag? Some bags were left by gates or strung in prominent positions on bushes, presumably to be collected on the return leg. If so, there is a considerable amount of poo amnesia around. I had found just about everything but a quarter milepost. I decided to try further along the track bed. Returning to my mark, I stood to attention and stared into the distance. 'One, two, three ... four-hundred and thirty-nine.'

I scraped a mark, looked around, nothing. But, at least my position tallied with our map estimate. The Viaduct hugged the hillside on one side and faced the river on the other. Its tall arches hidden behind thick cloaks of ivy. I eventually located the remains of the milepost, hidden in the undergrowth, only ten yards or so from my scraped mark. The remains of its triangular wooden block was still attached to a massive length of broad gauge rail buried deep in the viaduct. No one could have shifted it without an effort disproportionate to its scrap value.

Now that I knew the location of 159/1, I needed to find the next telegraph pole towards Ironbridge station. Simple really. Within ten metres, I had found what looked like the stump of a pole covered in ivy. To one side were the metal anchors that once helped to keep the pole upright. Pacing out 60 yards towards Ironbridge, I stopped and marked the ground before searching the undergrowth. Nothing. Maybe it was not 60 yards after all.

I gave up, and went back to the first pole and then paced 60 yards in the other direction. I found the base of the pole easily, confirming that 60 yards had been correct. Returning to the original mark, I made a more detailed search, kicking the undergrowth aside. Eventually I kicked something hard in the undergrowth, another anchor point but without the link. Looking at its angle I calculated where the pole should have been. Working back, I eventually found the pole just below the surface, covered in undergrowth. I now needed to calculate the probable height of the telegraph pole, in order to estimate where I should stand to get my head level with the top. Easy!

An old fence line running along the crest of the bank looked like the obvious place to start. I figured that Jack would have buried the treasure on railway property as a matter of convenience. What better place than near a boundary fence? If he were disturbed whilst digging there, it would appear to be a legitimate task. Standing with my back against the fence, I looked towards the pole's position and estimated its top would be level with my head if I stood about six feet further down the bank. I scratched a rough cross with my heel and scrambled down. Feeling elated, I strode purposefully back to the house collecting my thoughts as I went. I considered our best cover would be a combination of dog walking and Geocaching. Hopefully it could help explain why I had a spade and metal detector half way up a bank.

*****

I crawled around the hospital's main entrance congested by taxis and blue badge holders, but could not see Joan. I eventually spotted her sitting on her walker's seat by the sexual health clinic door. I abandoned the van in a cross-hatched area and ran across to her. I helped her up into the van and put her walker in the boot.

'What do you want with this huge thing?' she said. I tried to frame a response, but she beat me to it. 'Thought you'd have driven something sportier than this,' she said, with a dismissive appraisal of its vast interior.

*****

Joan beamed as we swung into the old station car park.

'How far from here?' she said.

'It's about half a mile down the old track bed. Don't worry it's a civilised path,' I said, as I pointed towards the far end of the car park. 'You see the bush over by the wall, well that's about where 158/111 would have been.'

'Well, surely it's not that far, we're at least 100 yards beyond 158/111 and then it's two poles up, which is towards us. So by my reckoning it's only 600 yards not a half mile,' she said, with a mischievous twinkle in her eyes. 'You go and get set up, I'll follow at my own pace, but don't start digging till I get there. Okay?'

Yes, ma'am anything you say ma'am.

Lucy and I set off, metal detector and collapsible spade in hand. I scrambled up the bank and rechecked my previous estimate. I felt confident that I had the right place and began to imagine Jack digging here over sixty years ago. Joan's voice dragged me back to the business in hand.

'He's geo catching,' she said, to a bemused dog walker watching me from the path.

The walker's dog exchanged pleasantries with Lucy, who adopted her usual sitting stance, as she waited for it to lose interest.

I had read all the instructions, but this metal detecting lark wasn't as easy as it looked on the box. I swung it from side to side in the approved style without even a "beep". So, I increased the sensitivity to maximum and crossed my figures. After a number of false alarms the VU meter began to twitch consistently as it passed a spot a metre or so from my mark. The instructions suggested that the needle movement could be either a small piece of non-ferrous metal or it could be a large piece of any metal. I didn't know which to hope for. Anyway, all the analysis would be worthless unless I found something.

I rechecked my position, which looked in line with the telegraph post stump and about nine yards above the track bed. Saplings peppered the bank, one of which grew just next to the spot. Moving to one side, I eventually dug a bucket shaped hole before bottoming out against solid rock. Searching the spoil, I found little that warranted the VU meter's interest. I rechecked and found the detector now bleeped next to the tree. Prodding the exposed roots produced a corroded buckle attached to fragments of what looked like a hessian bag strap. I soon found a matching buckle and strap ends all with small fragments of material attached. Digging slightly to one side I eventually found more of the decomposed bag. Stuck in what must have been its bottom corner seam I found a single Roman coin. The find hadn't been what we had been hoping for, but it confirmed we were probably digging in the right place.

I slid down the bank. Lucy showed pleasure in my return, wagging her tail as she circled me. Joan, though, had read my body language. She knew I had drawn a blank before I even spoke. Brandishing the coin, I rubbed it on my trousers and presented it to her along with the buckles. Joan turned them over in her hand wistfully.

'The coin looks like the one Tom gave you?'

'Did you see any pieces of pottery or something the coins were stored in?'

'No just bits of old bag, definitely nothing Roman, unless GWR meant something in those days.'

Joan crumpled with disappointment and bent towards Lucy.

'Let's finish your walk, shall we?' Joan said, to Lucy who wagged in anticipation.

'Shouldn't you get back to the home?'

'All in good time, first things first.'

'We could check the clues in the Bible.'

'No, I think this is the place,' Joan said, as she surveyed the bank blankly.

'It looks that way doesn't it, and the coin sort of confirms it,' I said, as Joan turned towards me.

'Or, maybe it's been a wild goose chase all along.' Joan looked disconsolately at her dirty shoes.

'I'd still like to look at the ....'

'Tomorrow. Tomorrow. It'll wait till tomorrow, won't it?'

A deflated silence marked our journey back to the home. I dropped Joan off as agreed, just around the corner, close enough for her to saunter in comfortably behind her walker, but far enough not to be seen getting out of the van.

Chapter 16: Harris' Confession

A sombre atmosphere of anti-climax hung over Joan's room. She sat in her wingback chair staring blankly. I searched for an oblique introduction, sensing Joan had little interest after the crushing disappointment of our find.

'Last night I looked through copies of those news articles I found at the library. The ones about Jack's death. It's only an insignificant point but, do you know what happened to Jack's dog? According to the papers she waited by his fishing tackle for him.'

Joan's face melted.

'Yes, as a matter of fact I do. The dog's name was Skipper or Nipper, something like that anyway. It was like that story of Greyfriars' Bobby. You know, the dog that wouldn't leave his master's grave.'

'The one in Edinburgh?'

Joan nodded her agreement, as she recalled the story.

'My Tom took it to Madeley with him. His adopted Dad was none too pleased by all accounts. Tom eventually took her back to Jack's cottage when he took it over. She lived there for the rest of her life, but she died before I met Tom.'

'That's a lovely story,' I said, staring blankly at the Bible in Joan's lap. My tinnitus screamed at me to close my eyes and relax, just for five minutes. I woke with a jolt as the Bible slid from Joan's knees and thudded to the floor. We had both apparently closed our eyes, though the crash had only woken me: Joan slept on. As I wrestled it onto my lap I noticed a page had become detached and hung out, corner first. I attempted to realign the page.

'Joan, look what I've found!' I said, holding the paper towards her.

She responded with the slow relaxed breaths of sleep.

Intrigued I started to read. It was a letter of sorts written by Harris. I read it through twice as I waited for Joan to wake up. It answered some questions I had never thought to ask.

'Sorry, I must have dozed off. What were you saying?'

'I found this letter in the Bible. It's sort of a confession written by Harris, shall I read it to you?'

'Have you read it?'

'Well, yes.'

'Read it to me then, please.'

8th May 1945

If you find this note before finding the second clues it will save you a considerable amount of trouble. If you have found the clues and are searching for the treasure, stop now, the coins are gone.

You may have met me, you may think that you know me, think again. You may have heard of me and think you know something about me, think again. Either way read on, if you will, I invite you to know a little more. This is a confession of sorts to cleanse myself, before I begin another life. You may find it conceited and boastful but it is the truth.

My first life had been a life of privilege at our family home in the Borders. My late father's bankruptcy ended my comfortable existence.

I recovered by stealth and cunning as a modern Robin Hood in Birmingham, until my merry men deserted and joined an East End Mob under the leadership of a maniac, leaving me exposed and surplus to requirements.

My third life has been a little life, allowing me to hide from my second life. Jack found me, believed my story and gave me a home. He also made it possible for me to continue living in his cottage after his death, until now.

My first confession is that I was responsible to an extent for his death. I did not kill him myself, but I could have saved him, had I warned him in time. I delayed my warning and arrived to find his cap floating on the river's surface. I had followed Jack and learnt of his many secrets, most involved other men's wives, girlfriends, sisters and daughters, but one in particular may have caused his premature end. She was my age, younger than Jack, she was not beautiful, but she was certainly not plain. Anything she lacked in beauty she more than made up for with pure animal attraction and presence. I knew her through my position, tutoring the estate children, a job Jack had won for me. I managed to kiss her once when her guard was down, I was confident there was more to come, given time. She was the only woman I thought about during my third life here in the Gorge. She was my passion, my obsession. Imagine how I felt, when I overheard a conversation between the estate's gamekeeper and her husband the owner. The gamekeeper was talking about her and her lover, I thought at first they were talking about me. I kept silent and hidden until I eventually worked out they were talking about Jack. I had no idea. A wave of hatred and jealousy washed over me. It was difficult to listen, my head spun, but listen I did. Soon I understood it all, the meeting place, the time and date. The husband ended the conversation by instructing the gamekeeper, saying: 'I'm due up in London tomorrow, I'll leave the problem to you, if you catch them, warn him off. Use some rough stuff if you need to, I'll deal with her later.'

My head ached with hatred and jealousy: Jack had stolen the prize without my knowledge, even though I lived under the same roof. I should have said fair play to him, but I could only see what I had lost. I hatched a plan on the spot, I would tell her what I had heard, but in my own time and too late for her to warn Jack. I would then offer to warn Jack but with no intention of doing so. I hoped Jack would be beaten up and give her up. She would see I had helped her in her hour of need and reward me. Well, that was the plan.

Jack set out from the cottage that night full of

anger, despite my attempts to persuade him to stay at home. That night Jack realised I was his enemy and not his friend. I gained the use of his house when he died and could have had his lady if the cards had fallen fairly. In the event, she died in a riding accident. I stuck it out at the school, though without the chance of seeing her, it lost its appeal.

My second confession is easily told. I knew where Jack had hidden the clues. I read them and resealed the envelope quite authentically I believe, though I could not act until Jack was out of the picture. The clues would be easily solved by anyone aware of Jack's love of Benthall Church, of Golden Syrup, and Sherlock Holmes.

The second part in his Bible stumped me, until I borrowed a pocket railway encyclopaedia from the Institute. I had obviously spotted the reference to Sherlock Holmes, which helped me put it into context. I'm sure the coins were meant for someone else but hey ho. I will put them to good use. Tomorrow I leave Ironbridge. The end of the war appears an appropriate time to start a new life.

John Calder

The letter abruptly ended our adventure. I didn't know what to say. I half-heartedly suggested we met again when I came to visit Mum and mumbled my goodbyes.

Chapter 17: Where's Joan?

I left Mum happily spooning soup and headed for reception. Joan had not been at the lunch table so I decided to check in her room. Her door stood slightly ajar, I knocked and went in. I thought for an instant that I had mistakenly stumbled into someone else's empty room. Her walker confirmed I had been right. The Bible and photos were missing and her personal things had been cleared from the bathroom. It had the feel of a dead person's room. I headed towards reception at the double. Waiting until the reception area cleared, I walked to the desk and asked the receptionist quietly.

'Hi, have you seen Joan about? Only I just looked for her in her room and it appeared to be empty. Has she moved to a different room or something?'

'I'm sorry, we don't know what has happened. It looks like she moved out during the night. Though quite how she managed it in her condition is a mystery.'

'But, her walker is there, in her room.'

'Yes, and clothes in her wardrobe.'

'If you can give me her address I could take her walker and clothes to her.'

'Well, that's the problem you see, we don't have her address.'

'Sorry, I don't understand.'

'Join the club, neither do we. We've been checking all the information we have but we've drawn a blank I'm afraid.'

'What information?'

'Well, her address for instance. The house she moved here from has different owners now. Apparently, they purchased it three months ago. Both the agent and new owners have Joan's address as the home.'

'Surely the Council have her address, I mean presumably they put her in here?'

'Well no, she organised it herself, privately. We were paid promptly every month.'

'So you have her bank details.'

'You'd think so wouldn't you, looks like we were being paid by a shell account which was closed yesterday.'

'The Manager rang the Council this morning on the off chance, but from what I hear, they appear to be none the wiser. We have absolutely nothing of any consequence about her on file. Anyone would think that she didn't exist.'

'How can I contact her then?'

'I know it's not much help, but even if we knew, we couldn't tell you. So, in a roundabout way, you're no worse off.'

'Any ideas how she managed to leave?'

'The smart money says by taxi during the night shift break. We think she took the back stairs. That way she could avoid being seen and, if she knew the code to the back door, well Bob's your uncle.'

'Have you reported it to the police?'

'That's an awkward one. We did think about it, but when we looked at it, she hasn't broken any laws as far as we know.'

'I meant, reporting her as a missing person.'

'We did think of that but we didn't really know who to say was missing.'

'Did she leave any message or anything?' I said, noticing an envelope in her hand.

'Yes. She left a thank you card for the staff and this envelope addressed to "Mary's son," that's you isn't it?'

I nodded and she handed me the envelope.

'In the card she thanked everyone and said she was checking out, as if it was a hotel. Fair do's to her, there aren't many who manage to check out of here.'

'Okay. I'll be in again on Wednesday to see Mum. If you hear anything, please ring me,' I said, stuffing the envelope in my jeans.

'And if there's anything in the envelope you'll let us know.' She said, to my back as I escaped. Truly rattled, I jumped into the van and set off.

The blare of a car horn jolted me into the present. The noise coincided with a small car's attempt to avoid the front of the van, as I attempted to turn into the main road. Where it came from, I wasn't sure but it certainly wasn't hanging about. The four occupants were sure, sure that I was an idiot, confirming their thoughts with one and two fingered salutes.

My button had been pressed. ~~Making~~ I made a hasty three-point turn and floored the van as I set off after them. I could just see their lights and a spray of sparks from the underneath of their lowered car as it veered sharply into a lane that headed into countryside. I followed them into the lane, though by the time I got there they were out of sight. From memory, there were no road junctions for a couple of miles; still angry I pushed the accelerator hard. I felt I must be gaining, though their tail lights were nowhere to be seen. Hedges whipped by, silhouetted against the night sky, somehow reminiscent of my schoolboy night time bike rides. At least now, I benefited from lights and brakes. Halfway round an innocuous corner, it tightened and tightened again. A hedgerow appeared out of nowhere, growing bright in the lights. Instinctively, I pulled hard on the wheel and simultaneously stamped on the brakes. The hedge disappeared fleetingly and then reappeared, first on my left then on my right. The van lurched to a standstill. The engine died. I sat there thanking my lucky stars I had not hit anything. Lowering the window, I stared back in the direction I had just come from. The van's hot exhaust ticked in the silence. Strident bass notes boomed in the distance as if mocking me. I began to question what the hell I had been doing. What on earth had I been planning to do if I had caught up with them? Give them a piece of my mind? I could hear my father's voice in my ear:

'The youth of today! They should bring back conscription.'

Had I become my father? I reminded myself that I had been young once.

*****

Once at home I pulled the envelope from my pocket and ripped it open. It contained a Roman coin and a note, which read.

'Thought you should have this coin

you found it. Check your phone

Joan.'

Finding my phone, I slid the lock off and entered my four-digit code: the home screen appeared. A message waited for me.

'Hi John, how are you?'

Stunned, I remembered conversations with Joan that indicated she had no intention of ever owning or using one of those new-fangled things. She had fooled me again and, anyway, how did she have my number? Noticing it was an iMessage, I replied

Me: You have an iPhone?

Joan: Got to move with the times!

Me: I'm at the home where r u?

Joan: You got my note?

Me: Yes, but where r u?

Joan: In my new home

Me: Where?

Joan: Can't say

Me: Uv left stuff, I'll bring it 2u

Joan: Charity shop stuff, don't want it

Me: Your walker?

Joan: Never needed it just a prop

Me: Your mints

Joan: Ha ha you suck them I don't like them

Me: Is that it?

Joan: Thanks for the adventure :)

Me: Joan what do you mean?

Me: Joan?

Me: Spk 2 me pls

290

Joan had blocked my number or she just refused to answer. Frustrated, I located her number in my history and dialled. Immediately "User busy" appeared. I redialled several times with the same result. Yes, she had definitely blocked me.

Chapter 18: The News

Visiting Mum gave me something to focus on now that Sarah had disappeared from my life. A local traffic report cut into the Radio 4 programme I had been half listening to, when something caught my ear. The traffic report concerned the stretch of road I would use on the way to see Mum. The traffic report ended, but the local station failed to transfer back to Radio 4.

"In our local news today, we hear about a Shropshire woman who hopes to hear the result of her long battle to keep a collection of Roman coins. More about this story after the main news."

Exiting at the next road junction, I avoided the jam. Congratulating myself, I made a mental note to listen to the local news, but soon forgot. I parked the van and clocked in at reception. While I was helping Mum into her wheelchair, she said 'hello' for the first time in ages.

She appeared in good form, commenting occasionally as we progressed around a familiar route. Returning for lunch, I sought out the duty nurse and enquired if Mum's medication had been altered. Nothing had changed, but they had noticed an improvement, which had started the day before. On my way out I went back to find Mum to say goodbye, she rewarded me with a smile and a wave. Brilliant.

Unfortunately, by the following day Mum had once more retreated into her solitary world.

*****

Lucy and I set off on our favourite Benthall walk, which involved passing the shops on the way to the Bridge. Experience taught me to walk Lucy on the riverside of the road, away from the pubs, coffee shops and cafés where she always found something to eat. It does not matter how old or dirty it is, she will gobble it up. As we passed the newsagents, I noticed the evening paper billboard from the day before proclaiming, "County Woman Loses Roman Coins Battle."

Lucy must be the only dog in the world that saunters along well behind their walker. Any dog worth its salt is ahead of its walker and being encouraged to come back. Not Lucy, she is constantly encouraged to keep up.

Passing the shop on my way back, curiosity got the better of me.

'Any of yesterday's evening papers left?' I said, looking hopefully at the bottom shelf.

'Only a midday edition I'm afraid,' the assistant said, bending to pick it off the bottom shelf.

'Does it have the billboard story?'

'Yes, I think so,' she said, flicking through it. 'Yes, here it is, it only made top story in the later editions.'

'I'll take it then, please.'

'You're lucky, it should have gone back. It's been saved for a regular, though I doubt if he wants it now.'

'Thanks,' I said, taking the paper. I got to the door when she called me back.

'You still have to pay for it. I know it's yesterday's news but it's still full price.'

'Oh, I'm sorry' I said, looking sheepish and fumbling for change in my pocket.

Lucy must have just sat there, as I hurried past her down the road with my head in the paper. She could have barked or something. Returning for her a few moments later, she looked at me warily, half-wagged her tail nervously. She appeared to have sensed it would be her fault, but could not quite work out why. I noticed from the corner of my eye the shop assistant giving me a knowing look.

Turning to page three, I scanned the article:

Shropshire Woman Loses Fight to Keep Roman Coins

A local woman learnt today that she had failed in her attempt to claim ownership of a collection of Roman coins. The Star understands the woman's late husband found the coins while walking near the old Roman City of Wroxeter. It had been hoped that a local collector or museum would purchase the coins so that they could remain in Shropshire. A Coroner's inquest ruled that the declaration period had been breached and disallowed the claim. The Star understands that an appeal is expected.

The woman in the story, *could she be Joan?* But, if it was Joan, why were we searching for the treasure her husband had already found? Or could this be another hoard? *Unlikely*, I thought.

I must have sat in front of the open paper for thirty minutes or so as a feeling of numbness bordering on paralysis gripped me. I failed to make any sort of sense of the story. Eventually I roused myself. I needed to speak to Joan, but how? I set about finding her contact details. I Googled 'Hailstone' with and without an 's'.

192.com came up with three Hailstones, but all resident in the South East. Northern Free Press announced a Joan Hailstone's recent wedding anniversary, obviously not my Joan. The surname Hailstone also came up on genealogy sites, but they were all families in the USA. Feeling stumped, I began to brainstorm.

I remembered the phone message conversation with Joan. Trawling through the phone's history, I found the records. I knew that just ringing or texting would not work as she had blocked my number. Slowly I remembered, the messages from Joan had been sent from an iPhone. I figured if she had an iPhone, there would be a good chance she still owned it, as it wasn't a throw away phone. I calculated that if I purchased a cheap "Pay as you go" mobile with a little credit, I could send a message to her that she would probably read, as she wouldn't recognise the number. I had one chance before she blocked me again.

Hi Joan it's John. Can you
help me for old time's
sake? Any chance you can
tell me your story, or the
part I played. I
guarantee I won't tell
Cheers John'

*****

After a couple of weeks, I had given up. I believed Joan had received my message but had decided not to play. Then, as I began to give up all hope, she confounded me by replying.

> John
> Ok I feel I may owe you an explanation let's meet at the square under frog clock 12 noon Sat.
> Joan

I knew exactly where she wanted to meet. I had watched the frog's performance many times when my kids were younger. The Telford Town Centre's square would fill with parents and children in anticipation of the frog show that played on the hour, every hour.

A strange place to meet, neutral territory and all of that, but hardly clandestine. *Perhaps her choice took into account the safety of numbers,* I thought, though quite why she should be concerned escaped me.

Chapter 19: Under the Frog Clock

I arrived early, telling myself I would browse the shopping centre while I waited for Joan, but found I had no interest beyond looking in a few windows on my way to the main square.

It's a light airy space but it can be choked by displays of the latest model cars, furniture and art. Today, however, shoppers strolled straight through it, using it as a thoroughfare between avenues of shops.

Staring at the clock, I debated what to ask Joan. I felt anonymous as transient fast food grazers, munched and littered next to me before moving on to fresh pastures. Twelve o' clock came and went. I began to consider giving up.

'John, is that you, mate?'

Looking up from my phone, I saw a half familiar face beaming down at me.

'You don't come up to the rugby club these days, the lads miss you.'

This helped but I still could not remember his name. 'When did we see each other last?' I asked, scrambling for any clues.

'About a month ago, in Wellington.'

'Are you sure.' *Don't remember that.*

'Very sure. We didn't speak or anything; I was on a stake out.'

'So that was you in the parked car, you were the policeman?'

'C.I.D. actually.'

'Thought you were a rep.'

'Most people do, I don't dissuade them'

'But why were you staking out the Nursing Home?'

'We weren't, we were watching a drug dealer across the road,' he said, with a pitying glance. 'I heard your partner left. Is that why you're looking so glum? What was her name?'

'Sarah.'

'Look if you're at a loose end these days and you fancy a pint or five, why don't you join the Morris Men Dance group I'm in?'

'Sorry not my sort of thing, still a bit gun shy after the Sarah thing.'

'Well if you change your mind it's great fun. I mean, you name another hobby where you can go in a pub blacked up, wear platform shoes, carry a big stick, shout and dance with men, to accordion music, in public, legally,' he said, with a wink and a shrug. 'Glad you can still smile, see you at the club for a pint one day.'

*****

Joan appeared, sidestepping dawdling shoppers as she homed in on our meeting place. She looked good; her clothes were colour co-ordinated, new and quite trendy. She looked ten, maybe twenty, years younger than when I had last seen her at the home. Maybe she had had a makeover or something.

'You keep strange company.'

'Old acquaintance,' I said, without enthusiasm.

'Old Bill,?' she said, eyebrows raised.

'No, Roger.'

Anyway, sorry I'm a little late,' she said, with a disarming smile. 'We did say half past, didn't we?' Without waiting for a reply, she continued. 'I'm only five minutes late then, I'm sure you'll forgive me, won't you?'

I had no answer.

'Now then, before we get started, why don't you do an old lady a service and get us both a coffee? I'll have a cappuccino and not one from one of those fast food places, a proper coffee. Meet you back here in five, I need to powder my nose.'

Hi Joan, good to see you. I'm well thanks, I thought. She had taken control already. As instructed, I set off in search of a proper coffee.

*****

'You took your time. Have you been roasting the beans?' she said, taking her coffee, as she absent-mindedly perused passing shoppers. 'Oh, that's good,' she said, with an approving glance. 'Aren't you having one?' she asked, looking at her coffee and then back to me.

I found it difficult to frame a polite answer.

'How's your Mum doing these days?'

'Oh, you know, up and down, same as ever but sort of okay.'

'How are you managing without Sarah?'

'Difficult to say really, depends on the day.'

'Anyone new in your life?'

'Let's change the subject.'

'Okay John, time's money and I don't have much of either,' she said, attempting a mock 1920s Chicago drawl, hoping I guessed, to lighten my mood.

'Let's start with the coins, you had them all the time didn't you?' I said, a little too forcefully. 'Sorry, I didn't mean it to come out that way.'

'When you say "all the time," then the answer's no. But if you mean before I involved you, then that's a different question and a different answer and the answer would be, yes.'

I had a sinking feeling that getting the information I wanted from our conversation would be difficult, if not impossible, but I pressed on.

'I guess what I would like to know is, if you had the coins in your possession, why did you want to find Jack's hiding place? Surely you knew its location, so why in God's name put me to all that trouble to find it?'

'Let's take this one step at a time. Yes, I had the coins but, no, I had no idea where Jack had hidden them.'

'Sorry, I don't understand. If you had the coins, why didn't you know the hiding place? And if you didn't know, why would you bother to find it if you had the coins?'

'I hoped to find a Roman pot or artefacts of some kind, that originally held the coins and had been left in the hiding place.'

'So, your disappointment was because we didn't find something like a pot and you didn't expect to find treasure at all.'

'Correct. If you remember, Harris's confession indicated he had cracked the puzzle and had taken the coins. The coin you found was a bit of a surprise to be honest.'

'But, we found his confession after we found the hiding place.'

'Correction, you found it then.'

'Why didn't we find Harris's confession when we looked in the Bible for the second set of clues or even when you took out the first clues in the envelope?'

'Because it wasn't there.'

'Come again.'

'It wasn't in the Bible until I staged dropping it.'

'So, I was supposed to find it.'

'Yes. The timing was important. Think about it, if you read Harris's letter in the beginning there would have been no need to search for the treasure. Reading it after you realised it had already been found, drew the whole searching phase to a neat conclusion, don't you think.'

'But, why the Roman bits and pieces?'

'I wanted to sell the coins, but I was having difficulty putting together a legitimate claim to them. I hoped to find a pot to recreate the way the Staffordshire hoard had been found.'

'So, did you have a plan "B"?'

'Yes, and a "C", but it looks like plan "D" will work. Watch this space, as they say.'

'What is plan D?'

'You will find that a local farmer will make a new find in the next couple of months.'

'More coins? What about the ones in the newspaper?'

'They were only a few of the total, sacrificed to test the market.'

'So how did you come by the coins, if you didn't find Jack's hiding place?'

'Tom had them. He kept them in an old railway snap bag in his shed. It's a shame really, they were beautiful coins.'

'I'm sorry, but I've lost the plot?'

'What don't you understand?'

'Well, in Harris's confession, he had found the coins and was going to start a new life with them the following day. So how did Tom come by the coins?'

'Okay, this is where it gets difficult. I'm not sure you need to know the rest of it. The truth could ruin people's lives.'

'Whose lives are we talking about?'

'For a start there's Jack, then there's Harris,' she said, looking into her cupped hands, 'and my Tom and me.'

'Well, we know Jack and Tom are dead and Harris would be about a hundred if he's still alive.'

I could have sworn a tremor ran through Joan as I mentioned Harris.

'Which leaves you, Joan. If anyone is hurt by the story it can only be you, can't it?'

'I suppose so.'

'I think you at least owe me an explanation.'

'Look, I'll tell you, but if you betray my confidence.' she said, with a withering flash of her eyes.

'I won't say anything, honest.'

Don't underestimate this woman, AGAIN!

'Believe me, I'll will keep it to myself. I swear I won't say a thing.'

'Woe betide you if you do,' she said, wagging a warning finger. 'Tom told me how he had gone to the Station Hotel for the VE celebrations. He'd been listening in to a group of men telling stories, each attempting to outdo each other. An extremely drunken gamekeeper started to tell a story of how he had been paid for killing someone. The story concerned the night Jack drowned a few years earlier. This gamekeeper fellow told his mates that he'd been given a job to rough Jack up a bit, the gaffer's orders etc., something to do with Jack seeing this rich chap's wife. They were to find him at the meeting place down at the river. Three of them set off to find Jack and do what they'd been paid to do.

Apparently, on the way to the meeting point, they bumped into Harris walking the other way, looking a bit shifty. A few minutes later, they found Jack's hat in the water and all his fishing gear and the dog on the bank. They hid and waited for Jack to come back, but after a while it dawned on them that something had happened but they weren't sure what. When Jack's body floated up a month or so later, they took the credit for disposing of Jack and got a bonus from the gaffer, for doing nothing. His mates were all impressed with the story and thought the gamekeeper a real wag, slapping him on the back and buying him more beer.'

'Did he hear anything about the wife of the industrialist? She went missing about the same time,' I said, as the thought jumped into my head.

'As far as I know it wasn't mentioned. Why do you ask?'

'I read about it in an old newspaper story when I was researching Jack's death. I think the gamekeeper was mentioned in Harris's confession, wasn't he? I wondered if the missing woman had been the same woman that both Jack and Harris were pursuing.'

'I suppose so.'

'Sorry, here I am going off at a tangent; please carry on.'

'Well, Tom went up to Jack's cottage to have it out with Harris. He wanted to know if Harris had been involved with Jack's death. When Tom arrived, he found Harris all packed with a suitcase and ready to leave.

Tom accused Harris of being involved and of course, Harris denied his involvement, he said he found Jack's hat in the water, just like the Gamekeeper did. Anyway, Nipper started to sniff round Harris's case. Harris toe-ended her away from it roughly and Tom took exception. Anyway, Tom and Harris got into a fight over Harris kicking Nipper, but I think Tom had also been fighting in his own mind because of Jack. They ended up crashing to the floor; Harris went down backwards with Tom on top, but Harris didn't get up again. Tom reckoned Harris hit the back of his head on the range or on the quarries. Apparently, Harris didn't bleed much, he looked like he'd gone to sleep.

Tom had killed him by accident of course, but he was scared that no one would believe him. The cottage would be Tom's when he made up twenty-one, or before, it was vacant. Everyone knew about Jack's will: you can't keep secrets in the Bridge. Tom thought the police would see it as a motive for killing Harris.'

'But, you told me that Harris had left by train and that Tom had confirmed it by asking at the station. But you knew all along that Tom had killed Harris.'

'I hardly knew you when that question came up originally. Why would I tell you that my Tom had killed him, even if it was an accident?'

'You didn't trust me, did you?'

'Look, it wasn't relevant at the time and anyway, it could have put you off. Or even worse you may even have been daft enough to tell the police.'

'But, Tom killed an innocent man. Harris didn't kill Jack. He admitted he contributed to his death by failing to warn him, but he didn't kill him.'

'Tom didn't kill Harris, it was an accident.'

'That's what Tom told you. He'd hardly say anything different, now would he?'

'Look Sonny Jim, I'm here to tell you as much, or as little, of the story as I please, and I don't intend to be cross examined. Comprende?'

'Sorry Joan, I understand. I just got a bit carried away,' I acknowledged, more than a little cowed. 'Please go on.'

'Where did I get to? Oh yes. Fortunately, Tom didn't panic. With all the celebrations going on, he figured there would be little chance he'd be seen. But, to make doubly sure, he decided to wait until the dead of night. He calculated that about three in the morning would be the best time to make his move. A steady drizzle had set in, no one in their right mind would have be out and about, so he got Harris and his case into an old wheelbarrow and took him down to the river along the back path.

As Tom laid Harris on the bank, he noticed he wore a ring that he remembered gathering dust on the mantelpiece. It was inscribed JC. Tom took it off his finger in case it helped identify him. He left his wallet and money in the jacket inside pocket so it wouldn't look like foul play. Tom slipped Harris into the fast flowing current and, as far as we know, his body has never been found,' she said, as if coming to the end of her story, before restarting reflectively: 'If you think about it, no one really knew who Harris was, so how could he be identified, even if they found his body? Nobody in the Bridge batted an eye when Tom moved into Jack's place and told everyone Harris had gone back to Scotland.'

'Where did the coins come from, then?'

'Well, while Tom waited for the dead of night, he went through Harris's case and found them,' Joan said.

Conversation stalled as we both took stock. Joan turned from gazing at the clock and smiled wearily.

'Time for me to go, I have a train to catch.' Joan's handbag beeped. She studied her phone briefly and returned it. Looking up, she noticed my quizzical stare.

'Just an alert, keeping an eye on some investments, the market's volatile at the moment, isn't it?'

'But I thought you didn't do technology?'

'Whatever gave you that idea? This is my third; good, aren't they?'

'But why make me do all that searching on the internet? You could have done it.'

'Yes, but you had to be convinced, not me,' she said, with a knowing nod.

'Have you time for one last question?' I said, still reeling.

'Okay, if it's short.'

'Well, I've two actually, how did you end up in the care home when you obviously didn't need to be there and why didn't Tom try to sell the coins?'

'The second one is easy. Tom didn't think they were valuable. I mean they didn't look very impressive all tarnished and mostly fused together. He left them in an old railway bag on a nail in his shed. I found them when I cleared out Tom's things, I realised they were valuable. Simple really.

The home. I used that to disappear, to become anonymous: a bit like Harris, maybe? He hid behind amnesia, I chose to hide behind twenty-four-hour security and client confidentiality policies.'

'But why? Why go to those lengths?'

'My my, do I have to spell it out to you?'

'It looks like it, Joan.'

'Look, stories about treasure live long in people's memories and the chance of being rich drives people to do things they would not normally think of doing.'

'I take it you're talking about the coins, but I don't see the link.'

'Men would arrive at my doorstep trying to trick their way inside by claiming to be meter readers or gas men. They weren't locals, most had Birmingham accents. It started to get out of hand: they wouldn't take no for an answer. I decided to get myself somewhere under their radar and behind locked doors, hence the home. Once inside, I worked at reinventing myself. You are now the only person who knows, for certain, of my link to Jack and the coins,' she said, as she stood to go.

'Can I give you a lift? My van's outside.'

'Thanks for the offer, let's draw a line under it now, okay?' With that, she stood and half turned to walk away.

'Jack didn't drown, did he, Joan?' I said to her back as she strode away. I thought I saw her tighten her shoulders but she did not turn or respond as she merged with a pack of shoppers and disappeared.

I had set out to emulate Jeremy Paxman, but Joan had outmanoeuvred me, again.

Chapter 20: How may I help?

'One plus one dot com, how may I help?'

'Well, I've been with you for three months and I haven't had any interest.'

'No contacts at all?'

'None.'

'Do you have your membership number?'

'Yes: M 34 54 66.'

'And just for security purposes, what is your memorable name, please?'

'Lucy.'

'If you wait a moment sir, I'll call up your profile……. Ah yes. Do you mind if I call you John?'

'No.'

'John, I'm looking at your interest's section. You've indicated here that you're interested in heritage railways, bird watching, rugby, car boot sales, camping and writing; is that correct?'

'Spot on, yes.'

'Perhaps, if you don't mind me saying so, they are interests that a woman could be persuaded to take part in, once they were in a relationship, though possibly not interests that would encourage a woman to consider a date, if you see what I mean?'

'But, I answered the questions truthfully, as your company advises.'

'Yes, I agree, but perhaps some artistic licence is required here. May I suggest you consider some or all of the following: classical music, candlelit dinners, exotic holidays, London shows, weekend shopping excursions, that sort of thing?'

'I don't like any of those!'

'John, let's maybe look at this from the woman's perspective. Can I ask, have you viewed any of our female members' profiles?'

'Yes, I have actually. Quite a few.'

'Have you noticed their interests? Did you notice any of them with an interest in steam trains or camping? You may find the odd one or two interested in writing. But I do emphasise odd.'

'Okay, I think I get where you are coming from. I'll look at updating my profile. Maybe use some of your artistic licence.'

'Is there anything else I can help you with today, John?'

'No. Thank you. That's fine.'

'Glad to have helped John. Thank you for calling one plus one dot com.'

Who said you helped? There must be someone out there who likes what I like? But, maybe they're just not female, I pondered.

*****

In my youth, I earned pocket money as a paperboy delivering evening and Sunday papers around my neighbourhood in Cardiff. The evening papers were fine, it was the Sunday papers that I remember with horror. The papers were so cumbersome and heavy; we were forced to carry them in two separate bags, which strangled you with every step. I would be chased by dogs; berated by customers; miss my favourite TV; get wet and cold, and all that for ten and sixpence.

Today I take an electronic copy of our local evening newspaper, even though I would have preferred the paper version. I found it somehow gratifying to receive it electronically as it saved some poor kid delivering it, or me collecting from the local newsagent. The electronic paper kept me up to date with local news and events; without it, I would have missed a story concerning a large quantity of Roman coins: the successful sale of a hoard of Roman coins. The story expanded on the fact that the coins had been purchased for the county museum. The purchase had been won after a lengthy battle with other interested parties from outside the county. The story went on to say that the coins had been found on a farm near Wroxeter. The coins' substantial value would be split between the landowner and the lady who found the hoard. The story pricked my memory of an earlier article, which had been a filler buried at the bottom of the last page of local news. It described the unexplained break-in at a local archaeological dig. A lock had been forced and a few low value pieces of un-catalogued Roman pottery had been taken.

I wonder who could be behind this, then? I thought, smiling to myself. *Second time lucky then, Joan.*

Confident that this particular story had reached a conclusion, I offered silent congratulations to Joan.

Tomorrow would be another day, as they say, and the day after that, I enrolled for a WEA creative writing course. I felt it had fallen to me to complete Jack's story, to fill in the gaps and make it whole from beginning to end. I had done the research while looking for the treasure with Joan. The time had come to pull it all together.

Part 3

Around and around

Chapter 1: Warning – the beginning.
Twilight of the Roman Empire in Britannica

His nostrils flare as the odour of burning flesh fills his lungs; acrid smoke stings his eyes; screams and shouts ring in his ears. Swirling mist parted, a wide-eyed child shambles towards her mother, her faltering gait hindering progress. She stumbles, her pursuers close in, her mother is out of reach. He must act to save the child. He scoops her up, but they are on him. Hot, reeking breath in his face, the blows rain across his head and back as he protects the girl. Blood bubbles and oozes through his hair before smearing his eyes, he sees only red.

Watching the horror through closed eyes, cold sweat spurs him to wake. A flickering lamp tugs him towards consciousness. Hugging himself, realisation gradually dawns. *A dream maybe; but so real, too real for comfort.* Disoriented, he lies, torpid, as his brain races, searching for a meaning. His upbringing led him to believe there would be an explanation for every event. He finally understands, his Gods are sending him a warning in the form of a dream. The meaning had been plain; the Empire's enemies were closing in, heralding the end at Viroconium. He must protect the collection.

For twenty years, Lucius had dedicated his life to raising a magnificent statue to Venus, which would dominate the Temple Square. The collection would reach its target within a year. Lucius felt cheated, his life's work thwarted, a solution must be found. If Virocunium were taken, he would be unable to protect the coins. Should he carry them and risk losing them in battle or retreat? Should he bury them beyond the city walls and recover them later?

The facts were few but, if the Gods spoke true, the hordes would come and come soon. He had faith in the Gods and would ask them for a sign. Closing his eyes, he selected a coin from his bag, placing it in his palm. After a moment's contemplation, he spun the coin upward. Opening his eyes, he followed the sparkle of reflected lamplight as it arced upward, hung for an instant then fell. A puff of dust signalled the end of its flight. Confirmation lay there at his feet. The Emperor's head lay face down in the dirt. Lucius threw on his robe, thrust a pair of knives into a stout leather bag, grasped his staff and stepped into the night air. Rainwater formed sluggish streams in the gutters. Wet cobblestones glistened in the moonlight. Barks hurled by insomniac dogs punctured the silence. A rat scurried.

The air hung heavy with the stench of excess. Unobserved, he entered the temple. An oil lamp he took from the entrance cast a flickering glow around the vast chamber. His footfalls amplified, distorted and echoed around the vacuous void. His long robe trailed across the marble floor creating the swish of a giant snake slithering towards its prey. Lucius went straight to a tapestry hanging across a sidewall. Its once splendid colours were faded, anonymous, just part of the fabric of the building.

Lucius swung the tapestry clear of the wall, releasing dank air, which struggled to rise. Stepping into the musty void, he felt for the correct block. Narrow and insignificant, its only purpose had been to fill the gap between two more impressive blocks. Lucius lowered the lamp and, with a knife in each hand, levered at its edges. Flexing under pressure, the knife blades forced the block away from its larger neighbours. Gripping the protruding edge with his fingernails, Lucius worked it to and fro until it moved towards him to reveal the hidden coins. They caught under his nails as he scraped them towards the gaping bag; so many coins and all of them silver. Maybe all those years of collecting could still be worthwhile.

Lucius hung the lamp back on its hook, checking for prying eyes. He swung the bag strap over his shoulder so that the bag and coins were disguised by the swell of his belly under his cloak.

Viroconium's inhabitants had faded away into a drunken sleep. The festival had run its course. *What better time to move the collection*, Lucius thought. *The Gods are by my side this night and the omens are good.* He felt somehow liberated, master of his own destiny.

As he approached the River Gate set in the southeast corner of the city walls, a centurion stepped forward out of the shadows to challenge him. How had he overlooked the certainty of being challenged by the centurion on guard, especially at that hour?

'Who approaches the gate?' he said.

With a jolt, Lucius recognised the voice. Instinct inspired his response.

'Ah Marius, I did not expect to find you on duty this night.'

'Lucius, is that you? Pull back your hood, let me see your ugly face,' he said.

Lucius complied wearily.

'You old goat, what brings you here at this hour?'

'Did you pull the shortest straw?' Lucius said, spreading his arms and delaying his answer.

'What short straw do you speak of?' Marius replied, with a puzzled look.

'The one you drew to be here on a festival night my friend. Did you offend the Gods in some fashion?'

'I'm always the one to tread on authority's toes, you know as much.'

'Whom did you offend?'

'They say I insulted the consul's wife.'

'She has duck's feet, I understand.'

'Enough small talk, why are you here at this hour? Why aren't you asleep in your bed, old man?'

Lucius stuck close to the truth: 'Violent dreams woke me, I saw the blood of Romans upon the feet of Celts,' he said, studying Marius's face hoping to read his mind. 'The Gods warned me that our time here will soon end. The Celts will reclaim their lands.'

'Are you drunk or mad, or both?'

'The warning is real, Marius.'

'You worry too much old man. There is life in the empire yet,' he said, blocking Lucius' passage.' Tell me what really brings you to the gate at this hour?'

'I fear I must go down to Sabrina's waters and sooth my troubled brow.'

'You are mad then. Be careful old man, the Celts may hide beyond every bush and rock. Take a lamp, to see them better.'

Uncertainty gripped Lucius, *was he jesting or was he serious?* A lamp could be followed and that was the last thing Lucius wanted. He craved the anonymity of darkness to cover his actions. Turning towards Marius with a broad smile, he took the offered lamp. *Raising Marius's suspicions would be foolish,* he thought. *He would humour him.*

Marius appeared taciturn, but he knew him to be a hot-headed young man, with deep animal cunning. The knowledge unsettled him. The priest and the centurion appeared an odd combination. Their friendship had been built upon the bond of a common birthplace. Lucius dared not test its strength with a secret of this magnitude.

'I see you've added bulk to your frame old man, you step with stiffness?' Marius said, with a questioning glance towards his midriff.

'I am tired and vexed, nothing more my friend. Return to the comfort of your post. Concern yourself no more on my account, after all I'm only an old man as you say.'

The two men nodded their farewells, Marius returned to his position as Lucius stepped out into the darkness beyond Viroconium's walls.

An ominous, biting, bone chilling wind blew from the Celtic west. The familiar path, an old friend in daylight, had become a stranger, hidden in impenetrable darkness. As his eyes adjusted to the blackness, he picked up the reflection of the dim lamplight from the path's smooth surface.

Babbling shallows reached his ears, a subtle warning: Sabrina's impenetrable depths lurked a few strides away. Stumbling down the slope, he reached the shallows. Moonlight briefly sparkled and reflected from her ripples and eddies, as she swept passed him on her hundred-league journey to the sea.

Once oriented, he hung the unwanted lamp from a tree, not wishing to betray his change of direction. Turning away from the well-trodden paths radiating from the ford, he faced downstream. With the wind at his back, he sounded out the hidden river path by tapping his staff against its compacted surface.

A burst of insistent ticking punctured the silence as a wren, hidden in a nearby bush, heralded the dawn chorus. The blurry horizon glimmered without real promise as a watery sun appeared, daubing the world in insipid shades of grey, brown and green. Moments later, it rose into a welcoming blanket of cloud and disappeared.

He had been happy in Britannia, yet he longed to feel the warmth of his native sun caressing his chilled back. Cold air ruffled Sabrina's warmer surface, creating thin strands of curling mist, which floated, skyward and vanished. Sheltered by the curve of the river's sandy banks he rested and took stock. Estimating the city walls to be a good league behind him, he began to feel safe.

Lucius searched the flood plain for landmarks. He considered a bank side willow, but decided against it as he recalled the power of the river in flood. Sand and time slipped through the hourglass as he nervously searched for a suitable place. Indecision dogged him as he prevaricated about which of the few possible sites he should choose. He decided upon a heap of stones, boulder clay and brush piled in the corner of a wide clearing. Deep in his bones, he sensed the coins would be safe, their value hidden by discarded rubble. Working with speed, and surprising strength for his years, he hauled boulders into position, forming a void behind them. Taking a solitary coin as a keepsake, he placed the bag reverently into the void. After packing the hole with clay and stone, he disguised it with brush. He picked out and memorised what few landmarks he could find. Looking down at the coin in his palm, he wondered when he would return.

Satisfied, Lucius turned his back to the river and headed northwards, uphill towards the valley ridge. He decided to return through the North Gate fearing further interrogation from Marius. Climbing through rough pasture, the wind blasted and buffeted him, chilling his left side. Lucius watched a Raven fly languidly across the valley below, its ragged black silhouette reminding him of the empire's enemies. He hurried on towards the North Gate, tramping in a wide arc through thistle-peppered meadows and wind-blown copses. Gusts of wind clattered naked branches, filling the air with the sound of rattling bones. The pungent aroma of wild garlic invaded his senses as his feet strayed from the path.

Approaching the Gate, he attempted the look of an early riser out for exercise, forcing his knotted body to look nonchalant. Lucius thought the guard looked short for a centurion, though his muscular build and malevolent glare more than compensated for his stature. One glance into his menacing eyes convinced Lucius he would rather be his friend than foe.

'Have you wandered all the night?'

'Sleep would not take me, my son, evil dreams drove me beyond the city walls.'

The centurion's puzzled gaze worried Lucius.

'What of the leagues of city roads, why roam beyond the walls?' he asked.

Lucius glanced at his feet, avoiding eye contact. After a moment's consideration, the centurion waved Lucius past, with a pitying glance at his dew-sodden feet. Lucius tugged his hood over his eyes as he passed bleary citizens starting their day.

Exhausted he lay down, unconsciously his eyes slid closed. He soon climbed weightlessly through scudding clouds, which parted to allow him sight of the familiar ground below. A blurred figure glided into view and briefly focused. Uncomfortably, he watched himself moving tentatively toward the river. A second figure appeared but refused to focus. It followed him, neither gaining nor losing ground. He called out to himself, 'Watch your back,' but the warning went unheard. The figure in the dream turned and stared menacingly back at Lucius. He could so nearly recognise its face though it remained stubbornly at the edge of recognition.

*****

Weeks passed as Lucius's belief in his god's message began to unpick at the seams.

'Wake yourself, Lucius.'

The voice possessed a dream like quality, did it speak to him? His cautious eyes blinked towards a face so close to his own it blurred. Could it be a dream? No, its foul breath denied the possibility of it being a dream.

'Lucius,' the face said, shaking his shoulders until recognition glimmered in his eyes.

'What do you want with me at this hour?'

'What hour? The sun rose some time ago, good citizens are about their labours!'

'Forgive me. I sleep fitfully since the dreams started earlier this moon.'

'It's my duty to inform you of bad news.'

'Your news must indeed be bad. Someone of your rank would not deliver a message of little importance,' Lucius said, gesturing for him to begin.

'It is with a heavy heart that I must inform you that your friend Marius is no more.'

Lucius stared uncomprehendingly through squinted eyes.

'Marius died in a climbing accident on patrol three days ago. He is buried some thirty leagues to the west'

'But, how?'

'His dying wish was that his tunic be presented to you with the following message "Forgive me"'. Lucius took the tunic with shaking hands.

'Why blood?' his eyes travelled between the dark stain and the Centurio's face. 'I ask once more, how was his end.'

'You know the code, Marius was carrying out his duties to the Empire. I am not at liberty to inform you', he said. His erect demeanour barred further questions.

'One more thing, and this is a direct order. Report at the North Gate before the sun reaches its full height. Bring only what you can carry on a three-day march - that is all,' he said, before nodding severely and swivelling on his heel, leaving Lucius in puzzled silence.

He recalled shared scenes from his friend's life as he pulled the tunic edges through his fingers as if handling a string of beads. Back and forth, the tunic's edge passed through his hands. As the pain subsided, his fingers began to register five lumps at regular intervals around the tunic's embroidered edge. The bumps were invisible but could be found by touch; pinching them between thumb and forefinger, he discovered them to be hard and circular.

Hidden buttons, he supposed, *But why?*

He found his knife; its blade flashed as he withdrew it from its leather sheath. Working carefully, he cut the stitching along the inside edge hoping to avoid damaging the tunic. Released from its hiding place, the shape turned into a coin of the same denomination as the ones he had buried only weeks ago. He calculated that the five coins hidden in the tunic were equivalent to a Centurion's annual wages. How had Marius amassed such wealth? In life, his coins were soon spent, he saved nothing. The hammer blow of realisation struck Lucius, as the coins and Marius's last words gelled in his head. His dreams had probably become reality once more.

*****

Lucius presented himself at the North Gate as ordered. He had with him his stout bag, his stave and a bundle under one arm. He carried a few coins from the temple and those from the tunic, a few clothes, some small mementos and food for three days. Appraising the assembled group, he realised they were all Romans; native citizens were to be left to their fate. He hoped they would accommodate their new masters as they had done before, but only time would tell.

Formed into a snake-like column with Centurions at the head and tail, they moved forward. Few looked back as they marched away. It had been several years since many in the column had marched behind the standard; the pace took its toll. As luck had it, the road to Deva had been well maintained and the weather fair. Oblivious to the muttered complaints and curses of his fellow marchers, Lucius strode forward consumed in thought as he attempted to unravel the puzzle of recent events. Rumours circulated that their overnight campsite would be reached within another league, but like many good rumours, it transpired to be false.

Chapter 2: The beginning of the End
Saturday evening 3rd October 1942

She stretched awkwardly, straightening the stiffness from her arms and legs. Daylight diffused into dusk settling eerily across the landscape. Time to move out of her hiding place. She moved cautiously through the copse towards the road at the brow of the hill. Standing half hidden at the bus stop she stared into the gathering gloom as myriad uncertainties closed in. She must anticipate its lumbering approach with sufficient time to break cover and flag it down. She couldn't risk standing in the open and being recognised by someone in a passing vehicle.

Several cars had passed; their dull lights glimmered and flickered as they negotiated the pitted road. She assumed she would recognise the bus by its engine noise, its lights or speed. She did not know exactly what would identify it, but believed something would.

Eventually, a pair of lights set higher than the cars before, flickered their way towards her. *This must be the bus, it sounds like a bus.* She stepped forward onto the stones and loose tarmac at the road's margin, her arm stretched out, her face set determinedly. Her heart sank as the bus neither altered course nor slowed. Stunned, she glimpsed the glow of the driver's face, as he looked out towards her. In glare of brake lights and protesting brakes, the bus eventually came to rest in a haze of steam. Stepping cautiously across uneven tarmac she made for the open door and stepped gratefully aboard.

Attempting a nonchalant look in an oversize gabardine Macintosh, she flashed a smile of thanks to the driver and moved unsteadily towards the rear as the bus jerked reluctantly into life. Peering down the dimly lit bus, she searched for her seat. Slumping into a seat at the back, she turned to her fellow passenger, but before she could speak, a soft voice said, 'I thought you would never come!'

He placed a finger to her lips stifling her reply. He held her with his eyes as he withdrew his finger and kissed her tenderly.

'Jackson, you gave me such a fright, you look like a tramp.'

'Thanks, I've been living rough.' He elbowed her gently in the ribs. 'Look, I have a plan, but we can't talk here,' he said, smiling a crooked smile.

They sat in silence, holding hands in the dark as the bus took its circuitous route around outlying villages that loomed out of the darkness. A tide of passengers ebbed and flowed at each stop. Jack fought to control his feelings of exhilaration and terror. Hand in hand, they had willingly jumped into an uncharted chasm, free-falling towards their new life.

The bus ground to a halt in the deserted terminus.

'Do you know anyone here?' he said, looking through the windows, as they moved cautiously towards the door.

She looked confused.

'Would anyone recognise you here, in Wellington I mean?'

'No, I don't think so.'

'Let's talk in the pub over there.'

They crossed the road trying to look as inconspicuous as a tramp accompanied by a woman in an oversize Macintosh, riding boots and windswept hair could manage. They sat at a quiet corner table and sipped their drinks warily.

'You go first,' she said, nervously.

'Okay. I have a plan, but if it were a jigsaw there would be a few pieces missing.'

'We'd better look under the rug then,' she said.

They shared a brief grin.

'The plan is to put as much distance between the Bridge and us as we can. How about Australia? I have a twin brother Robert living out there.'

'It sounds wonderful.'

'He's in the back of beyond on a sheep station, he'll see us right. I thought we'd travel to a port tonight and lie low; then trick our way aboard a ship sailing that way. That's where the pieces are missing!' Jack searched for her hand under the table. 'Everything will come right, though I'm not quite sure how.'

'I think so too. You know I have this wonderful feeling that we've known each other for ever. I feel comfortable with you Jackson, please don't betray my trust in you.'

He knew exactly how she felt as his stomach knotted with an intense longing that everything would work out well.

'I think I may have some of your missing pieces,' she said, preening herself.

'I'm all ears.'

'Well, since I found your note, I've been planning our escape.'

'How many missing pieces do you have then?'

'Some, if not all of them.'

'Tell me.'

'I have money, quite a lot actually,' she said, smiling proudly and patting her bag. 'We have clothes in a trunk at Crewe Station. I also have my passport and my husband's, plus his travel authorisations.'

'What if he misses them?'

'He's in London on business, I doubt he will notice for at least a couple of weeks. By which time we'll be far from here. Anyway, as long as we fool everyone else, I don't think it will trouble him. If he doesn't lose face, I don't think he will pursue us. It may just suit him.'

Jack looked at her with delight and wonderment.

'You're chocolate, that's what you are, chocolate.'

'I know,' she said, with a cheeky grin. 'Let's get the trunk and change into our new lives.'

They endured an uncomfortable journey to Crewe; concerned they would be exposed before they recovered the trunk.

Chapter 3: Different people?
Saturday night 3rd October 1942

A feeling of relief swept over them as they recovered the trunk and set about changing their appearance from down-and-outs to respectable middle-class citizens. Jack struggled to shave days of stubble in cold water. He then hid their old clothes, as Eleanor purchased tickets, singles, with no thought of return.

'First class is a bit rich, isn't it?'

'Not at all, we need a compartment to ourselves don't you think? After all, we have masses to say and do,' she winked as she attached a note to the door and pulled down the blinds. The note read 'Just Married'. Jack settled back against the plush seats and savoured his surroundings. For all of the years he had worked on the railway he had never travelled first class.

'What shall we do with the money?' she said as she opened her bag. 'We can't take this much currency out of the country, can we? Unless we hide it.'

'Well, I could make a suggestion,' he said, with a sparkle in his eyes.

'I hope it's not rude.'

'Well, you could do with a bit more up top, if you know what I mean.'

He put his arm up, protecting himself from a possible assault. She playfully slapped him while smiling broadly at his pretence of fright.

'I'll go and spend a penny and see what I can do,' she said, stepping into the corridor.

A few minutes later she swept into the carriage looking extremely pleased with herself.

'What do you think?'

'Worth every penny, I'd say,' Jack said, with a stage wink in admiration for her inflated bosom and received another whack for his cheek.

'At the risk at getting whacked again, you appear to have put on a few pounds on your hips as well.'

'I spread it about a bit. At least the dress fits now. Not bad considering I borrowed it from my sister. Maybe you would like me to grow into this size permanently?'

'I probably shouldn't answer that. I'm bound to say the wrong thing.'

He pulled her close and kissed her. She pulled away and became serious.

'Why are you doing this Jackson? Why are you running away with me? I hope it's for the right reasons. I wouldn't want to be jumping from the frying pan into the fire,' she said searching for reassurance in his eyes.

'I'm hoping to make up for lost time. As we're asking awkward questions, how do I know you're not just running away and I'm the first ticket you found?'

'Jack, never question that again for as long as you live. I'm here to be with you, no other reason. As you say, time for awkward questions. Do you have any regrets, Jack?'

'How many can I have?'

'Oh, as many as you need, as long as they don't spoil our future.'

'Well there's leaving Tom. Hopefully he will be fine, he will have my cottage and a legacy if everything works out,' he said, while absentmindedly watching the darkness beyond the carriage window. 'Maybe one day, when we're settled, where ever that is, I'd like to ask him to visit,' he said, taking her hand.

'And Nipper?'

'Nipper. I don't think she'll be able to come,' he chortled. 'You know, yesterday I saw Tom and Nipper from my hiding place. They were together on the river bank, if you'd seen them you would have thought that Nipper and Tom had been together all their lives. They looked so happy, the sight of them eased the pain of leaving them both.'

'Any more regrets?'

'Well yes.' He paused and fixed her with one of his winning smiles. 'I most regret not meeting you under the Albert ten years ago.'

'You can't regret that, it might never have happened for us then. Besides, we have to make the most of our future together, now. Regretting the past is only wasting precious time.'

They settled down to tell each other the stories of their last few momentous days, as they thundered through the night towards an uncertain but passionate future together. Jack sensed she needed to tell her story first, which would suit him as it gave him time to organise his jumbled thoughts and tell his story coherently.

She told him how Harris had sought her out and warned her not to meet Jack. Jack's face screwed up with anguished puzzlement.

'Why didn't he warn me, the bastard?' he said, a flash of anger in his eyes. 'Sorry, please carry on,' he said, as he checked his anger and forced an apologetic smile.

She then explained how talk of his drowning had reached her by the following morning. The discovery of his fishing equipment, the rowing boat and Nipper by the riverbank, added weight to the gossip. She explained how an inexplicable sense grew in her until she was certain he had not drowned. It went against all logic, but her whole being knew her version to be the truth. She reasoned that if he were still alive he would make contact by leaving a note at their hiding place by the Albert. Biding her time, she chose her moment to slip away unnoticed. His note had almost melted her with the combined heat of relief, joy and love.

Run away with me

Meet me on the 8pm Madeley

to Wellington bus.

Any day, any stop.

As soon as you can.

x

*****

The note had been the invitation she had waited for, throughout her adult life. Logically she listed the requirements for their escape. It came down to money, clothes and the ability to travel. She explained how her near panic had only been controlled by her unshakeable faith that she wanted and needed to escape with him. Jack listened to her intensity. Her ability and her poise impressed him so greatly he almost burst with pride.

She had packed a travel trunk with her husband's older clothes, gauging that they would fit Jack. Her husband had put on weight and acquired a new wardrobe. She had not understood at the time, but she had taken the best clothes and hidden them, saved for a rainy day.

Money had been more difficult as she had none of her own. She wanted for nothing, as she could buy anything, within reason, but only through her husband's accounts at London stores. She had felt ambivalent about her mother's legacy, until his note galvanised her into action. She arranged to visit her sister in Birmingham, taking the trunk of old clothes along on the pretence of taking the clothes for her sister's husband. Within hours of arriving at her sister's door, she repacked the trunk with some of her sister's clothes and then took it to a local station and forwarded it to Crewe. Having dealt with the trunk, she caught the next train to London where, over the following three days, she liquidated her mother's shares and bonds. Returning to the Bridge without comment, she set about finding passports and travel authorisations amongst her husband's papers. At last, everything had fallen into place.

Rising at first light, she crept down through the house as the dawn chorus announced her departure. She wrapped her newfound wealth and documents in her trust old gabardine Macintosh and hid it deep in the woods beyond the house. She would collect it after breakfast as she rode out never to return.

She then explained an unnerving feeling that the gamekeeper was watching her again. She wondered if she had been seen or followed to the woods. Eventually, she decided to challenge him. He had watched her from a distance as she mounted her new stallion. She walked the horse towards him as she stared him down, her head steady and focused.

'Is there something amiss?' she said, as haughtily as she could.

'No, nothing at all, everything is fine and dandy.'

'You see, I get the impression you've been watching me. I feel unnerved by your attention. Should I speak to my husband?'

'There is no need, I assure you. My apologies if I caused you discomfort, I didn't mean anything by it,' he said, staring at the fields behind her. 'Please excuse me, I have pheasants to find.'

She felt she done enough to deflect him. Now was the time to act. Riding out she confidently smiled and greeted anyone she passed.

She rode towards an ancient mining area that hid numerous worked-out bell pits and shafts. Riding her mount around the slopes, gullies and open airshafts, carefully leaving horseshoe impressions that would easily be found. She then impaled her scarf on a prominent gorse bush. Pointing her mount in the direction of the house, she slapped its flank. The horse cantered away. Stepping across broken countryside she cautiously moved towards the desolate bus stop. Jack silently gazed at her, humbled by thoughts of the risks she had taken to be with him. She stared at him expectantly. 'Your turn.'

Eventually he began, explaining that as he sat disconsolately waiting for her on the riverbank. How he had come to believe that she would never meet him there or anywhere, it was over between them. How he saw the faces of the people he had betrayed, the people who hated him, distrusted him and even those he had helped. How the voices in his head had driven him to take his own life.

How the crushing chill of the river had broken through the trance that demanded his destruction. Thinking quickly, he laid an oar in the river and placed his prize hat between the boat and the bank. Scrambling up the far bank, he collapsed exhausted into the long grass and pondered his next move. He then explained that, as he lay looking back towards a puzzled Nipper, Harris had appeared, his familiar walking style easily recognisable in the gloom. Seizing the opportunity, he raced under cover back to his cottage. Still dripping river water, he dared not enter the cottage for fear of giving the game away. He contented himself with a quick look at the old place through the dirty windows on his way to the shed. He grabbed a jar of rainy-day money hidden behind his tools, picked up an old pair of overalls and a duffle coat and closed the door. As he reached the garden gate he heard the tell-tale click of the latch and squeak of the hinges as the front door opened and heard Harris say.

'Hello, is someone there? Jack, is that you?'

He reached the woodland path before Harris could catch a glimpse of him. His first night had been spent in a wayside hut where he plotted his next steps. It had been dawn before he slept, but by then, he had a plan.

Chapter 4: All aboard
12.01 Sunday 4th October 1942

Standing arm in arm at the stern rail they watched the glimmer of Holyhead's blacked-out buildings disappear into the night sky as their vessel headed towards a gale out in the Irish Sea.

'We said there would be no secrets between us, Jackson.'

He nodded solemnly, expecting more difficult questions, but none were asked. She looked deep into his eyes and said, 'I'm illegitimate, a bastard'

'It doesn't matter to me.'

'It matters to me, somehow. It's so strange: it never entered my head to question my parentage, until Mother died.'

'Sorry, you've lost me.'

'Jack, do you remember the summer of 1913? It's when I was born.'

'No, not really, I would have been nine or ten.'

'How long have we known each other?' she said looking up into his eyes.

Jack thought that this might be some sort of a test. He felt he knew the answer, but pretended to consider it carefully, before announcing: 'I don't remember the exact date but we first met at about two o'clock on a sunny Saturday afternoon in 1932 at the Summer Fair.' Jack flashed her a cheeky grin of triumph. Her answer surprised him.

'We actually first met less than three months ago and look how far we've come. We only saw each other at the Summer Fair, we didn't really meet until I saw you from my horse on the railway.'

'What are you saying?'

'I faked losing control of my mount. I wanted to see if you recognised me and if you were interested…'

'Well you had me fooled, I thought ….'

'Isn't it right that we both feel we've known each all our lives? Not that we know the details, but we feel so comfortable with each other.'

'It's as you say, but I'm dammed if I can see how we've met before. Believe me, I would have remembered your eyes if I'd seen them before.'

'I bet that's what you tell all the girls.'

'Yes, but in your case, it's true.'

Jack hunched up in a boxing pose, hoping to evade the playful blows that would surely land.

'How would you feel if I told you a story that I have just learnt about myself. A story that questions even who I am.'

'You're being very mysterious, but let's go below first, you must be getting cold.'

They settled in a quiet corner of the lounge. Eleanor relaxed into her chair and began her story. Jack listened, his eyes watching her intently.

'When mother died, she left me the shares and bonds I told you about. What I haven't mentioned is that amongst the documents passed to me by her solicitor was a letter addressed to me in my mother's handwriting. The envelope carried directions that it should not be opened before mother's death. I have it here,' she said, producing it from her handbag and passing it to him with a tremulous hand. 'Please read it. I found it a profound shock, though you may not see it that way.'

Jack took the letter from its envelope with growing concern. His lady had been speaking in riddles, where usually she spoke directly. She appeared to be searching for an answer in his words or his actions. He began to read, as much to stop himself from saying the wrong thing as to understand its message.

To my daughter Eleanor,

I hope you will not hate me for keeping this from you for so many years and only revealing it after my death. My only excuse is that I am a coward at heart and wished to avoid the myriad questions you were bound to ask once you knew your story.

The fact is that you are not my daughter by blood. We adopted you as a baby, at the time it appeared that as a couple we could not have children. You were our lucky charm as soon after you came into our lives I fell pregnant. The rest is history. Before I come to the missing parts of your life, I need to assure you that you have always been loved and cherished as our child.

We were never able to establish your parentage. You were found by the railway line, at Chunes Crossing. You were placed out of harm's way, away from the rails but in full view, guaranteeing that you would be quickly found. You were snug and safe, wrapped in blankets inside a box. Your clothes were clean; you were well fed and very bonny. A note pinned to the box asked that you be taken care of and that you were called Eleanor.

Exhaustive enquires were made at institutions, hospitals, hostels and many other organisations, but we found no trace of your mother. You had been taken to Wenlock hospital and then to the orphanage, from where you were swiftly adopted by your father and me.

There is little more that I can tell you, other than a boy found you by the name of Hailstone. The orphanage mentioned him when they told us what they knew of your story. We never met him, though I believe he lived in the Gorge somewhere.

It only remains for me to advise you not to delve into your roots, as I believe it will be a painful and fruitless search. The intervening years will have covered any remaining tracks with the sands of time.

Please always remember, you were loved and cherished as our daughter.

*****

Jack stopped before the end and handed the letter back as tears welled and streaked his cheeks.

'Do you remember now? You were that boy, weren't you?'

'Yes, that was me.'

'So, I have known you all of my life, Jack,' she said, as she gently wiped away a tear.

'Jack, was one of the faces you saw China's,' she said, studying his face as she asked.

'No. Why do you ask?'

'Well we must be able to trust each other. It's us against the world.'

'But, why China?'

'Jack, it's only gossip, but …'

'What's the "but"? Tell me.'

'Okay,' she said, screwing up her eyes, willing herself to speak. 'Jack, did you kill China?'

'No! Why?'

'The rumours say, China had been shouting his mouth off about getting back at "June's fancy man",' she said, looking at him pointedly as she said "June's fancy man".

'So?' he said, regaining his composure.

'The rumours also say that you and June were close and that the gun that killed China was taken from your cottage,' she said, trying to read Jack's reflection in the dark widow. 'This isn't the reason you're running away, is it Jack? It's to be with me, isn't it?' she said, her eyes pleading. 'You're not just running away from justice?'

Jack continued to stare blankly, not meeting her eyes. After what seemed an eternity, he turned slowly away from the window and searched for her hand.

'Well, now it's time to put your trust to the test,' he said, his face surprisingly expressionless.

'Yes, the rumours are right about me to June, but, before you ask, it was over long before we met under the Albert.'

'I believe you, but what about China's death?'

'You need to be patient while I tell you what happened. As I sat alone in the railway hut on that first night thinking what my next move should be, I remembered what you said about disappearing without trace. Anyway, I suddenly saw an opportunity to manufacture my disappearance.'

'What's this to do with China's death?'

'Hold your horses and hear me out. You know I told you about moving the coins and leaving them for Tom.' She nodded cautiously. 'Well what I didn't tell you was that I came across a motorbike accident, the rider had been killed, his head and face mangled. Because I had the coins, I couldn't report the accident, so I was forced to leave him where he fell, hidden in thick bushes. I couldn't risk the Police or anyone else quizzing me, because of the coins. So I rode off and left him.'

'That's not like the Jackson I know.'

'One day, I hope you will understand. Unfortunately, the story gets worse.'

She looked troubled as she tried desperately to trust him.

'So, as I hid in the railway hut, it occurred to me to dress the dead man in my clothes, push him in the river and allow him to be found as me. All I had to do was drag him out of the cover and down the riverbank, then fix it so he wouldn't surface before he had decomposed. By the time, he is found they will hopefully only identify him by my Granddad's watch.'

'Jackson! How long had he been dead?'

'Four-days. I was lucky, though, the body was shaded and half submerged in a shallow pond, and so he wasn't too bad. But, here's the thing as I undressed him I found this silver whistle in his pocket. It's China's from the Great War.'

'How did it get there?'

'It had me puzzled for a moment,' he said, 'Until, I discovered a tattoo on the man's bicep. I knew the tattoo it belonged to Chas, remember me telling you about him? The lad on leave from the army. The thing is I remembered him getting it done, him and his mate did it for a dare, drunk as skunks both of them. They both had each other's names tattooed on their arms, mates for life sort of thing. Only a few of us knew about it. Chas kept it covered, "Ted" it said, you could imagine the ribbing he would get having a tattoo of another man's name!'

'What are you saying?'

'Well, Chas had been on leave in the Bridge when China went missing. It's hush hush, but Chas was in the Commando's or SAS's. He was a killing machine, with a few screws loose into the bargain. I reckon he could have been AWOL when he had the motorbike accident. He was in civvies, no papers, just a couple of coppers in his pocket. He must have stolen the army motorbike and been on his way to visit June, he was that callous.'

'But why did Chas have China's whistle.'

'He probably took it as a trophy, he's that mad.'

'Then why did you take it?' she said, narrowing her eyes.

'I didn't want to leave it on the body, my body.'

'Why keep it, why not throw it away?'

'I don't know really, I suppose I had some hope of using it in some way to pointing the finger at Chas. I hadn't worked it out.'

'What about the gun.'

'Chas took it to the cottage knowing I was out and gave it to Harris as a trophy for me, it's a German officers Luger. The problem is Harris didn't tell me about it, so it sat in the junk draw where Harris put it. Until that is Constable James came sniffing around.'

'Why did Harris give him the gun.'

'Well, Harris isn't Harris, He's a gangster called JC. I think he saw an opportunity to get rid of me and take the house.'

'My head is spinning, why did Chas give you the gun?'

'To get rid of it and to implicate me in China's death.'

'But why?'

'It's another long story but to cut it short, China had an older sister called Grace, who he thought the world of. She worked at the bakers, I bought bread most days and we became friends. Before you get any ideas, she had discovered she batted for the other side. As you can imagine that would have gone down like a lead balloon in the Bridge. So, she kept it under her hat. She persuaded me to pretend she was my girlfriend. It worked fine, it just looked like I was playing the field. People were scandalised that I was running around behind her back, they would even try to warn her. We just laughed.

When she made up twenty-one, she left for London. No one could stop her. The trouble was people believed I had put her in the family way and she had run away through shame. Chas blamed me, but I couldn't explain or defend myself. As he grew up he appeared to get over it, but I'm not really sure he ever did.

Then she was killed in the blitz a year ago. Chas had never seen her since she left the Bridge. I think it all came back in spades when she died. The gun was his way of setting me up for China's death, his way of paying me back.'

'Can you prove any of this?'

'Not a word,' Jack said, staring at his boots. After a few seconds which had felt like minutes or even hours, he turned and stared into Eleanor's eyes, then took a deep breath.

'You asked me if I was running away because I had killed China.'

'Yes, you said "No"' Eleanor said, guardedly

'Well I lied. I am running away. Not because I killed China, but because the Police believe I did. And I have no way of proving I didn't. I think the real killer is dead. And even what's worse is that sometime soon the real killers body will float to the surface of the Severn, disguised as me.'

Epilogue

Within weeks of Lucius's warning, Celts overran Viroconium, signalling the decline of the Roman Empire in Britannia. Lucius found himself ordered to return to his native land, with no opportunity to recover the coins. Not that he knew whether Marius had found the coins and reburied them or just taken a few. "Forgive Me" Marius had asked. Lucius did. Lucius was much venerated by his neighbouring citizens who enjoyed his eccentric stories of hidden treasure in Britannia. He died in his sleep as an old man.

*****

Bill and George raised countless pints at Jack's wake. They continued to drink to his memory on the first Friday of each month, though without Jack and his stories the evenings were never the same.

They continued to work happily as railwaymen until the line closed in 1963 but neither had the stomach for a transfer or to drive the new diesel trains. Fishing soon became their full-time occupation. They abandoned their favourite pegs up river, preferring to fish closer to the Bridge and drink in the pubs nearby. Unspoken, but subliminally understood, had been their concern that their accusations may have contributed to Jack's death.

They died within a few weeks of each other, never having breathed a word of the hoard to another living soul.

*****

Eleanor's husband remained a widower, preferring on this occasion to garner sympathy by mourning her loss, which provided an excellent disguise for other exploits. The advent of peace proved disastrous for his manufacturing businesses. He attempted to diversify without success. As his wealth and influence declined and without friends on high to protect him, he was forced to run the gauntlet of the sodomy laws.

*****

Paul and Annie, or Errol and Cinderella, whichever they preferred, arrived home safely to their mother in Manchester. They happily told stories of catching fish and train rides, having never once understood the problems they had caused; sorry, though, that the penny-a-fish man had drowned.

*****

Constable James, John to his friends, married his childhood sweetheart, Jane the barmaid. The couple were blessed with a boy, born five months to the day of their wedding. They eventually produced a family of five children, four of them girls. John loved Henry his first child but in certain lights he could not help thinking he had a look of Jack about him. He resisted the temptation to ask Jane the question that haunted him; a sage decision, as he certainly would not have appreciated an honest answer.

*****

Joan set off for a holiday in Australia; her luggage included Tom's ashes. She found Jackson and Eleanor lying side by side in a bush community graveyard. Such a tiny district in such a vast country, not easily found you would have thought, but Joan and Tom had visited before. They had told their neighbours they were going to South Wales, forgetting or mumbling 'New'. They travelled for three days in uncomfortable trains and planes, before a final, bumpy, fifty-mile ride along dirt roads. It had been worth every second though to bask in the reflected warmth of Jackson and Tom's embrace.

It had been easier this time. She had flown first class to Sydney in twenty-four hours and five hours later, she had arrived in a hire car. Yes, she could drive: there was always more to Joan than met the eye. She gazed over randomly spaced headstones and across a sea of swaying grasses towards a blue haze clinging to a stand of Eucalyptus. Gradually a hazy memory emerged. Set in an orange landscape beneath an azure sky, she sees Jack and Ellie sitting comfortably on a veranda facing the outback. Jack and Ellie wave to Robert across a sea of sheep as he rides steadily towards them. Reality and imagination merged.

One question remained unanswered: should she leave Tom with his Father or take him home to the Bridge?

Joan eventually came home to the Bridge, to Tom's cottage; she had purchased it before leaving for Australia. There had been no doubt that she would come home, as she did when Jack and Eleanor had invited them to stay all those years ago. Their decision had more to do with the pull of the Bridge than her dislike of the heat and flies.

Joan and Skipper, her Jack Russell settled happily at the cottage. The Bridge is different now, so many incomers. No one remembers Joan or the part she played.

*****

Gazing across the vast expanse of Fistral beach, I watch surfers catching the last waves of daylight. Behind them, the setting sun paints clouds in shades of red and orange. Wetsuits spread across tufted grass drying in a gentle breeze that carries distant chords played on an acoustic guitar.

Lucy and I sit side by side, her paws and my feet hang out through the van's sliding door as we soak up the view. We look past the new woman in my life towards the fading sunset, hoping to see beyond its colours and glimpse tomorrow. Languidly, I allow my eyelids to close. A beautiful blue floods my mind's eye. Powerful waves break before washing lazily across golden sand.

We have known each other for some time now, but never like this. Her skin contrasts wonderfully with her white costume. As I gaze at her, that music begins to play again. That same saxophone riff grows louder in my head as I watch her wonderfully liquid movement towards me

Hopefully, this is not a dream.

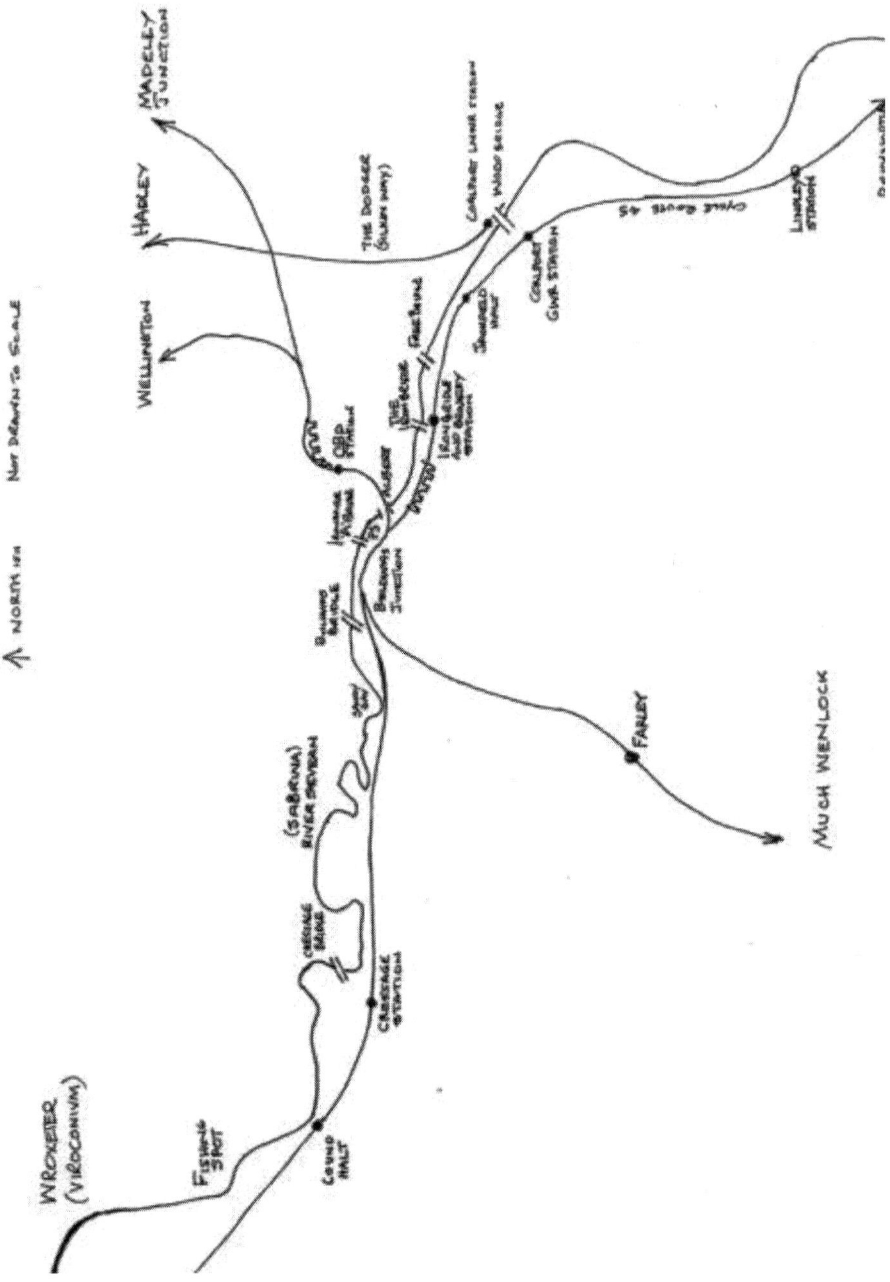
NORTH
NOT DRAWN TO SCALE
WROXETER
(VIROCONIUM)
FISHING SPOT
COUND HALT
CRESSAGE STATION
(SABRINA)
RIVER SEVERN
WELLINGTON
HARLEY
MADELEY JUNCTION
THE DODGER
(SILKIN WAY)
BUILDWAS JUNCTION
ALBERT
COALPORT GWR STATION
COALPORT LNWR STATION
WOOD BRIDGE
FARLEY
MUCH WENLOCK
LINLEY STATION

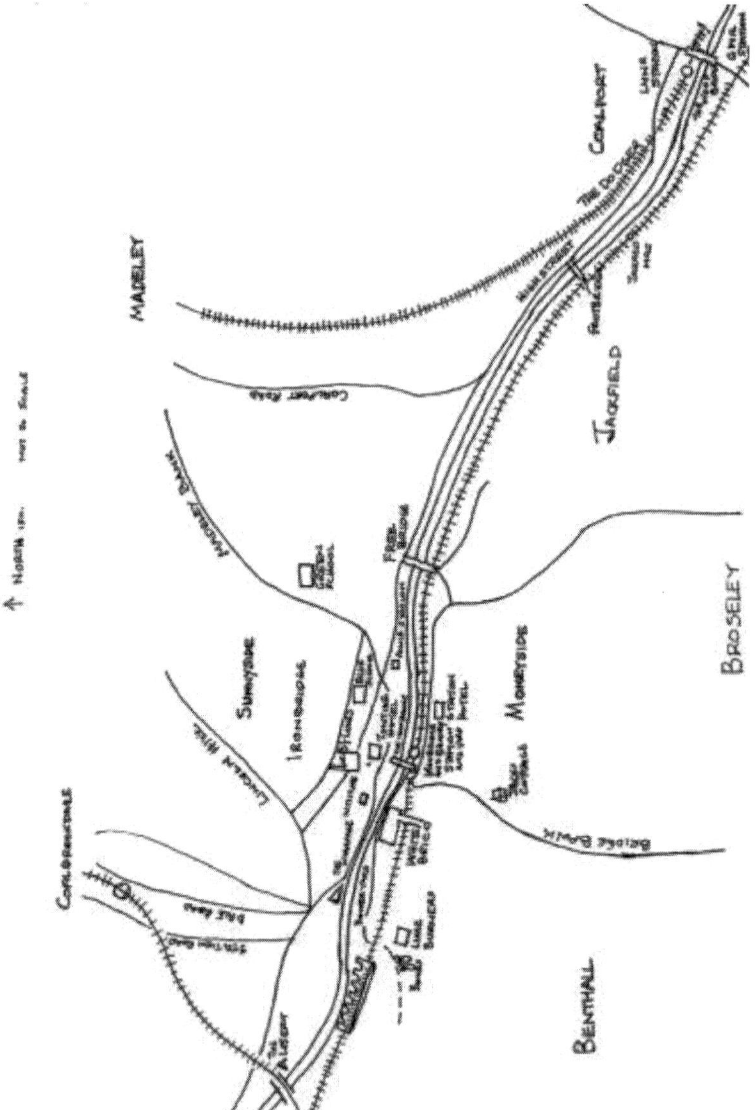
NORTH
MADELEY
COALPORT
JACKFIELD
BROSELEY
BENTHALL
COALBROOKDALE
IRONBRIDGE
SUNNYSIDE
MADELEY BANK
COALPORT ROAD
BRIDGE BANK

Printed in Great Britain
by Amazon